RAVES FOR STUART WOODS

HEAT
"High melodrama and unexpected twists make this teflon-coated blockbuster business as usual in Woods's practiced hands."

—*Publishers Weekly*

"A high-concept action thriller."

—*Kirkus Reviews*

DEAD EYES
"A masterfully paced thriller. . . . Woods is a pro at turning up the suspense."

—*Publishers Weekly*

"*Dead Eyes* keeps you reading."

—*Cosmopolitan*

L. A. TIMES
"Relentlessly paced . . . Pulse pounding . . . Vinnie Callabrese is . . . the most fascinating protagonist Woods has yet created in this long string of highly successful and imaginative thrillers."

—*The Washington Post*

"A slick, fast, often caustically funny tale."

—*Los Angeles Times*

"Stuart Woods is a wonderful storyteller who could teach Robert Ludlum and Tom Clancy a thing or two."

—*The State* (Columbia)

IMPERFECT STRANGERS

STUART WOODS

HarperTorch
An Imprint of HarperCollinsPublishers

The book *Imperfect Strangers* by Stuart Woods is available on tape from HarperAudio, a division of HarperCollins*Publishers*.

This is a work of fiction. Names, characters, places, and incidents are products of the author's imagination or are used fictitiously and are not to be construed as real. Any resemblance to actual events, locales, organizations, or persons, living or dead, is entirely coincidental.

❦

HARPERTORCH
An Imprint of HarperCollins*Publishers*
10 East 53rd Street
New York, New York 10022-5299

Copyright © 1995 by Stuart Woods
Cover illustration by Kirk Reinert
ISBN: 0-06-109404-8

First HarperTorch paperback printing: November 2000
First HarperPaperbacks printing: October 1995
First HarperCollins hardcover printing: January 1995

HarperCollins®, HarperTorch™, and ♦™ are trademarks of HarperCollins Publishers Inc.
Avon Trademark Reg. U.S. Pat. Off. and in Other Countries,
Marca Registrada, Hecho en U.S.A.

Printed in the United States of America

Visit HarperTorch on the World Wide Web at
www.harpercollins.com

20 19

This book is for
Harold and Lauren Cudmore

IMPERFECT STRANGERS

CHAPTER

1

As the sun rose over Berkeley Square, the May sunshine drifted through the blinds in the Mount Street flat, two blocks west. The rays fell across the face of Sandy Kinsolving, waking him as if they had been the bell of an alarm clock. He lay on his back, naked, and blinked a couple of times. Oriented, he turned to his right and moved toward the woman next to him. He shaped himself to her back and pressed his groin against her soft buttocks, and he felt the stirring come.

She gave a soft moan and responded, pushing against him. In a moment she was wet, and he entered her, moving slowly, enjoying the early morning moment.

The phone rang, the loud, insistent jangling that only an older British phone could make. He cursed under his breath and, without stopping the motion, reached across her and lifted the receiver.

1

"Hello?" he said hoarsely.

"It's Joan." She waited for him to respond.

He still did not stop moving. "Yes," he said, finally, then he became more alert. "What time is it in New York?"

"Nearly two A.M."

"What's wrong?"

"Daddy has had a stroke."

He stopped moving, wilting like a violet in hot sun. "How bad?"

"They don't know, yet, but at his age—"

Jock Bailley was ninety-one. "I'll get myself on a flight as soon as the office opens. Where is he?"

"Lenox Hill. I'm calling from there."

"I'll let the New York office know what flight I'm on."

"Albert will meet you."

"You all right?"

"Tired."

"You'd better go home and sleep. There's nothing you can do there."

"I suppose you're right. Laddie and Betty are here, anyway."

"You should all go home and sleep."

"I will; I can't speak for Laddie."

"See you this afternoon."

She hung up without saying good-bye.

Sandy replaced the receiver. A little ball of apprehension had made a tight knot in his belly.

"*Sandy,*" the woman said accusingly. "You stopped."

Sandy rolled onto his back. "Sorry, luv. I've just been put out of commission."

"Bad news?"

"Yes, bad news. Illness in the family."

"I'm sorry."

"Thanks. I'd better get dressed. Do you mind break-fasting at home? I have to go to New York."

"Certainly, dear," she said, rising and heading for the bathroom. "I'll just get a quick shower."

"Thanks." Sandy stared at his ceiling and tried to put a good face on all this. Jock wasn't dead, yet; that was something, at least.

Sandy took the lift down at eight o'clock and let himself into Cornwall & Company, the wine shop on the ground floor. He stood for a moment and watched the sunbeams cut little swaths through the dust in the air, which was in the process of gathering on the hundreds of bottles that lined the walls of the large shop.

He walked to the rear of the shop and climbed the old circular staircase to the offices above. He set his briefcase on the desk in his little office and sat down heavily. As he did, the door from the first-floor landing opened and Maeve O'Brien stepped into the offices.

"Maeve," he called out.

She came to his office door. "Yes, Mr. Kinsolving?"

"Would you get me a seat on a flight to New York? The earlier the better."

"Of course. I thought you were staying until next week, though."

"Old Mr. Bailley has had a stroke."

"Oh, I'm sorry to hear it. I'll call the airlines." She hung up her coat and went to her desk.

A few minutes later, Maeve was back. "You're on the eleven o'clock; it was the earliest. I'll pick up your ticket from American Express."

Sandy suddenly couldn't tolerate the office anymore. "I'll pick it up myself; I could use a walk."

"As you wish."

He let himself out the front door of the shop, locking it behind him, and walked slowly past the Connaught Hotel and toward Berkeley Square. Even if Jock was still alive, at his age he couldn't come out of this whole. What would happen if he couldn't communicate, couldn't make his wishes known? Oh, Jesus.

Sandy circumnavigated Berkeley Square and started back up the south side of Mount Street, past the poulterer's and the antique shops, past the tobacconist and the chemist, past his tailor's. He remembered he had a fitting that morning. He stopped at the little American Express office as the manager was letting herself in.

"Good morning, Mr. Kinsolving," she said pleasantly.

"I'd like to pick up a ticket for New York," he said. "The reservation's already made."

"Certainly; I won't be a moment."

He stood outside the agency and watched the morning light fill the elegant street, with its pink granite buildings, lately sandblasted of the decades of London grime, looking new in the moist air. He loved this street. He could get almost anything done within the block—have a suit made; lunch at the Connaught or Scott's; pick up a packet of condoms from the Indian chemist, then forget to use them; be measured for a brace of shotguns at Purdy's on the corner; or select a case of good port at Cornwall & Company, his London base. It jarred him that he was leaving this to go back to New York before the appointed time. He didn't know what awaited him there, and he didn't want to guess.

After a passable airline lunch, he ordered a single malt whisky, uncharacteristic for him at this hour. He wasn't sleepy, but he wanted to be. An announcement came that the movie was about to start. The airplane was equipped with the new individual movie screens; he flipped up his screen and adjusted the headset.

As he did, someone came forward and took the empty seat next to him. "My seatmate snores," a man's voice said. "Hope you don't mind."

"Not at all," Sandy replied, smiling politely, not bothering to glance at the man.

The titles came up on the screen, and Sandy prepared to lose himself in whatever the movie might be. It turned out to be the Alfred Hitchcock classic *Strangers on a Train*.

Peter folded away the screen and put away the headset, then accepted his third Scotch from the flight attendant. He turned to the man beside him out of automatic courtesy. "Join me?"

"Don't mind if I do," the man replied. "What is that you're drinking?"

"Laphroaig."

"Oh, yes, the same for me, please."

Sandy looked at his companion for the first time and found him to be very much like himself. Hardly identical in appearance, but about the same age, mid-forties, the same good clothes, good haircut, good teeth. His hair was sandy, going gray, as Sandy's was dark, going gray. He noticed the three-button cuff at the end of the man's sleeve and knew that they went to the same shirtmaker. His accent was hard to place; something English in it, but not English; mid-Atlantic, maybe.

The man offered his hand. "I'm Peter Martindale," he said. "Peter will do."

"Sandy Kinsolving." They shook hands.

Sandy's drink arrived. "Your good health, Peter," he said, raising his glass.

"And yours, Sandy." Both men drank.

"God, that's good! You can taste the peat. Too many of them wouldn't do your liver any good, though."

"Certainly wouldn't," Sandy replied. "Not unless you were laboring very hard in the vineyard, sweating it out."

"And what vineyard do you labor in, Sandy?"

"Wine. I buy and sell it. You?"

"Art. I buy and sell it. In San Francisco."

"I'm in New York and London. I can't place your accent."

"California Brit, I guess," Peter said. "Born in Liverpool, been out on the coast for twenty years."

"How's the art business?"

"Good. And wine?"

"Good and getting better. I'm glad to see the recession behind us; I've got a lot of good claret in the cellars that I'd like to have sold two or three years ago."

"But you can get more for it with the extra age, can't you?"

"Yes, but it's less nerve-wracking to sell it young, keep it moving."

"Your clothes are English, but your accent isn't."

"Grew up in Connecticut; lived in or around New York all my life."

"School?"

"Amherst."

"I was at Oxford, probably about the same time."

"I envy you the experience. I tried for a Rhodes scholarship, but didn't make it."

"You're the right age for Vietnam."

"Missed it; had a wife and child by the time I left Amherst."

"What did you do right out of university?" Peter asked.

"Went into advertising, like my father."

"When did the wine trade come along?"

"Not for some time; it was liquor, at first. My wife's father has had a large distributorship since Prohibition ended."

"Sounds like he might have been in the business before it ended," Peter said, smiling.

"Right. His family were distillers in Scotland. He was the second son, so they shipped him to Canada to see if he could move some of their goods to a thirsty America."

"And did he?"

"Oh, yes, and the goods of a lot of other distillers, too. By the time he was twenty-one, he was driving fast motorboats down the Bay of Fundy to the coast between Boston and Portsmouth. He knew Meyer Lansky, Lucky Luciano, the lot of them. They convinced him he should stick to importing, rather than distributing. They had that well in hand."

"So, when Prohibition ended, he went legal?"

"That's right. His father died about that time, and his older brother inherited. But he had the distribution rights to the family brands, and he was well connected with other distillers, as a result of his recent activities. He poured his illicit profits into the business, and pretty soon he was leading the pack."

"And how long did he run the business?"

"Right up until yesterday. He had a stroke last night."

"That's a long run; how old was he?"

"Ninety-one."

"So you'll take over, now?"

"That remains to be seen," Sandy sighed. "Old Jock had a son and a daughter late in life. The son's in the business; I'm married to the daughter." He sighed again.

"You don't make it sound like the happiest of circumstances."

"I'm sorry, I didn't mean to whine."

"Oh, nothing like that, Sandy, but I can see how that sort of family could be difficult to live in."

Sandy pulled at the whisky again and began to relax. He found he needed to talk, and he had the ear of a sympathetic stranger, someone he'd never see again after this flight.

"It was difficult at first," he said. "I married Joan the summer after my junior year at Amherst; she was at Mount Holyoke, and she was pregnant, if the truth be known, and I wanted to do the right thing."

"Were you in love with her?"

"Yes, and I was, oddly, very happy when she told me she was pregnant. Old Jock, her father, thought I was after his money, of course, so I made a point of not taking a penny from him. I worked two jobs my senior year, and we lived in a garage apartment. I don't think I've ever been happier."

"Why advertising? You said your father was in the business?"

"Yes, he was an old-timer at Young and Rubicam, and I joined the trainee program there. Did well, too. Jock had assumed I'd want a job with him, so I managed again not to meet his worst expectations. He liked that. Before long, he was insulted that I hadn't come to work for him, and he began to press me hard. When I thought I had played hard-to-get for long enough, I gave in. Since I was by that time a successful account executive at Y and R, I thought he'd want me to take over his marketing." Sandy laughed ruefully at the memory. "Let me tell you something, don't ever go to work for a Scotsman without a contract."

"I take it you did."

"I did. He put me to selling booze, and do you know what my territory was?"

"Not good?"

"The Bowery! One day I had a nice office and a secretary on Madison Avenue; the next, I was in and out of every gin joint from Eighth Street to Houston, in the regular company of what used to be called bums—that was before they became the homeless."

"I don't guess you sold much single malt whisky."

"Not much. Sixty percent of my sales were in cheap gin and rye. We weren't in the wine business in those days, so I didn't have to sell muscatel."

"Was it tough work?"

"I worked my ass off and never made a squawk, either; Jock was waiting for that. Meantime, his son, John Junior, or Laddie, as he's always been called, was working the Upper East Side, lunching at 21 every day and getting his suits made at Dunhill's. If I'd showed up on the Bowery in a Dunhill suit, I wouldn't have lived through the first week. I worked in coveralls, out of a panel truck."

"I take it this didn't last forever."

"No, after two and a half years, Jock brought me uptown and put me in marketing—as *assistant* marketing manager, working for an old rummy who didn't know a third of what I did about marketing and advertising."

"And how long did you take that particular form of abuse?"

"Not long. After about two weeks, I walked into Jock's office and, more or less, told him to go to hell. I told him I wouldn't work for him another day, that he didn't have sense enough to use talent where it would do some good."

"And what was his reaction?"

"I don't think anybody had ever talked to him that way before, but he took it surprisingly well. Cunningly, he asked if I had another offer somewhere. I told him the truth—I didn't, but I'd go out and make a job for myself. Advertising was in something of a depression at the time, and Jock knew it, but he knew I wasn't bluffing, either, so he surprised me."

"He gave you the marketing job?"

"No, he asked me what I'd like to do in the business."

"And what did you tell him?"

"I hadn't expected the question, so I didn't have a ready answer. Rather impulsively, I blurted out that I wanted to start a wine division. Jock didn't know anything about wine; I mean, he drank single malt scotch with his meals. Not that I knew a hell of a lot about it, either, but I had the advantage of knowing more than Jock did, and to my surprise, he took me up on it. 'Okay,' he said, 'I'll give you a hundred thousand dollars of capital and a thousand square feet of warehouse space. Go start a wine division of Bailley and Son, and let me know how you do.'"

"That was quite an opportunity."

"I was flabbergasted, really. I walked out of his office in a daze. I don't think I slept for a week; I read every book about wine I could get my hands on, I visited every wine shop on the East Side, and I found an empty storefront on Madison Avenue and rented it. I invested most of my capital in California wines, and I took full page ads in the *Times* and sold at steep discounts. It was my only way into the market, and it worked; I turned a twenty thousand dollar profit my first year, and I established some invaluable contacts with growers. The business grew rapidly.

"Then, three years ago, I heard from a friend that Cornwall and Company, an old established London shipper and retailer, was about to go on the block. The last Cornwall was on his deathbed, and he had not done a good job with the business when he was healthy. They had a golden reputation and a severe cash-flow problem, and I persuaded Jock to go for it. I bought it from the widow a week after Cornwall died, and it's been the most fun I ever had."

"That's great," Peter said. "What happens now?"

Sandy finished his drink and signaled for another. "I don't know. If Jock had stayed healthy for another month, I'd have been a major stockholder in Bailley and Son."

"You mean you're not?"

"I own about three percent of the stock, but Jock was finally ready to do the right thing. The success of Cornwall finally convinced him that I was indispensable, I think, and he made me some extravagant promises."

"Which now, he may not be able to keep."

Sandy started on the new drink. "Right. I don't know why I'm telling you all this."

"Can I make a guess about something? The marriage to Joan isn't what it once was."

"Hasn't been for, I don't know, twelve, fifteen years."

"And Jock has a grandson?"

"Our boy, Angus."

"Is he in the business?"

"No, he opted for medicine; he's a resident in cardiology at Lenox Hill Hospital."

"Is Joan in the business?"

"Not up to now," Sandy replied.

"Suppose Jock dies tomorrow? What will Joan do?"

"She and her brother, Laddie, will inherit Bailley and Son. Except for my three percent, of course," he said ruefully. "And then I think it's likely that Joan will divorce me."

"Ahhhhh," Peter moaned softly. "She's got you between a stone and a very firm surface, hasn't she?"

"She has."

"Well, you're not alone, Sandy. I've been building my gallery for eighteen years, and it's become a regular cash cow. However, my wife of three years has just announced her intention to divorce me and marry a painter who I made into a giant of the art world."

"I'm sorry, Peter, that's a tough break."

"Tougher than you know. California is a community-property state."

Sandy let out a short, ironic laugh. "Believe me, if New York were a community-property state, *I'd* divorce *Joan*."

"It gets worse," Peter said. "Her new husband, the painter, will take most of my good artists with him, once the divorce and settlement are final. She'll take half the business, and then, together, they'll gut my half."

The captain came onto the loudspeaker system and announced their approach into Kennedy Airport.

"Sandy," Peter said, "did you enjoy the movie?"

"*Strangers on a Train*? Loved it. I must have seen it half a dozen times."

"Tell me, what went wrong with Bruno's plan for him to murder Guy's wife and for Guy to murder Bruno's father?"

Sandy thought for a moment. "Two things, I think; first of all, Guy didn't take Bruno's proposal seriously until it was too late, and second, and most important, Bruno was crazy."

"What do you think would have happened if Guy *had* taken Bruno's proposal seriously, and if Bruno *hadn't* been crazy?"

"Well, I think they would have pulled off two perfect murders." Sandy stopped talking and looked at Peter with new, if somewhat drunken awareness.

"Sandy, do you think I'm crazy?" Peter asked.

"I don't believe you are," Sandy replied.

"Do you think I'm a serious person?"

Sandy looked at Peter for a long time. "I believe you are," he said, finally.

The airplane touched down and taxied to the gate before anyone spoke again.

Peter stood up and stretched. "Perhaps we should talk again," he said.

"Perhaps we should," said Sandy.

CHAPTER

3

S andy sat next to the hospital bed and looked into
Jock Bailley's clear blue eyes. The two of them
were alone.

"Jock, can you understand me?" Sandy asked.

The eyes gazed into his, innocent, childlike, expres-
sionless. Jock's face had relaxed from its usual hauteur
into the soft, unworried face of an infant.

"Jock, I just wanted you to know that I'm here, and
that we all want you to get well," Sandy said.

A doctor entered the room and walked to the bedside. "I'm Stan Warner," he said, offering Sandy his
hand. "You're Mr. Bailley's son-in-law, aren't you?"

"Yes, I'm Sandy Kinsolving. Doctor, is he conscious?"

"He is, but he's aphasic."

"What does that mean?"

"He's unable to move very much or communicate in
any way."

"Does he understand what I say to him?"

"I'm afraid I can't give you a definitive answer on that. He may very well understand everything, or he may understand nothing; he may not even know who you are."

"Is he likely to recover to any extent?"

"Again, there's no definitive answer. He could improve dramatically over the next few weeks, or he could remain as he is until death."

"Is he out of danger?"

"He's stable for the moment, but at his age anything could happen."

"What is your experience of people his age recovering from something like this?"

"Let's step out into the hall, shall we?"

Sandy followed the doctor from the room.

Warner motioned Sandy to a bench and sat down beside him. "I'm told that Mr. Bailley was an extraordinarily vigorous man before his stroke."

"That's perfectly true," Sandy said. "I know sixty-year-olds who aren't as acute."

"That stands in his favor, of course, but you asked what my experience of this condition was in people of his age."

"That's what I want to know."

"Not good. Of course, few people his age are in as good a condition, so it's hard to apply my experience. I just haven't had a patient like Mr. Bailley before."

"I see."

"I wish I could give you more solid information, but the statistical likelihood is that he will decline over a period of weeks or months, then die peacefully. Of course, he could have another stroke at any moment, and another one would likely kill him immediately.

However, there's no accounting for the human will. From what I've heard of Mr. Bailley, he could still have the resources to make a significant recovery and live for years more. There's no way to tell how much brain damage he's suffered, so he might need considerable rehabilitative therapy in the event of a partial recovery."

Sandy looked up and saw his wife and son coming down the hallway. He stood up, kissed Joan on the cheek and hugged Angus. "You've both met Doctor Warner?"

"Yes," Joan said.

"I came straight here from the airport," Sandy said. "I was afraid—"

"Have you seen him?" Joan asked.

"Just for a moment. He's awake, but—"

"Aphasic," Angus said.

"Yes, Doctor Warner has been explaining his condition. It seems that it's difficult to predict what will happen."

"His heart's still strong," Angus said. "I'm betting on some kind of recovery."

"I hope that happens," Dr. Warner said. "Well, if you'll all excuse me, I have some patients to see. Page me if you need anything at all." He walked away down the hall.

"He seems like a good man," Sandy said.

"The best," Angus agreed. "Grandad's lucky to have him."

"There doesn't seem to be anything I can do here," Sandy said. "I think I'll go home. Joan, will you come with me? Albert's still downstairs."

"Yes, I think so," his wife replied. "Angus, you'll call us the moment there's any change?"

"Of course, Mother."

Sandy took his wife's arm and walked her to the elevators.

• • •

Albert, Jock Bailley's longtime servant, stopped the car in front of the Fifth Avenue apartment and opened the trunk for the doorman to collect the bags.

Sandy greeted the doorman and the lobby man, then got into the lift. Joan was silent all the way to their floor. The elevator opened directly into their foyer, and Sandy used his key to let them into the large apartment. It had been bought with money from a trust that Jock had established for Joan when she was born. Although Sandy was well paid at Bailley & Son, he never would have managed anything on the scale at which they were now living. There were fourteen rooms in the apartment, and three maid's rooms. Today, the servants were nowhere to be seen.

Sandy followed Joan into the bedroom, undoing his tie and getting out of his jacket.

"You must be tired," she said solicitously.

"Yes, I think I'll sleep for a while."

"You should have taken the Concorde," she said. "You'd have been here earlier and you'd have been a lot fresher, too."

"Tell you the truth, it never crossed my mind. Anyway, Jock would have had another stroke if he'd thought I'd spent that much money on a flight to see him."

She smiled. "You're right about that, I guess."

He sat down on the edge of the bed and untied his shoes. "I still can't believe it's happened."

"Neither can I."

"How's Laddie taking it?"

"Like a Scot. He's worried, of course, but he's at the office today."

"I guess I'd better go down there tomorrow and talk to him about what to do."

"What to do?"

"About the business; how to divide up the responsibilities. With Jock out of the business, it's going to take some redrawing of the lines of authority. I mean, Jock was doing as much as ever, you know, running the place with an iron hand."

"Yes, I suppose he was. Well, Laddie can handle it, can't he?"

"He won't have to handle it all, you know. I can take up a lot of the slack."

"Mmmm, I suppose," Joan said absently. "You get some sleep. Shall I wake you for some dinner?"

"No, let me sleep straight through, if I can. I'll be fine tomorrow."

"As you wish." She left the room, closing the door silently behind her.

Sandy hung up his suit in his dressing room, stuffed the trees into his shoes, got into a nightshirt and went to bed.

His last conscious thought was of Jock's shining infant's eyes.

Sandy woke in a dark room and got up to go to the bathroom. He didn't notice until he returned that Joan had not been to bed. He picked up the bedside clock and looked at its luminous face. Just after 3:00 A.M. He switched on a lamp and saw a folded note on his bedside table.

I'm at the hospital. J.

Sandy started getting dressed.

As he got off the elevator Sandy saw the little group standing in the hall outside Jock's room. Joan, Laddie and his wife, Betty, and Angus, still in his white coat.

"What's happened?" he asked as he walked up to them.

Nobody seemed inclined to reply.

"Daddy had another stroke," Joan said, brushing away a tear.

"Why didn't you wake me?"

"I didn't think it was necessary."

"Well, how is Jock?"

Angus spoke up. "Dad, the stroke cost Grandad even the most basic functions; we had to put him on a respirator."

"Oh, no," Sandy breathed.

"We disconnected the respirator ten minutes ago. Grandad died almost immediately."

"What?" Sandy said.

Joan spoke. "Daddy had a living will; it expressly said that he wanted no dramatic measures to keep him alive. We all talked about it and decided to honor his wishes. Doctor Warner agreed."

Sandy sank onto a bench and stared at the wall opposite him. "Poor Jock," he said.

Laddie spoke for the first time. "He had a long and productive life, and he was never ill, until the end. I think this is exactly how he would have wanted to go."

"Perhaps you're right," Sandy agreed.

"I think we should all go home and rest," Laddie said. "I've already phoned the funeral directors, and they'll collect the body in the morning. Let's meet tomorrow for lunch and discuss the arrangements."

"Fine," Sandy said.

"Come to lunch at our place," Joan said.

Laddie nodded his agreement and bade them goodnight.

Sandy stood and put a hand on his son's shoulder. "If your shift is finished, why don't you come home with us and stay for lunch tomorrow? You should be in on this."

The three of them took a cab back to the Fifth Avenue apartment. All the way, Sandy tried to think about the future, but he couldn't manage it; he was too sad.

The following morning, Sandy rose early, slipped into some jeans and went for a walk. A couple of blocks away he stopped at a pay phone and dialed a number.

"Hotel Pierre," the operator said.

"Mr. Peter Martindale," Sandy said.

"Hello?" Peter's voice.

"It's your traveling companion of yesterday."

"Oh, yes, how are you?"

"I'm not sure. Perhaps we could meet? Very discreetly?"

"Of course," Peter replied. "I'm looking out the window at Central Park. If you enter the park from the corner of Fifth Avenue and Central Park South, you come to a long row of benches. I'll be sitting on one at four o'clock; you sit at the other end and read a newspaper; don't acknowledge me at all."

"Four o'clock, then," Sandy said. He hung up the phone and walked slowly back to his apartment house.

CHAPTER

They sat down to lunch at one o'clock. When the food had been served the servants left the room and the family was alone. They ate nearly silently, and when the dishes had been cleared and coffee served, Laddie, who sat at the head of the table, in Sandy's usual place, took a document from his pocket.

"Father left explicit instructions," he said. "They're brief; I'll read them to you: 'I wish my body to be cremated as soon as possible after my death and my ashes to be buried in my family's plot in Aberdeen, Scotland, without ceremony. If my family and friends wish to hold a memorial service at a later date, they may do so. All my other intentions have been outlined in my will, which is in my office safe, and a copy of which has been deposited with my attorney.' It's signed and dated January first of last year."

Laddie laid the document on the table. "I have already given the funeral directors their instructions. The ashes will remain with them until I can get away to take them to Aberdeen. I'll try to do it next week.

"I went to the office this morning, and in the presence of Father's secretary and two other employees, opened his safe and removed the will." He removed another document from his pocket and laid it on the table. "I don't know that we need a formal reading, as its instructions are very simple. There are approximately a million and a half dollars in bequests to servants and charities. Apart from that, there is a bequest to Angus of five million dollars, in trust until his thirtieth birthday, and one to Sandy of half a million dollars, to be paid outright. He left the company to Joan and me in equal shares. I am his executor. I will set up your trust as soon as possible, Angus, and I'll disburse your bequest as soon as the will has been probated, Sandy. Does anyone have any questions?"

Everyone was silent.

"The will is here, if anyone wishes to read it," Laddie said. With that, he rose. "If you'll excuse me, I think I should get back to the office to begin overseeing the necessary changes there." He nodded to them all and left, his wife on his arm.

Angus rose and kissed his mother on the cheek. "If you'll excuse me, Mother, Dad, I have to be back at the hospital." He left Sandy and Joan sitting at the table.

Joan spoke first. "I expect this must come as something of a shock to you, Sandy."

"What?" Sandy said, popping out of a daze.

"The will, and the bequest to you."

"Well, it wasn't what he had intended to do as recently as last week," he replied.

"What do you mean?"

"I mean that he called me into his office and said that he was grateful to me for my loyalty to him and the company, and that he intended to leave me the wine division. He said he would be making a new will shortly."

"Did anyone else overhear this conversation?" Joan asked.

"No, but he said he would tell Laddie about it. And, of course, his lawyer."

"Laddie has said nothing of this, and when I spoke to the lawyer this morning, he made no mention of it, either. Not that it matters, of course. That document there," she pointed at the will, "is his last and very legal testament."

Sandy folded his napkin and placed it on the table. "I'd better get down to the office and help Laddie." He started to rise.

"I don't think that will be necessary, Sandy," Joan said.

Sandy sat down again. "What do you mean?" he asked.

"Laddie and I talked this morning. We feel that you should leave the company with immediate effect."

"*What?*"

"We both feel that it would be best if Laddie managed the company alone. I'll be joining the board. We'll buy your three percent of the company at book value, or you can keep the stock and collect dividends, if you wish. We would prefer to buy you out and keep all the stock in the family."

"Am I no longer in the family?" he asked, as calmly as he could manage.

"Sandy, our marriage has been an empty one for both of us for years; it's my very strong feeling that we should end it as soon as possible."

"And how long have you been planning this, Joan?" he asked.

"It's been on my mind for some time. I'm sure it's crossed yours, as well. I've been seeing someone else for some months."

"Oh? And who would that be?"

"Terrell duBois," she said.

"Holy Christ," Sandy said. Terrell duBois was the chairman of the wine division's principal competitor, duBois & Blanche. "Isn't Terrell married?"

"Yes, but that will come to an end in due course. Sandy, I would very much like all this to be as amiable as possible. You needn't move out of the apartment immediately—shall we say, the end of the month? I haven't told anybody about this, not even Laddie or Terrell, in any specific terms, and I think it would be in your best interests if we handled this calmly."

"In my best interests?"

"Laddie and I are inclined to be generous in the terms of your leaving the company, if you are cooperative. Should you decide to make a fuss, either over the divorce or over this alleged plan of Daddy's, then we will do only what is required of us by law. I hope I make myself clear."

"You certainly do," Sandy said.

"Please don't mention this to Angus just yet. Around the end of the month we'll formalize our arrangements, and Angus can be told then. I don't mind if you sniff around for another job between now and then. I'm sure you will find something suitable."

"You're planning to sell the wine division to duBois & Blanche, aren't you?"

"It crossed my mind. Laddie, as you know, has no interest in wine, and I can't see him paying some expert a lot of money and stock to run a division that has always been something of an embarrassment to him. He was very hurt when Daddy agreed to let you start a new division, you know."

"He never said anything but congratulations," Sandy said.

"Laddie always did hold in his emotions," Joan said. "By the way, although you will be, for all practical purposes, a free man at the end of the month, I do wish you to keep up appearances until that time."

"What sort of appearances?"

"Well, we do have some dinner invitations this month, and, you will recall, on Saturday night we have the Hamptons Hunt Ball, at the Waldorf. Since we are both on the board of the recipient charity, I think it would be proper to appear there. Do I have your agreement? Will you behave, just until the end of the month?"

"All right."

"Thank you, Sandy; I knew you would behave well about all this." She rose and left the room.

Sandy sat at the table, still stunned. He thought he had been prepared for the worst, but this went far beyond anything he had imagined. They were going to sell his wine division to Terrell duBois, and he was going to be on the street. True, he'd have a million or so in his pocket, from Jock's bequest and the sale of his stock, but that was a fraction of what he'd have had if Jock had lived to keep his commitment. Everything would be gone—his business, the London life, the grand apartment, the social status. He was out, and that was it.

He got to the park early, picked a bench and pretended to read his paper. He did not want to look despondent should he be seen by someone he knew. He sat there, running his situation over and over in his mind. He had made up his mind not to keep this appointment. He had been sure that, whatever happened between him and Joan, he could, somehow, make it right, or, at least, acceptable. Then he began to think about something else.

"Good afternoon," a voice said, and he jumped. "Don't look at me; just concentrate on your paper. We can hear each other very well."

Sandy resisted the temptation to turn and look at Peter Martindale. Instead, he folded his paper back to expose the crossword puzzle, took out his pen, and pretended to do it. Surreptitiously, he glanced around to see who might be within earshot. The park was by no means deserted, but the benches on either side of them were empty.

"You got here first," Peter said. "May I take that to mean that you are eager to get on with this?"

"You may," Sandy replied.

"You were pretty drunk on the airplane; do you remember what we discussed?"

"I do. We discussed removing the errors in *Strangers on a Train*."

"Yes, we did. Now we have to face what that means; it means that you and I are contemplating each committing a murder on a stranger. Do you think you can actually do that?"

"All I have to do is pretend she's my wife," Sandy said. "What about you? Can you pull this off?"

"Oh, yes," Peter said. "I can absolutely pull it off. I'll need your help, though, in planning it."

"And I yours," Sandy replied.

"Of course. All we have to do is pretend that we are murdering our own wives, then have the other step in and do it."

"That's about right, I'd say."

"Have you ever killed anyone, Sandy?"

"No, but I believe I can do it, especially if it's a stranger."

"We each have to do it without getting caught."

"Of course," Sandy replied. "That's understood. I don't believe either of us is interested in getting caught."

"Our best defense, even if suspected, is that we are completely unacquainted with our victims. And with each other. That last point is extremely important. We must never be seen in the same place again; we'll have to communicate through other means."

"What means?"

"I had in mind public telephones. You pick a couple of telephones in New York and memorize the numbers. I'll do the same in San Francisco. If either of us wants to contact the other, he calls from a public telephone, asks for, say, Bart, and is told by the other he has the wrong number. Two hours after the call, he goes to the appropriate pay telephone and waits to be called there. Mind you, even on public phones, we have to be circumspect. You can never tell when someone might accidentally be cross-connected."

"That sounds like a good plan. Who goes first?"

"I don't think we need flip a coin," Peter said. "If you're ready to proceed, well, I'm already in New York. If you can plan something the next few days, I'll stay on and do the deed."

"How about Saturday night?"

"The day after tomorrow? Ideal, but what's the plan?"

"She and I are attending a charity ball that night. We've done this a hundred times, and it's always the same; we leave the apartment at eight and take the elevator to the ground floor of our building. She stays in the elevator, continuing to the basement, while I ask the doorman to get a cab for us."

"Why would she go to the basement?"

"Each apartment in the building has a storage room in the basement. I keep some out-of-season clothes and some wine in ours, and she keeps her furs there because it's cool, and her major jewelry is kept in a safe in the storeroom."

"It's always the same?"

"Always, for an event like this one. She won't need a fur at this time of year, of course, but she will certainly want her diamond necklace, and that's always kept in the safe. The insurance company insists, and we're not covered if it's stolen from the apartment."

"Very good, I like it," Peter replied. "How do I get into the basement?"

"I had extra keys made an hour ago," Sandy said. "One to the outside door, and one to the storage room. I'll pass them to you before we part company." He gave Peter the address of the building.

"That's up near the Metropolitan Museum, isn't it?"

"Right. On the side street, there's a flight of stairs leading down to the basement door. A black, wrought-iron railing conceals the stairs from the street. Every evening around six, the janitor brings out the trash from the building and stacks it in the gutter nearby. Often, he doesn't close the door properly, so you may not even need the key. He's always finished by six-thirty, because he wants to get home for dinner. Watch the stairs for him and the block for foot traffic; sometime between six-thirty and seven-thirty, let yourself into the building. Our storage room is the one nearest the door, on the right. Let yourself into the storage room and wait there for her. I'll leave the rest to you, but when it's done, don't linger; get the hell out of there, and don't let yourself be seen on the street. That's all there is to it."

"Let me see," Peter said, and he went over the whole thing aloud again. "Why would the janitor be putting out rubbish on a Saturday night? Surely the city doesn't collect on a Saturday."

"We have a private service, and they pick up seven days a week. The basement doesn't have enough room to store the trash for more than twenty-four hours."

"Good. Do you want me to get the keys back to you?"

"No, dispose of them immediately in a way that they can't possibly be found. They could tie you and me to the event."

"Of course. How about San Francisco Bay?"

"How about the East River? Don't hang on to them a minute longer than you need to. And be sure you don't leave any trace of yourself—fingerprints, fibers, anything."

"Right. When I'm back in San Francisco, should I call you at your office to leave the phone numbers?"

"I won't be going to the office. Call the apartment." He gave Peter the number, and then told him to call only if it was absolutely necessary. "And don't say anything unless I answer. Ask for Bart, then recite the number twice. When I come to San Francisco to keep my part of the bargain, I'll do the same. It would be better if we didn't talk at all again until I come out there."

"I think you're right about that," Peter said. "But I want you to call me on Saturday afternoon at the Pierre and confirm our arrangements. If it's a go, just say, 'This is Bart, everything is fine'; if not, say 'This is Bart, everything is off,' then hang up. If I shouldn't be in at that moment, leave the same message with the operator. The Pierre is very good about messages."

"All right," Sandy said. "Anything else?"

"I think it would be good if we considered the worst. Suppose one of us is caught or suspected."

"I won't implicate you," Sandy said. "If I'm caught, it'll be my own fault. It wouldn't go any easier for me if I incriminated you, and vice versa."

"I agree," Peter said. "I wish we could shake hands on it, but I think we'd better just leave. You go first, and leave the keys on the bench."

"Right; good-bye and good luck."

"Same to you."

Sandy eased the keys from his pocket, wiped them carefully on his coattail, and set them on the bench. He got up and walked away, tossing his newspaper into a waste bin. At the corner, he looked back. The bench was empty.

CHAPTER

5

Sandy left the park feeling as though he had just performed some daredevil stunt, and lived. He walked slowly up Fifth Avenue toward his apartment building, taking deep breaths, his heart pumping furiously.

Joan deserved this for treating him as she had; she thought she could walk away from the marriage with his business in her pocket, probably to sell it to Terrell duBois, and that that would put a dagger through his heart, retribution for his unfaithfulness. But who was responsible for his being unfaithful for all these years? Who but Joan? She had been loving, then after Angus was born, she became cool, then icy, then simply rock hard. His role in her life was to escort her to social events, a role he would play for the last time on Saturday evening.

By the time he reached the building his heart had returned to its normal rate after a walk, and his breathing was steady. He greeted the doorman and the lobby man and took the elevator to his apartment. It was Joan's, of course, but soon it would be his.

For two more days Sandy held his secret in his heart, feeling no doubt, anticipating the event. He felt this way until the moment he heard his son's voice on the telephone.

"Hi, Dad, I've got a day off, believe it or not." It was Saturday, the morning of the big day. "How about some tennis?"

"Sounds good," Sandy said automatically. "Meet me at the Racquet Club as soon as you can get there; I'll ring for a court, and we can have some lunch afterward."

"I'm on my way."

The voice had introduced a note of complexity to his feelings, and when he saw his son, standing in the lobby of the venerable club on Park Avenue, things got worse. Angus was taller than he, like his grandfather, and with Jock's prominent nose and receding hair. The strange science of genetics had skipped a generation, bypassing Sandy completely. For the first time Sandy thought of old Jock and what he would think of all this. Jock, the strict moralist, in his way, would be ashamed of him, he knew. They hugged and headed for the elevators.

Sandy had given up squash after Angus had read in a medical journal of the deaths of a large number of fit, middle-aged men on squash courts who were unable to tolerate the wild bursts of cardiorespiratory action required by the frequent spurts of activity during squash. He had taken up tennis again, after an absence of fifteen years from the sport, and he enjoyed playing with his son, who, although younger, was less crafty on the court. The two were, therefore, about evenly matched.

They changed in the locker room and walked out onto the court. The club was not crowded on a Saturday in May, the members mostly being at their country homes on Long Island or in Connecticut, and they had not had to wait for a court.

Sandy parried his son's power game with lots of spin, drop shots, and wily ball placement, and their match was close, but Angus took him in two straight sets. Two was enough for Sandy; some of his energy had gone elsewhere.

They sat in the grill and ate unhealthy bacon cheese-burgers, washed down with Dutch beer, and Sandy mostly listened. Angus was excited about the approaching end of his residency the following month.

"I'm thinking about establishing a practice of my own right away," he said.

"Wouldn't it be wiser to get some more experience with an established doctor?" Sandy asked.

"Ordinarily, yes. But I'm thinking about a new kind of cardiology, one that starts with a group of patients my own age and concentrates on fitness and diet. I'd rather keep well people healthy than treat sick ones," he said.

"How will you attract your first patients?" Sandy asked, interested.

"I'll advertise in the *New York Times* and the *Wall Street Journal*. Doctors can advertise, now, you know, and my generation is a lot more fitness-oriented than yours. My inheritance will make it possible for me to find good office space and fund the ad campaign right away, without waiting. Mom and Uncle Laddie are my trustees, and I'm sure they'll go along with the plan."

"I'm sure they will."

Angus suddenly looked embarrassed. "Dad, I'm sorry about the will; I don't know why Granddad treated you the way he did, after all your years with him."

"He told me a couple of weeks ago that he was going to leave me the wine division," Sandy said. "He died before he could execute a new will, I guess."

"That's terrible. What are you going to do?"

"Well, I don't think I want to work for Laddie. He's a good fellow, but he's never cared anything about the wine division. If anything, it's always been something of an embarrassment for him, I think, because his brother-in-law thought of it and made it work."

Angus nodded. "I had figured something like that. I'm planning to budget a million dollars for my practice—that will include an extensive athletic facility—and as far as I'm concerned, you can use the other four million to start a new wine company, if that's what you want."

Sandy was unable to respond for a moment. He fought tears, and cleared his throat to make sure it was still working. "Son, that's a very kind offer, but to tell you the truth, I don't know what I want to do. I'm a bit at sea."

Angus placed a hand on Sandy's forearm. "Just remember, I want to help. I'll make Mom and Uncle Laddie see it my way."

Sandy raised his beer mug in a mute toast.

"Dad, yours and Mom's marriage has always been kind of different, hasn't it?"

"Different from what?" Sandy asked, surprised. Angus had never before mentioned such a thing.

"Different from other people's marriages, I mean."

"In what way?"

"Well, I can't remember you and Mom ever showing much affection for each other, and to tell the truth, I've always enjoyed the company of both of you more when you weren't together."

Sandy stared down at the table. "I don't know that I could explain our marriage to you, Angus," he said. "I've never even tried to explain it to myself. The fact is, we both would have been happier if we'd ended it years ago."

"Did Granddad have anything to do with your staying together?"

"Not directly, but of course, I worked for him, and I loved my work, and I'm not sure I could have continued there if your mother and I had parted."

Angus nodded. "Well, I guess each of us does what he has to in order to do the thing he wants most to do."

"That's a very sage observation from such a new physician," Sandy said.

They both laughed, and soon Angus was on his way somewhere.

Walking back to the apartment, Sandy's emotions were in turmoil. In a few hours, he planned to murder Angus's mother, or at least, have her murdered, and tomorrow he would have to face his son and pretend to be sad about her death.

Sandy had never been very introspective, but now he looked inside himself and asked the hard question. Am I a murderer? Can I do it and live with myself? Can I do it and live with my son? He started to think about what life would be like without the wine division and the Fifth Avenue apartment and the house on Nantucket and the club memberships, but he stopped himself. Those things were not relevant to the kind of man he was. Could he be who he was and start being someone else tomorrow?

"I am not a murderer," he said aloud to himself. "I am not, and I never can be." He was not particularly religious, but he felt that criminals, especially murderers, received some sort of higher justice, something beyond the courts and prisons and various methods of ending the lives of those who had killed. He stopped next to a pay phone. "I am not a murderer," he said.

He put a quarter in the phone and got the number from information, then dropped another coin into the machine and dialed the number.

"Hotel Pierre," a woman's voice said.

"I'd like to speak to Mr. Peter Martindale," Sandy said.

"One moment." A ringing ensued, then stopped. "There's no answer from that suite; would you like to leave a message?"

"Yes," Sandy replied, "and it is most urgent that Mr. Martindale receive the message."

"It's our practice to immediately put the message under the door of the suite and to turn on the flashing message light," she said. "Mr. Martindale is unlikely to miss it."

"Good. Would you please tell him that Bart called," he spelled it for her, "and that the project has been canceled, everything is off."

"I've got that," she said. "Would you like me to connect you with the concierge? Mr. Martindale would have to pass his desk, and he could also deliver the message directly."

"Yes, thank you." Sandy repeated the message and its urgency to the concierge.

"I'll be certain that he gets it," the concierge said. "Mr. Martindale said he was going out for only a short time, so he should have it soon."

Sandy hung up and continued his walk toward the apartment building. He felt somewhat lighter on his feet and in his heart. On Monday, he'd see a good lawyer and find out what could be done to negotiate a better settlement with Joan and Laddie. After all, he wasn't stone broke; he had what he had saved and invested, that was around a million dollars, and he had the half million from Jock. He could get started again, at least in a small way. Maybe he could find some investors. His son had already expressed a willingness to help. He walked on, reflecting on how close he had come to ruining his life, to jeopardizing his reputation and his personal freedom.

He must have been temporarily mad, he thought, turning into the lobby. Well, he was sane now, and he would simply make the best of things.

CHAPTER

6

At seven forty-five Sandy knotted his black satin bow tie and slipped into his dinner jacket. He slipped the Patek-Phillipe pocket watch into his waistcoat pocket and ran the chain through its special buttonhole. Satisfied with his appearance, he left his dressing room and walked across the bedroom. Joan was on schedule, which meant she would be ready about ten minutes after he told her what time they must leave.

He went into his study and, dabbing a light film of perspiration on his forehead, sank into a chair and picked up the telephone. He had a slightly queasy feeling in his stomach, and he wanted to make it go away. He dialed the Pierre and asked for the concierge.

"This is Mr. Bart," he said to the man. "I left a message a couple of hours ago for Mr. Peter Martindale."

"Oh, yes sir, the urgent one. I handed it to him

myself half an hour later, so you may be sure he got it."

"Did he read it in your presence?" Sandy asked.

"Yes, sir, he did."

"What was his reaction?"

"He looked, well, relieved, I suppose. He asked me to get him on an evening flight for San Francisco, and he checked out about an hour ago."

"I see. Thank you very much indeed," Sandy said. He hung up the phone feeling elated. He had been afraid of some slip-up, of Peter's somehow not getting the message.

"Are you ready, Sandy?"

Sandy looked up, surprised. Joan was ready on the stroke of eight o'clock.

"Yes, let's go down. Albert is collecting us first, and we'll pick up Laddie and Betty on the way to the Waldorf."

"Fine," she said.

In the elevator she was quiet, primping in the mirror, making tiny adjustments to her clothing and makeup. The elevator stopped at the main floor.

"I'll go down with you," Sandy said suddenly.

"That's not necessary, Sandy."

"Well, it's dark down there, and you know that outside door doesn't always close the way it should."

"You're very solicitous this evening," she said.

"Just part of the service." He managed a smile.

The old elevator door took some time to close, and as it began to, Albert, Jock's longtime servant and driver, stopped it. "Excuse me, Mr. Kinsolving," he said, "but Mr. Laddie is on the car phone for you."

"He probably thinks we'll be late," Joan said. "You'd better reassure him."

"All right," Sandy said, stepping out of the car. Then he

had a thought. "Albert, will you go down to the basement with Mrs. Kinsolving? I'd rather she didn't go alone."

"Really, Sandy, I've done it a thousand times," Joan said irritably.

Sandy took Albert by the elbow and guided him into the elevator. "I'll wait for you in the car," he said.

Joan glared at the ceiling.

Sandy strode through the lobby and got into the back seat of the old Cadillac. It was an old-fashioned limousine, with jump seats, not the contemporary stretched job that took up half a block. He picked up the phone. "Laddie?"

"Yes, Sandy. I tried the apartment, but you were gone. I take it you're on time?"

"Yes, we are; we should be there in under ten minutes; Joan's just getting her jewelry from downstairs."

"Well, I'm glad I caught you. Betty is unwell; she's dressed and everything, but she's just tossed her cookies into a flower pot, and she's a distinct shade of green. Will you forgive us?"

"Of course, Laddie; tell Betty I hope she feels better soon. Get some Pepto-Bismol into her."

"Right," Laddie said. "See you later." He hung up.

Sandy replaced the phone on its cradle, and remembered what a hard time he had had getting Jock to install the thing. Once he had had it, though, he had begun terrorizing the office the moment he left home, and he started again the moment he drove away from the office. The staff had talked of sabotaging the car phone.

Sandy glanced at his watch: ten past eight. He looked out the open door of the car and into the building: No sign of Joan and Albert. He rested his head against the back of the seat and thought. Monday, he'd see a lawyer, then ask for a meeting with Laddie, to give him the opportunity of doing the right thing. He hoped there'd be no necessity for a lawsuit.

"Mr. Kinsolving?"

Sandy jumped. Barton, the doorman, stood at the open car door. "Yes, Barton?"

"Sorry, sir, I've just come off my break, and I saw you in the car. Can I get you anything?"

"No, thank you, Barton, but could you have a look in the basement and see what's keeping Mrs. Kinsolving and Albert? I'm deep in thought, here."

"Of course, Mr. Kinsolving." Barton disappeared.

Sandy returned to his reverie. If Laddie didn't make a better offer, perhaps he'd entertain a sale, at the right price, of course. He couldn't see Laddie paying a new executive a high salary to come in and run the division; neither could he see Laddie wanting to do it himself. Sandy closed his eyes.

"Mr. Kinsolving!" Barton's voice was urgent.

"Yes, Barton?"

"You'd better come with me, sir," Barton said. "I don't know what's happened."

"What?" Sandy asked, confused, but Barton was already headed back inside.

Sandy snapped back to reality and got out of the car. She's having trouble with the lock, he thought; that's happened before. But his heart was beating fast. He saw Barton whisper something to the lobby man, Jimmy, and Jimmy picked up the telephone. The elevator was waiting.

The doors closed and the old elevator crept downward. "What's wrong?" Sandy asked.

"I think it would be better if you saw for yourself, sir," Barton said.

Sandy led the way from the elevator. He turned a

corner of the corridor and strode toward the storage room. The basement was lit by twenty-five-watt bulbs to save the building electricity, and Sandy could see ahead only dimly. Then, as he approached the storage room, he saw something blocking the corridor, something like a laundry bag. A few steps more and Sandy could see that Albert was lying across the hallway, his cap several feet away. He knelt beside the elderly man.

"Albert!" he said. "Can you hear me?"

Albert moaned and opened his eyes.

Then Sandy noticed that one side of his head was a dark color, and something was seeping down the servant's neck.

"Good God!" Sandy breathed. "Barton, call an ambulance!"

"I've already asked Jimmy to do that, sir," Barton replied.

Sandy reached for Albert's cap, then lifted the old man's head and let it down gently onto the cap. "Come with me," he said to Barton. He moved on down the hallway more gingerly, afraid of what he was going to find. The door to the storeroom stood ajar, but no light came from inside. Sandy reached into the room for the light switch, then flipped it on.

Joan lay on her back, her eyes open, staring at the ceiling. Her arms were askew, and her mouth was open. There were dark bruises on her throat. Across the room, the door to the old safe was open.

"Joan!" Sandy cried, moving to her side and slipping his hand under her head. He withdrew it quickly, and it came away bloody.

"Is she all right, sir?" Barton asked from behind her.

Sandy looked for a pulse at her wrist, then at her throat. "No, Barton," he said. "I don't think she's all right."

CHAPTER

Sandy sat in the lobby anteroom, a small, comfortably furnished lounge where those who had not been admitted to the apartments above could wait to be dealt with at the convenience of the building's occupants. He pulled his bow tie undone and leaned his head against the back of the leather couch, sighing deeply. He was alone in the anteroom, but a uniformed police officer stood just outside—protecting him or preventing him from leaving?

Had he done everything he could to prevent this? He had thought so, but he had been wrong, of course. Through my actions, he thought, I have caused the death of a human being. My wife is dead because of me. If I had just this one day to live over, he thought. No, this one week. I could change everything. No scotch on the airplane; no meeting with Martindale in the park; no trusting a concierge to deliver a message.

But now it was too late; he was helpless to change anything.

"Mr. Kinsolving?" a deep voice asked.

Sandy jerked back to the present. A tall, neatly dressed, black man stood beside the sofa; a shorter, balder, red-faced white man stood slightly behind him.

"Yes?" Sandy managed.

"I am Detective Alain Duvivier," the black man said.

"How do you do?" Sandy said. This was very odd; Duvivier had some sort of accent. "You're a *New York City* policeman?"

Duvivier smiled slightly. "I was born in Haiti," he said, "but I have been an American citizen for more than twenty years, and a New York City policeman for nearly as long."

"I see," Sandy said.

Duvivier indicated the man behind him. "This is Detective Leary," he said. "He is probably more what you expected."

"I didn't mean—"

"I understand," Duvivier said kindly. "I wonder if we might go to your apartment and talk there?"

"Of course," Sandy said, getting to his feet. He led the detectives to the elevator and pressed a button. The old car rose slowly. "I'm sorry, but it's an old elevator. We manage to keep it running."

Duvivier nodded.

At the eighteenth floor Sandy led them into his apartment, to his study, and offered them chairs, then took one himself.

"Mr. Kinsolving, are you quite all right?" Duvivier asked. "Would you like me to get you someone? A doctor? A relative?"

"I'm all right," Sandy replied. "I'm just . . . I don't know, *stunned*, I guess."

"That's quite understandable," Duvivier said. "Do you think you are up to answering some questions?"

"I think so."

"Please let me know if you grow tired and want to stop. Can I get you a drink of water?"

"No, no; I should be offering you something," Sandy said.

"Thank you, that's not necessary. May we begin?"

"Yes. What would you like to know?"

"Can you please tell me everything that happened this evening? Take your time, and be as thorough as you can."

"We were going out to a charity ball at the Waldorf Hotel," Sandy said. "We left the apartment shortly after eight and took the elevator downstairs. I got off in the lobby, and Joan—my wife—continued to the basement."

"Had you done this before? Allowed her to go to the basement alone, I mean."

"Nearly always," Sandy said. "We have a storage room in the basement, and Joan's furs and her best jewelry are kept there—the jewelry in a safe. Usually, if we're going to something dressy, Joan will go down to retrieve what she needs for the evening, while I ask the doorman to get us a cab."

"But you didn't need a cab this evening, did you?"

"No, a car was calling for us. It's funny, but I was going to ride down to the basement with Joan, but when the doors opened to the lobby, the driver, Albert, said that I had a telephone call on the car's phone."

"Why were you going to change your routine and go to the basement with your wife?" Duvivier asked.

"I don't know, exactly; I just had a feeling . . . "

"Of danger?"

"Not exactly; I just suddenly felt that I should go with her."

"But the telephone call made you change your mind?"

"Yes. So I asked Albert to accompany Joan. She protested, said she'd been down there hundreds of times, but I made Albert go. I suppose if I hadn't, I might be the one with the broken head. Still, I wonder if it might have been different if . . . " His voice trailed off.

"And who was on the telephone?"

"My brother-in-law, Joan's brother, Laddie. That is, John Bailley, Junior."

"And how long did you speak with him?"

"I don't know exactly, a few minutes, I suppose. He had called to say that his wife had become ill, and they wouldn't be able to go to the ball with us, as had been our plan. We were to have picked them up on the way. I was still talking to him when Barton, the doorman, came to get me. He took me downstairs. No, wait—he came to the car and asked if there was anything he could do for me. I looked at my watch and saw that Joan and Albert had been downstairs for some time. I still hadn't finished my conversation with Laddie—we briefly discussed some business—so I asked Barton to go and see what was keeping them. I was still on the phone when he came back and asked me to come downstairs with him."

Duvivier nodded. "Did anyone else witness any of this activity in the lobby or in the car? Any of the other occupants of the building?"

"Jimmy, the lobby man, was there. I suppose he might have."

"Why is the safe in your storage room, instead of in your apartment?"

"We forgot to provide for a wall safe when we were remodeling, years ago. Then quite a large old safe became surplus at my office, and I bought it and had it delivered to the storage room. It was too large for any convenient place up here."

"Mr. Kinsolving, had the building ever had intruders in the basement before tonight?"

"Yes, as a matter of fact. Late last year—November or December, I think—the custodian found two boys trying to break into one of the storerooms. It seems that the outside door to the street hadn't closed properly, and they had sneaked in. They ran as soon as they saw him."

"Did this ever happen again?"

"I don't think so; I would have heard about it, I think. You see, I'm the president of the co-op board. The incident was discussed at our monthly meeting, and we authorized the purchase of a door-closing mechanism to make sure the door would close properly. My impression was that it worked pretty well. The custodian would know better than I."

"Perhaps you could tell me a little about the building and its tenants," Duvivier said.

"Well, it was built in the twenties; there are nineteen floors, with a single apartment on each floor. There are no tenants; each occupant owns his apartment. The owners are all people of substantial means—one of the board's requirements is that anyone buying an apartment must pay cash—no mortgages."

"That keeps the riffraff out, I suppose," Duvivier said.

"Not really," Sandy replied. "Quite a lot of riffraff can buy an apartment for cash these days. The board has other requirements."

"What sort of requirements?"

"Well, an owner may not conduct a business from his apartment; his financial statement must show that he can raise the purchase cash without borrowing on other assets; he may not have a criminal record or a history of fractious litigation; he must produce a number of excellent references, including some from his previous abode and neighbors. That sort of thing. Anyone who can meet all the requirements is very likely to be a good neighbor."

"Are there any restrictions as to race or religion?" Duvivier asked.

"No. Of our nineteen families, seven are Jewish, three are black, and one Hispanic," Sandy replied.

"And how do you determine if an applicant has a criminal record?" Duvivier asked.

"The building has nine employees. Three of them—the three lobby men—are retired New York City policemen, who are armed at all times. One of them makes enquiries about criminal records; I'm not quite sure how they go about it."

Duvivier smiled. "I see. How long have you lived in the building?"

"Fourteen years."

"May I ask, did you purchase your apartment for cash?"

"Yes, from my wife's trust fund."

"Your wife was wealthy in her own right, then?"

"Moderately so. When we bought the apartment we paid probably a fifth or sixth of what it would bring now."

"Are you independently wealthy, Mr. Kinsolving?"

"No. I mean, I earn a good living, and I have some investments, but my wife has always been wealthier than I."

"Mr. Kinsolving, forgive me for asking this, but have you and your wife recently had any domestic difficulties?"

Sandy took a deep breath. Who else had Joan told? Best to be frank. "Yes and no. I mean, no, we have had no quarrels or upheavals, but nevertheless, earlier this week my wife expressed the intention of getting a divorce."

"Did she say why?"

"She said she was in love with another man."

"And his name?"

"Terrell duBois."

"Is Mr. duBois known to you?"

"Yes, he is a business competitor of mine."

"What is your business, sir?"

"I am senior vice-president of John Bailley & Son, who are importers and distributors of wine and spirits. I run the wine division."

"And Mr. duBois is in the wine business?"

"Yes."

"Mr. Kinsolving, would a divorce from your wife make a material difference in the circumstances of your employment?"

"Possibly. Part of my conversation with Laddie on the car phone was directed at that. We both expressed a desire to meet and work out how the company would be run. You see, Joan and Laddie's father, Jock Bailley, passed away earlier in the week, so things were in a state of flux."

"I see," Duvivier replied. "I believe the scene in the basement has been cleared by now; I wonder if you would accompany us down there?"

"All right."

The three men got into the elevator and started down.

"May I ask, what is in the safe?" Duvivier asked.

"In the way of valuables, only my wife's jewelry. I only have a few things, and I've never bothered putting them in the safe. Other than her jewelry, there are various papers—insurance policies, some stock certificates, our wills."

They reached the basement and walked toward the storage room, stepping over a pool of blood where Albert's head had lain. The door to the storage room was ajar, and Sandy was relieved to see that Joan's body had been removed. There was, however, another pool of blood.

"Have you figured out what happened?" Sandy asked.

"This is preliminary, of course," Duvivier said, "but we believe the intruder was already in the building when Mrs. Kinsolving and the chauffeur got off the elevator. He probably stood in the shadows in that alcove, there, and waited for Mrs. Kinsolving to open the storage room and the safe."

"The safe was open?"

"I'll come to that in a moment. Apparently, Albert hung back a bit, and the intruder struck him in the back of the head with a fire extinguisher that was affixed to the wall in the alcove. He then went to the storage room and attacked Mrs. Kinsolving."

"I saw marks on her neck," Sandy said. "Was she strangled?"

"Yes, but her head also struck the concrete floor with some force, first. She was probably unconscious when she was strangled, so she would have experienced no distress."

"I'm glad of that," Sandy said, "but if her head had already struck the floor with enough force to leave that blood, surely she would have been unconscious. Why would he have strangled her? He didn't strangle Albert, did he?" It seemed best to ask the obvious questions.

"No, he didn't strangle Albert. Perhaps she saw his face, and he didn't want a witness left who could identify him."

"I see," Sandy muttered.

"Would you open the safe, please?"

Sandy knelt and, from memory, worked the combination, then swung open the door.

Duvivier pointed a small flashlight at the interior. "Would you see if there is anything missing, please?"

Sandy looked into the safe, then extracted a velvet-lined tray. "A necklace of diamonds and sapphires and a matching bracelet are both gone; they fit these indentations here. Joan had the trays made to accommodate specific pieces. I believe she was already wearing her diamond wristwatch."

"Then he waited until she had opened and closed the safe before he attacked her," Duvivier said. "Your wife was wearing no jewelry, so the pieces you mentioned were taken by the intruder."

"Oh," Sandy said, "she always wore her wedding and engagement rings. They were platinum and diamonds, and the engagement ring had a fine, emerald-cut diamond of about five carats."

"Is there anything special about these pieces that would make them easy to identify?" Duvivier asked.

"The rings had her initials, J.A.B.K., engraved inside, but I suppose the diamond could be extracted and sold. The watch had her name engraved on the back. But the necklace and bracelet have been photographed. They both belonged to the late Duchess of Windsor; Joan bought them at auction at Sotheby's some years ago. Both pieces appeared in the catalogue."

"That will be helpful," Duvivier said.

"Also, we gave the insurance company photographs of some pieces years ago, and I think the rings and the watch may have been among them."

Duvivier turned and faced Sandy. "Mr. Kinsolving, did you have anything to do with your wife's death?"

Sandy looked directly at the detective and all expression left his face. "Certainly not," he said firmly.

The two detectives got into their car and drove toward the precinct.

"Okay, Al, what do you think?" Leary asked.

"We still have to talk to the chauffeur and the brother-in-law and the custodian and the wife's lover and all the relatives," Duvivier said.

"Come on, Al," Leary laughed, "You got a famous nose. What does your nose tell you?"

Duvivier shrugged. "Kinsolving did it, but we won't be able to prove it."

"No shit?"

"*Pas de merde.*"

CHAPTER

8

Sandy sat and looked at his son and his brother-in-law. The three of them of them sat in the study, half-empty glasses of Bailley's Single Malt Scotch Whisky in their hands.

"I still can't believe it," Angus said.

"Neither can I," said Laddie.

"I know how you both feel," Sandy replied.

"What do you think are the chances of the cops catching the guy, Dad?" Angus asked.

"I don't know, really; the police didn't say anything about that. When he tries to sell the jewelry, though, that could get him caught."

Laddie shook his head. "He won't do that, if he has any sense; he'll break up the pieces and sell the stones separately."

"I suppose so," Sandy replied.

"God, as if one death in the family wasn't enough," Laddie said.

"Laddie," Sandy said, "since you've already been through making Jock's arrangements, I'd be very grateful if you'd do the same for Joan."

"Of course, Sandy. Do you have any preferences?"

Angus spoke up. "Why not just do the same as for Grandad? I'll volunteer to take the ashes to Scotland and bury them together."

"I think Joan would approve of that," Sandy said. "Thank you, son."

"I'll see to it," Laddie said, then made as if to get up. "I'd better get home and break the news to Betty."

"Before you go, Laddie, there's something I have to say to both of you." Sandy took a deep breath; he had been dreading this. "It's bound to become public knowledge, and I think it's better if you hear it from me."

Both men looked at Sandy expectantly.

"After our lunch of earlier this week, Joan told me that she intended to divorce me."

"*What?*" Angus blurted out.

"I know, it came as something of a surprise to me, too," Sandy said. "I think we had fallen into the usual ruts that so many long-married couples do, and that made Joan vulnerable."

"Vulnerable to what?" Angus asked.

"Another relationship. Joan told me that she had been seeing Terrell duBois, and my impression was that, after some interval, she planned to marry him."

"Is that the guy you compete with in the wine business?" Angus asked.

"Yes, that's the one." Sandy noted that Laddie had said nothing, had expressed no surprise. What he had to say next might make a dent. "The police asked me if

I had anything to do with Joan's death. I suppose they had to do that in the normal course of events."

A longer silence than Sandy would have liked ensued before Laddie spoke up. "But you were on the telephone with me," he said. "You couldn't have done it."

"I think that, after hearing of Joan's intentions, they thought that I, perhaps, had hired someone to do her in."

"That's ridiculous," Angus said immediately.

"Preposterous," Laddie agreed, after only a short pause.

"Thank you both for that, but I think you had better be prepared to see the possibility aired in the media. I'm assuming that they'll hear the details of the investigation; they seem to hear of everything these days."

"Well," Laddie said, "whatever has passed between you and Joan, I want you to know that no one who knows you at all could ever believe for a moment that you caused her death, and if I'm asked by anyone, I'll certainly say that."

"I appreciate your support, Laddie," Sandy said.

The three sat in silence for a moment, then Sandy spoke again. "Angus, you look all in; why don't you stay here tonight? Your room is always made up."

Angus rose. "Thanks, Dad, I'll take you up on that. All this has had the effect of exhausting me." He shook hands with his uncle, hugged his father, and went off to bed.

Laddie rose. "I'd better be off."

"Laddie," Sandy said, rising with him, "I expect Joan told you of some of this."

Laddie shrugged. "I was shocked, of course, but I didn't think I should say anything to you until she had spoken."

"She said the two of you wanted to buy me out."

"She said something about it to me, but I had by no means agreed; I would have talked with you first. I had planned to raise the subject on Monday."

"I think she would have asked you to sell the wine division to Terrell duBois."

Laddie looked guilty for a moment. "And undercut you? I'd never have done that."

Sandy didn't believe him for a moment. "Thank you, Laddie. I'll come in on Monday, and we'll talk."

"Of course, Sandy, but don't feel pressured to come in. I won't make any changes without consulting you."

The two men shook hands, and Laddie took his leave.

Sandy went to his desk and dug in the bottom drawer for copies of his and Joan's wills; the police had taken the originals from the safe. He sat down and read through Joan's document. It was the same one she had signed some five years before. He hoped to God that some lawyer would not come out of the woods with a newly executed document. That would make things very complicated indeed.

Then something else occurred to him, made his heart lurch. The pictures. Joan had said that she had pictures of him in the London flat with two women. He certainly did not want the police to have those. He went next door to Joan's study and tried the drawers of her desk. Locked. He thought of trying to pick the lock with a letter opener, but reconsidered; he didn't want scratches on the lock.

Worried now, he went to Joan's dressing room and began searching; the keys turned up in the box where she kept inexpensive jewelry. He went to the desk and unlocked it; immediately he recognized the brown envelope, the kind used in every office in Britain. He listened carefully to be sure Angus was not still about, then he shook out the photographs onto the desk. The first thing he saw was a closeup of his ass, the motion frozen. There were others, too, with the woman on top, with her head buried in his lap and a rather ecstatic look on his face, and there were, as Joan had said, two women. One was a countess, no less, the wife of his sometime dinner host, an earl—the sort of thing that divorce courts and the British tabloids would have loved. He looked into the envelope and found the negatives, and he was pitifully grateful to see them. There was also a slip of paper on which had been printed, "With the Compliments of the J. Morris Agency."

It took him a moment to figure out from where the shots had been taken, then he realized that, on at least two occasions, someone, probably Mr. J. Morris, himself, had been in the bedroom closet that Joan used when she was in London. The perfect vantage point; Sandy never opened that door.

He thought for a moment of the best way to dispose of these snapshots, someplace where the police would never find even a scrap of them. Not any of the fireplaces or trash baskets. He went into the kitchen, found a match and burned the pictures over the sink, turning on the garbage disposal to grind and flush away the ashes. He was tempted to keep one photograph—a lovely shot of the countess with his erect penis clasped in both her little hands—but, regretfully, he burned it with the rest.

He fell into bed, willing his mind to exclude any thought of what had happened that evening. He needed some time before he thought of that again.

Sandy slept solidly, dreamlessly until after nine in the morning, and when he awoke he felt the disorientation that he often knew in strange places, but never in his own bedroom. Then, before he could lift his head, the previous evening flooded back, and this time, he let it come. Best to face it, put it in perspective. He couldn't be blamed for what had happened to Joan, could he? After all, he had done everything in his power to stop it. Not exactly. He had started everything with the meeting in the park with Peter Martindale. But, of course, Joan, herself, bore some responsibility for what had happened to her, because of her treatment of him, didn't she. He considered that for a moment, then, with some effort, absolved himself of all guilt. It didn't work.

He found Angus in the kitchen eating cereal.

"Morning, Dad, how are you feeling?"

"All right, I think. Amazingly enough, I slept well."

Angus nodded. "So did I. It's a phenomenon called 'self-anesthetization,' I think; a defense of the mind."

"It really happened, didn't it?" Sandy asked.

"It did, I'm afraid. By the way, a Detective Duvivier called, asked that you phone him back. The number's on the pad by the phone."

"I'll call him in a little while," Sandy said, pouring himself some orange juice.

"Pretty fancy name for a cop, isn't it? Duvivier?"

"He's Haitian; a rather elegant fellow."

"Is he the one who thinks you had Mom killed?"

"I don't know if he really thinks that, or if he just had to ask."

"Don't worry, if he really suspected you, he'd have read you your rights first. If he didn't do that, he can't use anything you said against you."

"Why doesn't that make me feel better, I wonder?"

"About Duvivier?"

"Yes. I mean, although I had nothing to do with Joan's death, it's bad enough that a policeman might *think* I did."

"Never mind what he thinks," Angus said. "It's enough that *you* know you're innocent. If you didn't do it, he can't prove you did it, right?"

"How do you know all this police stuff, Angus? We didn't send you to law school, did we?"

"I never miss 'NYPD Blue'; it's an education."

Sandy nodded. "Are you on duty today?"

"I was, but I called in. Strangely enough, I think I could have worked, but I thought it might look funny if I came in only a few hours after my mother died."

"I appreciate your offer to go to Scotland; I don't think I would have wanted to make the trip."

"I was going to take a couple of weeks off after I'm certified, so I may as well start in Aberdeen."

Sandy finished his orange juice, went to the phone and called Duvivier.

"Good morning, Mr. Kinsolving," the detective said. "I hope you're feeling better."

"Thank you, yes; still a lot of disbelief, but I'm all right."

"I wanted to let you know that the medical examiner will release your wife's body on Tuesday morning. He will have finished his work by that time."

"Thank you. What do we do then?"

"Contact a funeral director; he'll know what to do."

"Detective, I spoke last evening with my son and my wife's brother; is there any reason why we should not have my wife's body cremated? We had planned to take her father's ashes to Scotland for burial in the family plot, and it occurred to us that Joan might have wanted her remains to be there, too."

"No reason whatever; once the ME has completed his examination, there are no restrictions on what you may do." He paused. "Mr. Kinsolving, I wanted to let you know ahead of time that I will be speaking with all sorts of people you know about this case. I didn't want you to find out from them."

"I understand. Speak with whomever you like; it's all right with me."

"Thank you, sir. Do you travel very much on business?"

"Yes, I'm in London about one week a month; I also visit the Napa and Sonoma Valleys from time to time, and I'm in France two or three times a year."

"When did you last travel, sir?"

"I returned from London last Monday, on hearing of my father-in-law's illness."

"And when do you plan to travel again?"

"Well, I had planned a trip to the West Coast this week, but under the circumstances that will be postponed until my wife's affairs are settled and some decisions have been made about the operation of the company without my father-in-law."

"So you plan to be in New York for at least another week?"

"At least. Detective, are you telling me not to leave town?"

"Oh, no, sir; I just wanted to know if you would be available if I should need to talk with you again."

"Of course. You can contact me at my office during the week, or at home at night. I hope very much to hear from you that you have caught the person responsible for this."

"I hope so, too, sir. Tell me, do you have any other telephone numbers at home—other than the one we're talking on?"

"Yes, we have two other lines, consecutive numbers; the third is for a fax machine."

"Thank you, Mr. Kinsolving; I won't keep you longer. Good-bye."

Sandy hung up the phone.

"He wanted to know all your phone numbers?" Angus asked.

"Yes."

"He probably wants to tap them."

"Tap my phones? Isn't that illegal?"

"Not if he gets a court order."

"Angus, you watch too much television." He was glad of it, though; he'd have to be careful on the phone.

● ● ●

After breakfast Sandy took Angus for a long walk in Central Park. He reflected that, although he lived only across the street from the park, he rarely went there. He resolved to take more walks. "How are you feeling about your mother?" Sandy asked.

"I guess the way I've always felt about her," Angus replied. "Removed. You and I were always closer than Mom and I."

"Did you resent being sent away to Exeter at fourteen?"

"No, not really. It seemed like the thing to do, I guess; so many other guys I knew were going off somewhere to school. Isn't it a little late to be asking me?"

Sandy shrugged. "From the moment you were born, Joan wanted you to go to Exeter. I'm not quite sure how she settled so firmly on that school. Over the years she would talk about it, and it became a done thing without any argument."

"I remember her talking about it. It's so strange; I'm not exactly sad about her death. I mean, I'm sorry that she had to go through that, but I'm surprised at how little effect it's had on me."

Sandy felt exactly the same way, but he didn't say so. "You may feel differently after a little time has passed; or, on the other hand, you may go right on feeling the same."

Angus nodded. "What are you going to do now?"

"Well, Joan's death changes quite a lot in my life. Or rather, it keeps my life from being changed the way it would have, if she'd lived. I'll see Laddie tomorrow, and we'll come to some sort of accommodation. Laddie has never liked confrontation, and he'll want to settle everything as quickly and as amicably as possible."

"I always felt kind of sorry for Uncle Laddie," Angus said.

"Why?"

"Well, he seemed so much under Granddad's thumb."

"Believe me, Angus, we were *all* under Jock's thumb. To tell you the truth, I never minded that much. I had a rather weak father myself, and having a man of such authority over me was something I didn't dislike. In fact, I think it made me better at my work. If I had an idea I wanted to try out, I thought about it very carefully before I broached the subject to Jock. I knew I'd have to be ready to defend it on all sorts of grounds, and it made me do my homework and not go off half-cocked." He stopped and looked at his son. "You never needed second guessing, you know."

"I didn't?"

"Not from somebody like Jock. You always knew exactly what you wanted to do. You resisted the idea of joining the company long before Jock or anybody else had even raised the subject. You wanted medicine, and all of us knew that it would do no good to try and persuade you to do anything else."

"I guess that's true."

"Fortunately, the idea of your being a doctor appealed to Joan. I can't tell you what hell she could have put us both through if she'd had her heart set on your doing something else."

"I can believe that," Angus said. "Well, I guess we'll lay her to rest in Scotland and try to get on with our lives."

"I guess we will," Sandy replied. And the two strolled on through the spring morning.

CHAPTER

10

The calls began on Monday morning and continued throughout the day. How awful! So sorry
to hear it! Anything we can do? Sandy accepted
them politely, but by noon he was weary of them. The
Monday morning *Times* had the story and was clinical
with the details. God knew what the *Daily News* had to
say about it, and Sandy didn't want to know. Late on
Sunday afternoon he and Angus had visited Albert at
Lenox Hill and had found the old man sitting up in
bed, watching a movie on television. Sandy felt grateful that Jock's driver had not been seriously hurt.

In the early afternoon, Sandy asked Angus to man
the phone, and he went to the office—not his own office
over the shop on Madison Avenue, but the company's
headquarters in the Seagram Building. He kept a small
room there. He got off the elevator and headed toward
his desk, and he nearly ran head on into Laddie, who
was coming out of his own office.

"Oh, Sandy," Laddie said, and he seemed a little flustered. His shoulders sagged. "I think you'd better come in here; there's been a development you have to know about."

Sandy followed Laddie into his office. A man in his shirtsleeves was seated opposite the desk, and he rose as Sandy entered.

"Sandy," Laddie said, "I don't know if you know Walt Bishop, from our legal department."

"No," Sandy said, offering his hand.

"Sit down, both of you, please," Laddie said. "Sandy . . . well, Walt, perhaps it would be better if you told Sandy what you've just told me."

"Of course, Mr. Bailley," Bishop said. "First of all, Mr. Kinsolving, I want to apologize for not being able to tell you this sooner. I was on vacation in the Caribbean, and, because of the airline schedules, I wasn't able to return to the office until just a few minutes ago."

Sandy shrugged. What was the man on about?

"You see," Bishop continued, "the week before last, I came into the office on Saturday morning to write some instructions for my secretary before I left town. I ran into Mr. Bailley, the elder Mr. Bailley, when I went to use the copying machine."

"Father often worked on weekends," Laddie said.

"That was when Mr. Bailley asked me to do it," Bishop said.

"Do what?" Sandy asked.

"Write his will."

Sandy froze. "Jock Bailley asked you to write his will?"

"Yes."

"I don't understand. Why didn't he just call his lawyer?"

"My impression was that it was a spur-of-the-moment thing," Bishop said. "But he was very insistent; he wanted it done that minute, and he wanted to sign it before the day was out. Anyway, he dictated some provisions to me, and I went back to my office to prepare the document."

Sandy looked at Laddie. "You didn't know about this?"

Laddie shook his head. "Remember, he had the stroke on Sunday night. I suppose he would have mentioned it on Monday morning, if he had made it to Monday morning."

"Fortunately," Bishop said, "we have a software package in the legal department that includes a sample will, so all I had to do was add the relevant paragraphs on the word processor, and inside half an hour, I had a will for Mr. Bailley to sign."

"And did he sign it?" Sandy asked.

"Well, we had some trouble finding witnesses. It was a Saturday, after all, and no one else was in the office but the two of us, and we needed three witnesses."

Sandy was having trouble containing himself. "And did you find them?" he asked, as calmly as he could.

"Well, what we finally did was, Mr. Bailley and I took the elevator downstairs to the Four Seasons."

The restaurant was in the lowest level of the building.

"Two of the restaurant's owners, a Mr. Margittai and a Mr. von Bidder, were there, and they and the bartender on duty witnessed the will."

Sandy's heart would not stop hammering against his chest.

"Then Mr. Bailley bought me the best lunch I ever had," Bishop said. "He said it was a load off his mind and his conscience. I put the will in my files and went off on vacation; I didn't hear of Mr. Bailley's death until I returned to work today."

Laddie held up a sheaf of papers. "I have the will here," he said. "I have no doubt that it's legal and proper and that it fully expresses Father's intentions."

"Thank you, Mr. Bailley," Bishop said.

"It's pretty much like the one we read last week," Laddie continued, "except Father increased the sums for the servants and for Angus's trust—that from five to ten million dollars."

Sandy wanted to hammer on the desk and scream at Laddie to tell the rest.

"And he left the wine division to you," Laddie said, finally. "Joan got a third of the remainder of the business, and I got the other two-thirds. That's it."

Sandy let out the breath that he had been holding, as slowly as he could. "Thank you, Mr. Bishop," he said. I would have thanked you a lot more last week, he thought, before I instigated the death of my wife. Christ, if I'd known, none of this would have happened. Joan and I would have been divorced, and I would have had the wine division.

Laddie spoke up again. "Walt, I want to thank you for coming to me immediately on your return. And now, if you'll excuse us, Mr. Kinsolving and I have some talking to do."

"Of course, Mr. Bailley," Bishop said. He rose, shook hands with both the men and departed, closing the door behind him.

"Sandy," Laddie said. "This is only my rough estimate, of course, but I think the wine division must account for about a quarter of the value of the company; Joan's third of the remainder would account for another quarter. And, of course, you already own three percent of the stock. Unless I'm greatly mistaken, you are now the majority shareholder of John Bailley & Son. Ironic, isn't it?"

A great deal more ironic than you know, Sandy thought. "He told me he was going to do it," Sandy said. "I thought he just hadn't gotten around to it."

"He must have had some sort of premonition of his death," Laddie said. "It was certainly unlike him to do anything precipitously, on the spur of the moment."

"Yes, that's true," Sandy said. He was getting his heartbeat under control, now.

"What do you want to do?" Laddie asked. "I'm at your disposal."

"Laddie, I don't want your company," Sandy said. "Tell you what: Let's get your accountant together with my accountant; the two of them can choose a third man, and the group can evaluate the company. I'll pull the wine division out of the corporation, and I'll sell you my share of the liquor company for whatever the three men say it's worth. The company has no debt; you won't have any trouble raising the cash for a buyout. That way, each of us will remain his own boss."

"Done," Laddie said, slapping his palm onto the desk top.

Sandy stood. "And now, if you'll excuse me, I think I'd like to take a walk."

"Of course."

The two men shook hands and parted.

Sandy walked up Park Avenue, the May sunshine in his face, the air unusually clear and crisp. He was his own man; he felt omnipotent. After a lifetime of toil for Jock Bailley, he had been paid off, and paid off well.

He'd have been happy with just the wine division, but now, as Joan's heir, he'd have enough cash from Laddie's buyout to expand the business, open a West Coast branch, maybe even buy a small vineyard or two. He'd always wanted to grow wine, to have his own vineyard's output sold in his own shop. Now he was going to have everything he'd ever wanted, and more.

He walked all the way uptown to his apartment house. As he let himself in, he heard Angus on the phone. He walked into the kitchen.

"Hi," Angus said. "You weren't gone long."

"I didn't feel like working," Sandy replied. "Many calls?"

"A steady stream," Angus said, handing him a handful of slips. "And one wrong number. We don't have anybody named Bart living here, do we?"

"Who?"

"Some guy called and asked to speak to Bart."

Sandy's feeling of omnipotence vanished.

CHAPTER

11

Sandy walked up Madison Avenue with a lighter heart. He had just left the headquarters of John Bailley & Son, where he had concluded the corporate separation of the wine division from the company and where he had sold his interest in the liquor division. He gazed idly into shop windows; for many years he had been able to walk into any establishment and buy nearly anything he wanted, but today he had a wholly new sense of wealth. He had a cashier's check in his pocket for twenty-eight million dollars.

What would he buy? A jet airplane for his coast-to-coast trips? Not his style. A Rolls-Royce? Nothing gaudy. A vineyard? Maybe; he would see. But none of those things offered the immediate gratification he sought. He reversed his course and walked down Fifth Avenue; soon he stood in front of Cartier jewelers. He had never owned much in the way of jewelry. He

71

walked into the store and was greeted by a beautiful young woman.

"May I show you something, sir?" she asked, her voice slightly French-accented.

The accent reminded him of Duvivier, who had been very quiet for the past month, and he dismissed it from his mind. "I'd like to look at a wristwatch, please," he said.

"Of course; this way, please." She led him to a long glass case filled with watches.

Sandy examined half a dozen, then picked up a Panther watch, in eighteen-carat gold with a matching bracelet. "How much?" he asked.

"This model is fifteen thousand dollars," she said. "Plus sales tax, of course. We also have the Panther with diamonds."

He shook his head. Nothing gaudy. "I'll take it," he said, and handed her his Platinum American Express card. He would get a frequent-flyer mile for every dollar charged to the card, and the little bonus pleased him.

The young woman slipped the watch onto his wrist, showed him how to work the hidden clasp, then disappeared with the instrument to have a link removed from the bracelet for a better fit.

Sandy wandered around the store, glancing at diamond necklaces and broaches in the cases. Nobody to celebrate with, he reflected. One of these days before long he would come in here and buy some bauble for a beautiful new woman. The saleswoman returned, and he considered her for a moment. She was certainly elegant looking, and under the expensive suit she wore was surely a nicely sculpted body. He fantasized how she would look, feel in bed. It was a pleasant thought, but no. No sales clerks. He could afford any woman, now, any woman at all. He signed the credit card receipt, then slipped on the new watch and handed her his Rolex. "Would you send this to my home, please?"

"Of course, Mr. Kinsolving, and thank you for shopping with Cartier. I hope to see you again soon." She folded her business card into the receipt and handed it to him.

Maybe, he thought, looking at her breasts; maybe for some spontaneous evening of good food and sex, if he began to feel randy. He didn't feel randy, not yet. It would come, though; it always did.

"Thank you . . . "—he glanced at her card— "Ms. Duval."

"Angelique," she said.

He gave her a little wave and left the shop. He had one more business call to make, but he wanted to feel the check in his pocket for a while longer. He strolled slowly up Fifth Avenue, enjoying the sunshine and the atmosphere. He looked at the faces of the people approaching him. Perhaps one in ten seemed nearly as happy as he on this fine day. The others seemed worried, hurried, and harassed. He took as long as possible to reach his next stop, a handsome stone building off Fifth Avenue in the Sixties, not far from his apartment house. He climbed the steps and was observed by a uniformed man on the other side of the heavy door of glass and wrought iron. After the briefest of examinations, the man opened the door and showed him in.

"May I help you, sir?"

"Yes, I'd like to open an account," Sandy replied. He was in a foyer with marble floors and walls. A pair of overstuffed sofas faced each other; excellent paintings hung on the walls.

"Did you have an appointment, sir?"

"No. My name is Alexander Kinsolving; you may say that your bank was recommended by Arthur Shields of Wayne and Shields, my accountants."

"Would you please take a seat, sir?"

"Thank you." Sandy sat on one of the sofas and glanced at his new watch: two minutes past the hour. Let's see how long this takes, he thought.

The guard spoke briefly on a telephone, then returned. "Mr. Samuel Warren will see you, sir; please follow me." He ignored the stairs and showed Sandy into a small elevator. "You'll be met at the top, sir," the guard said, pressing a button and stepping out of the car.

Sandy rose four floors and stepped out of the elevator to be met by a plump, middle-aged woman.

"Mr. Kinsolving? Will you follow me, please?" She led him to the end of the hall to double doors of mahogany and opened one for him. "Mr. Warren, Mr. Alexander Kinsolving."

Warren came from behind his desk and extended his hand. "How do you do?" he asked. "I'm Sam Warren; please call me Sam. It's Sandy, isn't it?"

"That's right," Sandy replied shaking the man's hand. "I didn't know you were expecting me."

"I wasn't, exactly, but Arthur Shields rang today and said I might be hearing from you. I'm glad it was sooner than later." Warren waved him to a comfortable sofa and sat down beside him. "Would you like some coffee or tea?"

"Tea would be nice," Sandy replied.

Warren nodded to the woman, who still stood at the door, and she disappeared. The two men chatted idly until she returned with a silver tea service, then Warren poured for them both. "Now, Sandy," he said, "how can I be of service?"

"Are you acquainted with John Bailley and Son?" Sandy asked.

"Of course. Fine people, I hear."

"I've just acquired the wine division of the company, which I started some years ago, and some cash for my interest in the liquor division. I've always banked at Morgan Guarantee, the company's bank, but now that Jock Bailley is gone, and since my wife recently passed away, I feel that it's better to reestablish elsewhere. Your bank comes highly recommended by Arthur Shields."

"That's very flattering," Warren said. "Let me tell you a little about Mayfair Trust: we're private, of course—very private; we're based in London, with branches in a dozen cities around the world, and we offer a range of services that are as personal as our clients wish them to be—investments, mergers and acquisitions, money management, practically anything you might require. We have a few customers who simply deposit funds with us and deal with their affairs themselves, but nearly all of our clients ask for a more complete service."

"That is what I had in mind," Sandy said. "I've always operated the wine division as a subsidiary of the larger company, but now I'm independent, and I will need a lot of advice."

"Do you have expansion plans?" Warren asked.

"I already have a London company, and I was thinking of a specialist West Coast branch, dealing primarily in California wines."

The two men talked for more than an hour, and Sandy was impressed with Warren's immediate comprehension of what he wanted to do, and with the off-the-cuff suggestions he made.

Finally, when they seemed finished with their discussion, Warren asked, "Shall I open both personal and business accounts for you, then?"

"Yes, please." Sandy took the cashier's check from his pocket and handed it to Warren.

Warren looked at it and chuckled. "And how long have you had this in your possession?"

"A couple of hours, I suppose."

Warren rolled his eyes. "Oh, dear, the earnings we've already lost! We must put this to work immediately!"

"I'd like a quarter of a million in my personal checking account and two million available for working capital. What would you suggest doing with the balance?"

"Well, I think we should keep you pretty liquid, since you're going to be expanding, and God knows, interest rates are way down at the moment. We have a short-term lending program for periods as brief as a weekend—department stores, race tracks, other businesses that need substantial cash on hand to do business. That brings in much higher rates than are available to the ordinary bank depositor at our competitors, and it's low-risk. I'll have a talk with some of our other people here, and we'll have a few other ideas ready for you, say, tomorrow?"

"Sounds good," Sandy said, turning over the check and endorsing it. "I'll have Arthur send over the corporate resolutions for the business account."

Warren went to his desk and came back with some forms. "We'll need your signature, of course, but don't worry about the rest of the information; we'll deal with that as we need to."

The door opened and the secretary entered. She handed Warren a small folder; he thanked her and handed it to Sandy. "Your checkbook," he said. "Temporary, of course; we'll order something to your specifications."

Sandy took the checkbook and examined it; it was made of black alligator, and the checks inside didn't look temporary; his name and address were elegantly printed on them. He stood to go, and Warren stood with him. The two men strolled toward the office door.

"Sandy, among our many other services we offer advice on large purchases—airplanes, yachts, real estate. Should you feel inclined to purchase any of those or almost anything else, please let me know. We can sometimes effect large savings. In general, if you want something done and don't know who to call, call me." He handed Sandy a card. "My home number's there, too; I'm at your disposal day or night."

"Sam, it's going to be a pleasure doing business with you."

CHAPTER

12

Sandy entered his Madison Avenue shop with a fresh sense of proprietorship. He greeted his employees and took the stairs to his second-floor office overlooking the street. His secretary handed him a number of telephone messages, and the first one read: Call Bart at 4:00 P.M. eastern time. A number preceded by the San Francisco area code followed. Sandy ground his teeth. There was no avoiding this, he supposed; best to get it over with.

At a quarter to four he left his desk, asked his cashier for some quarters and left the shop. He walked over to Lexington Avenue and found a pay phone. At four o'clock sharp he dialed the number and fed in a handful of quarters.

"Well," Peter Martindale's voice said immediately

on being connected. "Nice to hear from you; I said I'd wait a month."

"You didn't," Sandy said. "You called my home."

"Sorry about that," Martindale said. "I thought it best to inject a note of reality early on. By the way, congratulations on your business transaction; I read about it in the *Wall Street Journal* this morning. I expect my little contribution improved your position."

"I specifically asked you not to do it; I changed my mind, and I left the required message, as specified by you."

"Sorry, old fellow, didn't get the message in time," Martindale drawled.

"That's a bald-faced lie," Sandy said; he was trembling with anger. "The concierge told me that he handed it to you personally."

"A little white lie," Martindale admitted. "I thought it best to proceed as planned. Now it's time for your part of our deal."

"We have no deal!" Sandy nearly shouted. "I called it off, and you violated my instructions! I feel no obligation to you whatever! Is that perfectly clear?"

"My friend, you are very ungrateful," Martindale said. "Don't you understand? I've set you free! Now all you have to do is set me free! You'll feel better when you entirely understand your position."

"Position? What position? I have no position!"

"Oh, but you do, dear man, you do. You now have a personal obligation to me that must be satisfied, and if you do not satisfy it soon and in the required way, I will bring you badly to grief."

"I don't really see how you can do that," Sandy said, but he felt less confident.

"I think it's best not to explain it to you on the telephone," Martindale said, "but until I can make it clear to you personally, please believe me when I tell you that it is in your interest to believe me. I can pull that very soft rug from under you very quickly, and I will do it, if I have to."

Sandy thought for a moment. "You want to meet?"

"Yes, and in San Francisco," Martindale said. "Be here by the end of next week; make the call as agreed, and I will give you further instructions. Do you understand?"

"I hadn't planned to be in San Francisco."

"Be here by the end of the week," Martindale said, then hung up.

Sandy stared at the phone for a moment, then hung it up and walked away. He was damned if he'd communicate further with that man, not in any way.

Sandy walked slowly back toward Madison Avenue, numb with dread and oblivious of his surroundings. He had gone little more than a block when something struck him, hard, in the right kidney. He fell to his knees, gasping with pain, and he was yanked sideways into a loading dock and forced onto his belly. His left arm was wrenched behind his back, and something struck him in the back of the neck. Sandy lost consciousness.

"Mister!" someone was shouting at him. "You all right?" Someone turned him onto his back.

Sandy blinked at the face hovering over him. A black man in coveralls was holding his head off the cement floor. "What?" he asked, rather stupidly.

"Can you talk to me?"

"Yes, I can talk. What happened?"

"I dunno; I came out of the john, and you was lying on my loading dock. Hang on, I'll get an ambulance, or something."

"No, no," Sandy said, struggling to get to his feet.

The man helped him up, then leaned him against the wall. "You want I should call a cop?"

"No, don't do that. I don't really know what happened; I wouldn't know what to tell a cop."

The man began dusting Sandy's clothes, and Sandy noticed that the left knee of his trousers was torn. Damn! he thought; a good suit, too! He felt for his wallet and his checkbook; both there. "Nothing seems to have been stolen," he said to the man. "I'll just be on my way; thanks for your help."

"Well, if you're sure you're okay," the man said.

Sandy stepped back out into the sunlight and started toward his office. His back and neck hurt like hell, and he was a little light-headed, but he seemed to be walking all right. He glanced at his watch; there was no watch. He went back to where he had been struck and looked on the pavement, then it dawned on him: He had been mugged for his wristwatch. And he'd owned it for less than a day! He hadn't even added it to his insurance policy yet. Fifteen thousand dollars, right down the drain!

Back in his office, he told his secretary to hold his calls, then he took off his jacket, loosened his tie, and stretched out on the sofa under the windows. What had he gotten himself into? Now he was locked in with Peter Martindale. What was it the man had said on the plane? There were two flaws in *Strangers on a Train*— only one of the two men had agreed to the plan, and one of them was crazy. Well, *he* hadn't agreed to the plan, and Martindale couldn't be entirely sane.

He had to go to San Francisco, anyway; he'd lied to Martindale about that—he'd already postponed the trip for a month, and he had to buy wines. He was going to have to face the man and persuade him to drop this madness. He closed his eyes and dozed for a moment.

When Sandy woke the clock on the wall said nearly seven o'clock. He got gingerly to his feet and went to his desk. His secretary had apparently tiptoed into the room and left a Federal Express package there. He sank into his large leather chair and picked it up; he wasn't expecting anything from anybody. He tore it open and found another envelope inside, a padded one, the sort that books were mailed in. He opened that envelope and shook the contents out onto the desk. His wife's stolen jewelry lay before him.

There was a note, neatly printed in block capitals:

I DON'T NEED THIS, I JUST THOUGHT IT WOULD LOOK BETTER IF I TOOK IT. TO PROTECT YOUR POSITION, YOU SHOULD TELL THE COPS HOW YOU GOT IT BACK. DON'T WORRY, THERE AREN'T ANY FINGERPRINTS, AND THEY WON'T BE ABLE TO TRACE THE PACKAGE.

There was a good four hundred thousand dollars in jewelry on the desk. Sandy groaned.

Duvivier stood before Sandy's desk and stared at the pile of jewelry. "Is it all there? Everything?"

"Everything."

"And it came by Federal Express?"

"Yes," Sandy replied, "the package is on the desk; I'm afraid my fingerprints must be on it, but I haven't touched the jewelry."

"Well, my guess is we won't find any fingerprints on the pieces or the package." Duvivier poked at the envelope with a pen. "And the return address is likely to be fiction. It was sent yesterday from a Federal Express office on Sixth Avenue in the forties, a busy one, so it's unlikely that any of the counter people will remember who brought it in."

"I don't understand," Sandy said. "Why would he return all the jewelry? Wasn't it the reason he attacked Joan in the first place?"

"I can only speculate about that," Duvivier replied. "I suppose he could have had a bout of conscience, but I doubt it. More likely, he realized he couldn't unload it without greatly increasing his chances of getting caught."

"He could have just dumped it in a trash can somewhere," Sandy said. "He didn't have to send it back."

"It's odd, I'll grant you."

"To tell you the truth, I wish he'd kept it," Sandy said. "A month had passed, and I was becoming reconciled to what happened, and now this comes along and dredges the whole thing up again."

"Well, I'm sure the pieces would bring quite a lot at auction," Duvivier said. "Especially the ones formerly owned by the Duchess of Windsor."

Sandy shook his head. "I don't want to go through that. I'll put them away, and maybe someday, when my son marries, he'll want to give them to his wife."

Duvivier nodded. "And what has happened to you in the past month?" he asked.

Sandy shrugged. "Most of my time has been taken up with the business."

"I read that you'd bought the company."

"No, my father-in-law left me the wine division and my wife a part of the rest of the company. I sold her inheritance to her brother. That will give me the capital I need for expansion."

Duvivier frowned. "My information was that Mr. Bailley had left you half a million dollars and nothing else."

Sandy shook his head. "No, it turns out that Jock Bailley made a new will a couple of days before his death. We didn't know about it at first, because it was done by a lawyer in the legal department, not his personal attorney."

"I see," Duvivier said. "And what is the attorney's name?"

"Walter Bishop."

"Friend of yours?"

"No, I didn't know him. You see, for the past few years I've worked almost entirely out of this office and London. I've spent little time at the company headquarters; I only know the top executives there."

Duvivier regarded him solemnly. "You've been very fortunate the past few weeks, haven't you?"

"If you think my wife's being murdered was fortunate—"

"My apologies; I simply meant that out of that tragedy have risen a number of strokes of luck: Your wife's jewelry is stolen, but it is returned; your father-in-law mostly excludes you from his will, but then a new will turns up. Suddenly, you own the business and you're a very wealthy man."

Sandy was suddenly angry. "And you think I've somehow engineered all this? You think I hired somebody to kill my wife, and I forged a new will?"

"It seems a possibility, doesn't it?"

"Well, I want you to investigate the possibility, Mr. Duvivier. I want you to delve into everything I do, question everyone I know, find the answer to every question."

"Do you?"

"I certainly do. But let me tell you something else; if, while you're investigating me, it suddenly turns up in the press that I'm a suspect in my wife's murder, or if anything else untrue, but derogatory, is published, I'm going to hold you and your department responsible. I will answer every question you have, cooperate in any way I can, but if you defame me or cause me to be defamed in the process, you will find your department facing a very serious lawsuit."

"Mr. Kinsolving—"

"You've mentioned that I'm newly wealthy; well, it's true, and I will spend whatever part of that wealth is necessary to protect my good name."

"Please, Mr. Kinsolving."

"I mean it; I have nothing to hide from you or anybody else, but I will *not* become a Claus von Bulow for the nineties, do you understand me?"

"Mr. Kinsolving, I have no intention of making that happen."

"Good. Now take that jewelry and that package and start investigating. I'm exhausted, and I'm going home to bed."

"Mr. Kinsolving, are you quite all right? You seem to be moving rather stiffly."

"I slept on the sofa for a while; I woke up with a stiff neck."

Duvivier wrote out a receipt for the jewelry and left. Sandy got into his coat to go home, tired, depressed, and angry.

All the way home he kept looking over his shoulder, wondering if another mugger was there. He couldn't stop himself.

CHAPTER

13

S andy got off the airplane in San Francisco and
into the waiting car. He checked into his suite at
the Ritz-Carlton, unpacked, gave some clothes to
the valet for pressing, took a nap, then ordered dinner
from room service. He watched television for an hour,
then, a little after ten he consulted the telephone book,
slipped into a freshly pressed jacket, and went downstairs.

"Can I get you a taxi, sir?" the doorman asked.

"No, thank you, I think I'll take a walk," he replied.
He headed down the hill toward the main shopping
district, his hands in his pockets. It had been unseason-
ably hot in the afternoon, but with evening the temper-
ature had dropped. He walked more purposefully to
keep warm.

Half an hour later he had found the address, prominently located among a dozen other expensive-looking galleries. He window-shopped several of them before coming to a stop before the Martindale Gallery. It was past ten-thirty, now, and he was surprised to see all the lights on and a woman working at a desk at the rear of the big room. She turned a page of what seemed to be a large ledger. Sandy tried the door, but it was locked; the woman looked up and waved a hand. "We're closed," she mouthed.

Sandy waved back and walked on down the street, but not before he had had a good look at her. About thirty-five, yellow hair, fashionably done, a cashmere sweater and pearls. Hard to estimate her height when sitting, but she seemed not very tall. All in all, very attractive, he thought.

The following morning he telephoned the gallery and asked for Peter Martindale. "This is Bart," he said when the man came on the line.

"Ah, Bart," Martindale said. "Good to hear from you. Ready to meet?"

"Yes."

"Go down to the waterfront and take the boat for the Alcatraz tour; there's one at noon—that okay?"

"Yes."

"I'll find you." Martindale hung up.

Sandy took a taxi to the pier and bought a ticket for the tour. The morning was cloudy and cool. At the last moment before the boat cast off, Peter Martindale, wearing a light raincoat, a tweed cap and dark glasses, stepped aboard and took a seat at the opposite end of the craft from Sandy.

Sandy avoided looking at him on the trip out. When

they docked, he disembarked along with the twenty-five or thirty other passengers and allowed himself to drift toward the end of the strung-out group. The tour guide greeted them, said a few words about the history of the place, then set off into the prison proper. A steel door clanged shut behind them, echoing through the abandoned facility. As the group moved slowly through the building, Sandy caught a motion in the corner of his eye. Martindale stood a few feet away, in a cell. He beckoned. When the tour guide turned to continue on, Sandy stepped into the cell.

"I thought this would be an appropriate setting," Peter Martindale said. He indicated a steel bunk hanging from the wall. "Take a pew."

Sandy sat down, and Martindale sat on the opposite bunk.

"Well, here we are," Martindale said. "I suggested we meet here, because I wanted you to see the inside of a prison; find out what sort of place you'll end up if you fail to hold up your end of the bargain."

"*There was no bargain*," Sandy said heatedly.

Martindale held up a hand. "Please, Sandy, please; we're way past that, now; there *is* a bargain, because *I say* there is a bargain. Face up to it; you have no choice."

Sandy sat silently, staring at the gallery owner; he could not think what to do next; the man would not be dealt with.

"I see I'm going to have to convince you," Martindale said. He reached into a pocket of his raincoat, took out a plastic bag, and tossed it across the cell to Sandy.

Sandy caught the small bag, and it was surprisingly heavy. He held it up to a ray of sunlight streaming through the barred window; his Cartier watch was in the bag. He looked up at Martindale.

Martindale smiled. "This little exercise is to help you understand that you are vulnerable."

"How did you—"

"Really, Sandy, you're an intelligent man, but not a very clever one. Five hundred dollars in the palm of the nearest hoodlum took care of that bit of business. I watched the whole thing from across the street, you know."

"But I called you in San Francisco."

"Of course you did; call forwarding took care of the rest." He removed a small cellular telephone from his pocket and held it up to the light. "A service of your friendly telephone company. Put the watch on."

Sandy slipped the watch, still in its plastic bag, into his pocket. "If you're so good at hiring hoodlums, why don't you just hire one to solve your problem?"

"Because hired hoodlums will turn on one in the blink of an eye; they make some stupid mistake, and when they're arrested they're reeling off one's name, address, and social security number before the cell door is locked, trying to do a deal. I want someone who can't do a deal, Sandy, and that's you, old fellow."

Sandy shook his head.

"Think of what you have now, Sandy— the business is yours; a rather large chunk of cash is yours; you're in a new world—accounts at Mayfair Trust, and all that."

Sandy looked up at him.

"Of course, I followed you. Now, let's get down to business."

"I won't do it," Sandy said quietly.

Martindale sighed. "All right, I'd hoped this wouldn't be necessary, but there it is. Sandy, you've seen how easily I got to you? It would be just as easy for me to get to your son."

"Now, wait a minute—"

"Works all those nights at the hospital," Martindale said. "Walks home to his flat a few blocks away. Dangerous place, the streets of Manhattan—even the Upper East Side."

Sandy's shoulders sagged.

"Ah, I think I've finally gotten through to you," Martindale said.

"What do you want me to do?" Sandy asked, defeated.

"How long will you be in San Francisco?"

"Two more nights. I'll be up in the wine country all day tomorrow, and I'll leave the day after on a morning flight."

"You'll be back in the city tomorrow night?"

"I can be."

"Good; make your way to my gallery a little after nine in the evening. It's at—"

"I know where it is."

Martindale smiled. "Good man. I'll tell Helena that a client is coming in from New York to see the Constable, the big one on the east wall; late plane and all that. She'd do anything to sell the Constable. Big bucks, as you Yanks say. Now, let me describe her to you."

"I saw her there last night."

Martindale looked surprised for the first time. "Sandy, I've underestimated you; you were getting ready all along, weren't you?"

"She was sitting at the desk in the rear of the gallery about ten-thirty, going through a large ledger."

"That's my girl," Martindale said. "Attention to detail, always. What she was doing, of course, was looking for just the right moment—financially—to let the ax fall."

"She's still working in the gallery? In spite of your . . . situation?" Sandy asked.

"Oh, we're nothing if not civil," Martindale said, chuckling. "You see, I'm not meant to know about her . . . relationship. It's meant to be a surprise. Sort of makes me bulletproof with the police afterwards, you see. I didn't know, so it couldn't be a motive."

"She's very attractive."

"Of course. Did you think I'd marry some scrubber? She's the perfect picture of the well-born California girl." Martindale leaned forward and rested his elbows on his knees. "Down to business, now: The street is deserted after ten, as I'm sure you noticed last evening. Greet Helena, chat with her; look at the Constable. Then, wander over to the little Turner on the back wall. That will put you within a couple of feet of the desk; there's a loaded pistol in the top right-hand drawer. Have a look out the front windows to make sure the coast is clear, then take the pistol and use it." He pointed at his heart. "One here." He pointed at his forehead. "Then, one here, just to be thorough. I hope I don't have to remind you to wear gloves? We don't want any residue on your hands, do we?"

"I suppose not."

"Then, before you go, mess her up a bit—rip her knickers off, that sort of thing; stick the pistol up her cunt, if you're really into it. The money box is in the top left-hand drawer; leave the checks, but take the cash—have dinner on me! Leave the gun there—it's registered to me—and go out the back door. It opens onto an alley that runs into the street around the corner. Walk slowly, do some window shopping, don't get rid of the gloves until you're well away from the premises." He reached out and put a hand on Sandy's knee. "And then, old cock, you're a free man— very free and very rich. Go back to New York, live your life, enjoy! You and I won't see each other again."

Sandy reached out and put his hand on top of Martindale's. "Make very sure of that, Peter, because once she's dead, if I ever hear from you again I'll make it my business to kill you. Do you understand me?"

"Of course, dear chap," Martindale said, getting to his feet. "I'm surprised you hadn't thought of that before now; I certainly was ready for you to try. But you see, I knew you'd realize that you might as well kill Helena as me. Much safer, and you'd have my help."

"Let's get out of here," Sandy said.

"One more thing: In the event that you're still thinking about trying to kill me, you should know that I've handwritten an account of our little arrangement, complete with gory details, and had my signature notarized. That document, along with the keys to your basement and storeroom, are in an envelope in my lawyer's safe, and written upon the envelope is an instruction to open it in the event of my death. Once Helena is out of the picture, I'll retrieve the envelope and give it to you for disposal."

"Let's get out of here," Sandy repeated.

"You've got it all, then?"

"All of it."

"Good. You go back the way you came." He glanced at his watch. "The group should be back where they started in a couple of minutes; I'll catch them up from behind. You first."

Sandy left the cell and walked back toward the tour's starting point. He gazed up at the tiers of cells around him; his steps echoed around the abandoned prison. Truly, he thought, this would be hell on earth. He resolved not to end up in a place like this. Shortly, the group appeared from around a corner, and he joined the rear of the crowd and worked his way up to the middle. As he boarded the boat for the trip back he saw Martindale get on.

On the trip back, the sun came out.

CHAPTER

14

S andy stood in the dusty soil of a Napa Valley
vineyard and listened to Mario Scotti, its owner,
extoll the virtues of his latest vintage.

"I tell you, Sandy, it is the best I have ever made!"
Mario was saying.

Mario said this every year, of course, in his slightly
accented English. He had been born in Tuscany and had
come to California as a child, but he had never entirely
lost his accent. Sandy bought Mario's wines each year,
and in increasing quantities, but this year he had come for
advice, as well. "Mario, I will increase last year's order by
twenty percent if you will find me a vineyard to buy."
Sandy knew that if there was a vineyard in Napa to be
bought, Mario would know about it, and he was not dis-
appointed.

"Larsen," Mario said.

"Lars Larsen?"

"What would a Swede know about wine? Vodka, maybe, but not wine."

Sandy knew the property: it was a few miles south, well located, pretty. "Why does Larsen want to sell?"

"The same as anybody else; he's spent all his money. The difference is, Larsen has spent it replanting with phyloxera-resistant vines."

The phyloxera parasite, scourge of European vineyards, had come to California, and every vineyard was faced with the huge costs of planting and maturing new vines that would resist the pest.

"What's his equipment like?"

"Beautiful. The man is obsessive about having the best this, the best that; always has been. Larsen was never one to make do the way I have to."

"I've drunk a bottle here and there, and it was good."

"He makes a pretty good cabernet and a pretty good merlot. Larsen is a technician; I think he believes that if he could reduce the best wine to a chemical formula, that he could duplicate it endlessly, like ink. He has a good, young winemaker over there; an artist, if he wasn't working for a chemist."

"You know how much he wants?"

"I can find out."

"Find out."

Sandy sat in the walled garden of the restaurant, Tre Vigne, and sipped the Larsen cabernet. Larsen sat across the table from him, watching for his reaction.

"Very nice," Sandy said.

Larsen's face fell. "That's all? *Very nice?*"

"It's excellent," Sandy admitted.

"It's *superb*," Larsen said. "You won't get my price down by bad-mouthing my wines."

Sandy shrugged. "So why isn't the merlot living up to its potential?" He knew he had struck home by Larsen's expression.

"So, I haven't been making it as long," Larsen said grudgingly.

"Tell you what I want to see, Lars—the books, the machinery, the figures on replanting, the lot. I want you to put a package together and send it to my bankers in New York." He wrote down Sam Warren's name and address. "And in a couple of weeks I'll get back to you. If we like what we see, we'll make you a substantial offer—I'm not out to steal you blind, I just don't want to pay a dime too much."

"I guess I can live with that," Larsen said. "I'll introduce your banker to my lawyer; we'll see what happens. And now, if you'll excuse me, I have to go and labor in my vineyard." Larsen shook hands and left.

When Sandy was sure he had left the restaurant, he whipped out his portable phone and called Sam Warren.

"How are you, Sandy?" Warren asked.

"I'm wonderful, Sam; I've found a property in Napa, and it's a gem."

"So soon?"

"My contacts are good." He told Sam about Mario Scotti.

"So why doesn't Scotti buy it himself?"

"For the same reason nobody else around here can afford it at the moment—they're all investing heavily in replanting. I've asked Larsen to send you a complete package on the place, and I'd like you and your people to go over it as soon as possible."

"Of course. We'll research what other Napa and Sonoma properties have brought recently, too, and if you can get us the package quickly, we'll have a ball-park figure for you within a few days."

"That's what I wanted to hear," Sandy said. "Scotti could be of help to you in setting a price. Talk to you next week." He hung up and addressed the remains of his pasta; he could not believe his good fortune in locating such a good property so quickly. He looked up at the trees shading the garden and at the blue sky beyond. That particular bit of sky was the roof over one of the world's premier wine-growing regions, and soon he would own a piece of it—his life-long dream.

Then he remembered what he had agreed to do that night, and it was as if the sun had left the sky. He forced himself to consider going to the police. He could call Duvivier right now, from his table, and spill the whole story. After all, the concierge at the Pierre would back him up on the message he had given to Martindale.

And that was all. There wasn't another person in the world who could substantiate his story. Martindale could simply deny the whole proposition, laugh it off as the rantings of a madman, and Sandy could prove nothing. And he would still have Martindale to deal with.

The man was ahead of him all the way; he had known that Sandy would come around to thinking of killing him, instead of his wife, and he had taken precautions—or, at least, said he had taken precautions. It was a bluff that Sandy could not afford to call. Martindale had the upper hand all the way—he could incriminate Sandy, but Sandy could not touch him.

Suddenly, Sandy had lost his appetite. He passed up dessert and asked for his check. It was a ninety-minute drive back to his hotel, and he had a decision to make. He had to decide just what he was capable of.

On the way back, he stopped at a men's store in Napa and bought a lightweight, reversible raincoat, a tweed cap, and a pair of thin driving gloves.

CHAPTER

15

S andy picked at his room service dinner, washing small bites down with large swigs of Lars Larsen's cabernet sauvignon. He had always held his alcohol well, especially wine, so he didn't feel drunk. He was looking for a level of buzz that would make him reckless.

Not careless, however. A bottle of wine put him in a place where confidence was a given. He could say anything to anybody, take nearly any risk, meet any challenge on one bottle of red. Finally, he was there.

Sandy got into dark gray trousers, a black turtleneck cashmere sweater, and his blue blazer. As an afterthought, he took the bright red silk pocket square from the breast pocket and tossed it into his suitcase. Nothing distinctive, or memorable, to catch the eye of an unwelcome spectator. He stuffed a tweed cap into one pocket of the reversible raincoat and the driving gloves into the other, then he rolled the raincoat into a tight wad and tucked it under his arm. What else? If he'd had a false moustache he'd have worn that. Glasses. He rummaged into his briefcase and found an old pair of heavy, black-rimmed spectacles that he hadn't worn for years. He didn't much need glasses, except for reading in dim light. He slipped them on and regarded himself in the mirror. A sad but altered face stared back at him. He put the glasses into the breast pocket of the blazer and left his room.

On the street, he declined the offer of a taxi from the doorman and walked in the opposite direction from his last visit to the gallery. Moving quickly, he walked down the street, then turned two corners and doubled back toward the gallery. Half an hour later he had one more turn to make, one more block to go. He stepped into a doorway, unrolled the raincoat and put it on, plaid side out, then donned the tweed cap, the gloves and the glasses. His reflection in the shop window revealed a different man. Different than he had ever been.

He found himself short of breath. He stopped for a moment, took some deep breaths, and forced himself to continue at a slower pace. The streets were deserted.

He turned the last corner. In the middle of the block, where the gallery was, stood a little group of people, and one of them seemed floodlit. There were other lights, too; red and blue. He kept to the opposite side of the street and moved down the block. On the other side of the ambulance were two police vehicles, one a black and white, the other an unmarked car. Mesmerized, Sandy stopped across the street from the gallery and watched. Inside, a clutch of men stood talking, and there was the flash of a camera. The photographer was shooting down, at something behind the desk.

The television crew began moving toward the ambulance, and Sandy caught the eye of the cameraman. "What happened?" he asked.

"Lady got herself snuffed," the man said without slowing down. He positioned the camera at the rear of the ambulance, and after a moment, he was able to photograph a stretcher covered by a blanket as it was slid into the rear of the vehicle. Sandy started walking again, keeping it slow, not wanting to attract attention by seeming to hurry away. When he had gone a couple of blocks, he removed the raincoat, the cap and the gloves, wadded them up and stuffed them into a wastebasket. A find for one of the homeless. He put the glasses into his breast pocket again.

Back at the hotel, Sandy waited impatiently until the eleven o'clock news came on. The story did not run until just before the weather. Sandy recognized the reporter from the scene.

"Police are withholding the name of the victim pending notification of next of kin," he was saying. "All they will say at the moment is that a gun was used."

A police detective blinked into the bright light. "The victim was a Caucasian female in her late thirties," he said. "There was a single gunshot wound to the head."

"Will the position of that wound make identifying the body difficult?" the reporter asked.

"Probably not," the policeman answered. "We have identification materials from a handbag that had been emptied onto the floor. The perpetrator was probably looking for money; the desk had been rifled."

The reporter faced the camera again. "The owner of the gallery, Peter Martindale, did not answer the phone at his residence, and his car was not in the garage. A neighbor said he believed that Mr. Martindale had gone to Los Angeles earlier in the day for a speaking engagement at a university there."

The weather report came on, and Sandy switched it off. What had happened? Had Martindale killed his wife in a fit of anger? Surely not, not when he was expecting Sandy to do it for him later that evening. This was baffling. Had Martindale contracted with more than one assassin, just to be sure? Made no sense at all. What the hell was going on?

The telephone rang. Sandy picked it up. "Hello?"

"It's Bart."

"Yes?"

"How was your evening?"

Sandy hesitated. "I think you must have the wrong number," he said.

"I was calling a pay phone," he said.

"This is not a pay phone; it's a hotel room."

"Will I find it necessary to call again?"

"I should think not," Sandy replied.

"All is well, then?"

"That depends on your point of view."

"Don't play games with me," he said.

"The game is over," Sandy replied, then hung up.

It was, he thought; it was over. And he was not a murderer.

CHAPTER

16

Sandy walked out of the front door of the hotel into the bright sunshine, rested, fresh, and looking for his car.

"Mr. Kinsolving," the doorman said. "Your driver has just phoned in; he's had a flat on the freeway, and he looks to be a good half-hour late. Shall I phone for another car, or will you take the hotel car with our compliments?"

Sandy looked at the stretch limousine with the back door open. "That will do nicely," he said.

"I hope you won't mind sharing with another guest."

"Of course not."

The doorman put the luggage into the trunk, and Sandy climbed into the forward rear seat, just to have the experience of riding backward. A moment later a long female leg entered the car followed by a tall woman. She gathered herself into the rear seat and opened a *New York Times*.

Sandy looked her over quickly: mid-thirties, auburn hair to the shoulders, hazel eyes, good clothes. He thought of saying something, but she seemed purposefully absorbed in her *Times*.

Sandy, himself, was more interested in his San Francisco paper, which he had just bought in the hotel lobby. He flipped through the pages impatiently, looking for the story. It was on page three, and small; nothing much new from the earlier evening's television report, except that the police had disclosed that a cash box had been found in a wastebasket two streets away. Sandy hoped it wasn't the same basket in which he'd deposited his disguise. The gallery's owner still had not been located and thus not interviewed. The woman across from him finished the first section of her *Times* and placed it on the seat beside her.

"Excuse me," he said. "May I have a look at your *Times*?"

She glanced at him briefly and nodded.

"Thank you." He dove into the newspaper and remained there all the way to the airport, except for an occasional surreptitious glance at his distant traveling companion.

Sandy checked in at curbside, but the woman followed her bags inside the terminal. Probably off to Europe or Asia; the last he would see of her. He realized, to his surprise, that she was the first woman he had found attractive since the moment he had heard about Jock Bailley's stroke.

He reached the gate just as first-class boarding was announced, took his seat and ordered orange juice. He was pleased, a few moments later, to see the woman from the car pass his seat and enter the tourist compartment. Pity she wasn't flying first class, he thought.

Twice during the flight he got up to go to the john and caught a glimpse of her in a seat a few rows back, her long legs spilling over into the aisle. He noted that she was not wearing a wedding ring.

At LaGuardia the limo driver was waiting with Sandy's name scrawled on a piece of cardboard. He beckoned the man to follow him to baggage claim, and the wait was nearly half an hour. The woman stood across the carousel, waiting just as impatiently as he. Her bags came a moment before his, and he hurried to catch up with her as she walked toward the taxis. As he had expected, there was a long line, and she looked annoyed.

"May I offer you a lift into town?" he asked. "Seems the least I could do, since I shared your car in San Francisco."

She turned a looked at him. "Where are you going?"

"Madison and Seventy-fourth, but the driver will drop you wherever you're going."

"Thank you, yes," she said, offering him a tiny smile.

He held the door of the car, a sedan this time, as she got in. Neither of them had a newspaper now.

"My name is Sandy Kinsolving," he said, offering his hand.

She took it. "I'm Cara Mason."

"Where are you headed, then?" he asked as the car pulled into traffic.

"Sixty-third, between Park and Madison."

"Nice block; have you lived there long?"

"A while."

"What brings you to New York?"

"I live here."

Oops. He was nervous. "Of course. What do you do in the city?"

"I'm an interior designer."

"With a firm?"

"With a partner."

"What do you specialize in?"

"Everything from the domestic to the industrial."

"Are you any good?"

She turned and regarded him coolly. "I'm very good indeed."

"As it happens, I'm in the market for a designer."

She looked doubtful. "Really?"

"Are you available?"

"For design work?"

Sandy reddened. "Just that."

"When?"

"Immediately."

"Why are you interested in me? As a designer, I mean."

"As it happens, you're the only interior designer I know, and I have to start looking somewhere. Do you think you could show me some examples of your work?"

"I suppose so."

"Not if it's an imposition," he said, looking out the window.

"What sort of work are you looking to have done?"

"I have a fourteen-room apartment that was decorated by my late wife. Our tastes didn't agree."

"I expect I could give you a few ideas."

"I also have a wine business on Madison Avenue that needs attention. Some years ago I bought an old shop in London that looks simply wonderful. What I had in mind was making the New York shop look more like the London one."

"Do you have a business card?" she asked.

Sandy fished one from his wallet and handed it to her. "And you?"

She rummaged through her purse. "I'm afraid I don't have a card with me," she said. She produced a pen and scribbled her name and number on a sheet of paper, ripped it from her notebook, and handed it to him.

They rode the rest of the way in silence. Sandy would have asked her to dinner, but he had the feeling that the invitation would blow his chances with her. Best to start with business.

"When could you bring over some photographs of your work?" he asked.

"Would this evening be convenient?" she replied.

Sandy smiled. "Around eight? I can probably rustle up something to eat."

"I may be busy later," she said. "Let's make it seven; by then I should know more about my schedule."

Sandy handed her another card, this one with his home address. "Seven it is."

"Just there, driver," she said, pointing to a slim brownstone with heavily lacquered front door and a huge brass knocker.

The driver opened the door, and Sandy got out to say good-bye. He was taller than she, just. "See you this evening."

"Thanks for the lift," she said, following the driver to the door. She unlocked the door and disappeared inside.

When Sandy got back into the car, he discovered that he was short of breath and trembling. Had it been so long since a woman had done this to him? He nodded.

It had. He began thinking about the evening and how to put Ms. Cara Mason at her ease in his home. It had been a long time since he had had a date that wasn't simply an assignation. He was going to have to rediscover some social skills.

CHAPTER

17

Sandy got a couple of hours' work done, then went home to prepare for his guest. He left her name with the lobby man, so she wouldn't be detained while he called upstairs, then he made a quick tour of the apartment to be sure the maid had done a good job; the woman had been slacking off since Joan hadn't been around to make sure she did her work. He plumped a few cushions, wiped the fingerprints off a glass coffee table, and pronounced the place ready.

He took a shower, dried his hair, and got into casual clothes—a soft flannel shirt, cavalry twill trousers, and a pair of alligator loafers that he hadn't often worn, because Joan hadn't liked them. He was nervous, and he considered having a quick drink, then decided against it.

The doorbell rang at seven promptly, and he saw that Cara Mason had dressed down a bit from her business suit, too. She was wearing a beige cashmere dress that suited her coloring very well.

"Come in," he said, showing her into the living room. "Can I get you something to drink?"

"Some mineral water, if you have it; fizzy, please."

Sandy left her standing in the middle of the living room looking around, while he went to the wet bar for a bottle of San Pellegrino. He poured two glasses and handed her one. "What do you think?" he asked.

She looked at him. "Is there a room in the place that was done the way *you* wanted it?"

"Yes, my study; come with me." He led her into the room and watched her take it in.

"Yes," she said, "this is more like you."

"How can you tell? We've just met."

"I can tell," she said. "It's what I do." She seated herself on the sofa and opened a portfolio on the coffee table. "Come and look through my work, and see if there's anything in particular that you like."

He sat next to her and slowly flipped the pages. He stopped at a color photograph of a San Francisco living room, with a view of the Golden Gate Bridge. "You've worked in San Francisco, too?"

"I grew up there," she said, "and until a year ago I was employed by a firm of architects. I did some independent work, too; this was one of the jobs."

"I like it very much."

"Would you like to live in it?"

"I don't think so."

"Keep looking."

He continued through the portfolio, looking at both San Francisco and New York rooms, and he was impressed. "I'm impressed," he said.

"But you didn't see anything that made you want to move in."

"No."

"Do you have some particular style in mind?"

"Not exactly; it's hard to explain."

"May I take a leap in the dark?"

"Of course."

"You'd like it if the apartment had the air of the most elegant, most comfortable men's club in the world."

He smiled. "You've nailed me."

"Just look at this room," she said. "It wasn't done hurriedly; everything in it looks chosen particularly, and you can't do that overnight. And it all works together."

"Thank you, I'm glad you like it."

"I think it would probably be best to order some traditional upholstered pieces—sofas and chairs—from a good house as a base and then pick out the accompanying pieces at good shops and auctions. I'd go for the best antiques you can afford."

"What sort of money are we talking about?"

"I haven't seen the dining room or the bedrooms, yet."

He spent half an hour showing her the rest of the apartment.

"I'm going to have a drink, now," he said, when they had returned to the study. "Will you join me?"

"I'll have a Scotch on the rocks," she said.

"Do you enjoy single malts?"

"I've never drunk one."

He poured them both a Glenlivet. "What do you think?" he asked when she sipped it.

"It's very . . . *big*, isn't it?"

"Actually, that's one of the lighter ones. It's an acquired taste."

"I think I could acquire it." She took another sip and set down her glass. "Now, you asked about money."

"I did."

"It depends a lot on what you're willing to spend for antique pieces and for pictures. Quite frankly, there's not a picture in the house I can stand, except what's in this room; they're mostly nautical, and I love them."

"Thank you; I agree about the other pictures. What does good antique furniture cost?"

"There's practically no limit, but I think we can find good pieces for, on average, between fifteen and thirty thousand dollars."

"And pictures?"

"Again, no limit, but if you're willing to spend, say, fifty thousand for four or five superb ones and five to twenty on a lot more, you'll be all right."

"Give me a total, ballpark figure."

"Between half a million and a million, depending on the pieces and pictures you choose."

"And your fee?"

"Ten percent of everything, furnishings and labor; but I'll save you at least that much with discounts and judicious buying."

"Agreed."

"We should be able to get you some money back, too. The things your wife chose—both the furniture and the pictures—while maybe not to your taste or mine, are auctionable. She obviously wasn't stupid."

"No, she wasn't. What do you think I could get for them?"

"Two or three hundred thousand, I should think."

"Whatever you can get for them at auction, I'll add to my budget."

She smiled broadly. "I like your style, Mr. Kinsolving."

"Sandy."

She raised her glass. "Cara."

"Cara, would you like me to fix us some dinner here, or would you rather go out?"

"I'll take my chances with you."

"Come into the kitchen; I'll see what's in the larder."

Sandy found some smoked salmon and eggs in the refrigerator, and some caviar, too. He scrambled the eggs with the salmon, made some toast, and served the caviar as an appetizer, straight, with little silver spoons. "Would you prefer champagne or vodka with your caviar?" he asked.

"Champagne, please."

He went to the wine cabinet and found a bottle of Krug '83. "This should have enough age on it to make it interesting," he said, working the cork from the bottle.

She tasted it. "Mmmmm," she breathed. "What's the word I'm looking for?"

"Yeasty," he said.

"Yes. You *are* in the wine business, aren't you?"

"I am, for my sins."

"Well, you must have sinned a lot to be doing this well at choosing drink," she said, raising her glass.

"Thank you, ma'am."

They ate the caviar, then the eggs and salmon.

"It all goes together so beautifully," she said.

"Thank you; it was meant to."

"Tell me something about your background," she said.

"Grew up in Weston, Connecticut, went to Exeter and Amherst, met my wife in college, got her pregnant, married her—in that order—produced a son.

Advertising for a couple of years, then joined my father-in-law's liquor business and eventually started the wine division. He died six weeks ago and left me the wine division."

"When did your wife die?"

"Five weeks ago."

"How?"

"She was murdered."

Cara put down her glass. "Do you mind telling me about it?"

He related the events of that Saturday night.

"That's terrible," she said.

"Yes, it was."

"Were you devastated?"

"I was numb. I have, in fact, remained numb, until tonight."

"What do you mean?"

"I mean that this dinner is the first pleasant social interaction I've had with another human being since it happened."

"Were you and your wife very close?"

"We had grown apart over a very long time."

"Do you miss her?"

"No, I do not. I'm glad to have my son, though; he's finishing up a residency in cardiology at Lenox Hill Hospital."

"You're a very direct man, Sandy."

"It's a waste of time to be any other way. Now you."

"I told you I grew up in San Francisco. Went to Berkeley, studied architecture, but discovered I was more interested in the inside of buildings than their structures. Joined my father's firm as a designer; when he died and the firm closed, I went to another."

"Ever married?"

"Once; for three years. A mistake."

"Whose?"

"Mine."

"You're pretty direct, too, Cara."

"We're in agreement on that point," she replied.

"Good. Cara, I'm very attracted to you. In fact, I'd be very pleased if you would come to bed with me right now."

She shook her head. "Too soon," she said. "But please don't think that's a flat turndown. You're a very attractive man."

"Thank you."

"I want your job, Sandy, but I won't sleep with you to get it."

"You've got it, on your qualifications and what you've suggested to me. As beautiful as you are, I wouldn't spend a million dollars just to get you into the sack. You can decide whether you want to sleep with me quite independently of the job."

She smiled, but said nothing.

"Would you like some coffee?"

She glanced at her watch. "Thank you, no. I've had a long day, as you have, and I could use some rest." She stood up. "Do you mind if I go now?"

"Yes, but I can live with it."

"I'll come back tomorrow when you're not here and make a floor plan and some rough sketches. Will you tell the doorman to let me in?"

"Yes, of course."

"I'll have something for you to look at in a week or so."

"I wouldn't like it to be that long before I see you again. How about dinner this weekend?"

"Saturday is good for me."

"And for me."

He retrieved her portfolio and walked her to the door.

"Good night," she said, offering her hand.

He took it. "Good night, and go safely. I'll look forward to Saturday," he said.

"So will I," she replied.

CHAPTER

18

S andy sat in Sam Warren's office at Mayfair Trust and listened to the presentation prepared by a younger associate at the bank, on the acreage, buildings, equipment, replanting and stock at the Larsen Winery. When the young man had finished, Warren took over.

"Here's where we are," the banker said. "Larsen wants twelve million for the property."

"What's it worth, in your opinion?" Sandy asked.

"Like anything else, it's worth what somebody will pay for it. Fortunately for you, because of the costs and uncertainties involved in replanting with phyloxera-resistant vines, the industry is in a period of retrenchment, and there's not likely to be a lot of bidding on the property. Our research has uncovered what Larsen actually has invested in the property, and, of course, what he owes, and I think what we need to come up with is a maximum amount we're willing to offer that would get him out of the business without a loss on his investment; actually, a small profit."

"And what is that number?"

"Eight million eight; we think that's about right."

"I see."

"I'd suggest offering eight, then working your way up in negotiations. It's important for him to understand right off that you're not going to pay anything near his asking price."

"I agree."

"There's another important consideration," Warren said.

"What's that?"

"Larsen employs a man who is, by all reports, a very fine winemaker. His name is Bernini, Italian-American, forty-two, good track record. He and Larsen have not hit it off, Larsen being so technically oriented, and in order for the vineyard to be worth the eight million eight, you're going to have to be able to sign him to a long-term contract at very good money. We feel that Bernini is very important to the operation."

"Has anyone talked to him?"

"Not yet. I think it would be best if you did that personally. We can structure an earnings and stock option package for him that would make it attractive for him to stay, if you can offer him a lot more freedom to pursue his own methods."

"Did you say stock options?"

"Yes. He's going to have to have the prospect of participation down the line somewhere. It's manageable, and we recommend such a course of action. The autocratic, one-hundred-percent owner is a thing of the past; if you want good people you're going to have to allow them to buy in."

"All right."

"My suggestion is that you contact Bernini, tell him you're interested in buying, then hand him off to us; we'll talk with his representative and structure an offer to the man, then we'll be in a position to negotiate seriously with Larsen." Warren handed him a slip of paper. "Here's his phone number; it's your call as to whether to go out there and see him, or just talk to him on the phone."

"Okay, I'll think about that," Sandy said. "If I pay eight million eight for the property, is that going to leave me enough capital to expand into San Francisco and operate the combined businesses?"

"We feel you can do it without incurring debt, but we think that we should set up a line of credit, just in case. We don't want you to feel pinched. Personally, my advice would be to acquire the vineyard, consolidate the operations and identity of the London and New York stores to the maximum extent possible, then establish good cash flow and operating profits before going into San Francisco. We're only talking about a period of a year, possibly two, before you make the San Francisco move."

"That sounds like good advice," Sandy said. "I'd want to devote some time to bringing the vineyard up to speed in terms of the quality of the output and reidentifying it with me and my company. Opening in San Francisco at the same time might be too much to bite off."

"That's our view," Warren said.

Sandy stood up. "Sam, thanks for your recommendations. I'll give all this some thought, contact Bernini, then get back to you in a few days." He shook hands with his bankers, then left.

He walked over to Fifth Avenue and took a taxi down to Fifty-seventh Street, then walked a few yards west to the Rizzoli bookstore. In the rear of the shop was a newsstand that handled foreign and out-of-town newspapers, and he picked up a San Francisco paper.

He went to a deli across the street, ordered a sandwich and iced tea, then opened the paper. The story was still on page three. It began:

GALLERY OWNER FOUND

Peter Martindale, owner of the Martindale Gallery, where a killing took place earlier this week, was located in Los Angeles by detectives from San Francisco Homicide. Mr. Martindale had left for Los Angeles on the day of the shooting to make a scheduled speech at UCLA on nineteenth-century English art, and the gallery owner was speaking at the university at the time the murder occurred in San Francisco.

Well, thought Sandy, he certainly covered his own tracks well enough. But what the hell happened at the gallery? He read on.

Police theorize that the killer entered the gallery through an unlocked rear door, shot the woman, and stole the cash box and a pistol from the desk. The cash box was recovered from a street wastebasket two blocks away and is being examined for fingerprints and other evidence; the pistol has not been recovered. Police believe it may have already been sold on the street.

So it was simply a run-of-the-mill crime? Some street kid had gone into the gallery and, unknowingly, had done Sandy's work for him? It seemed too good to be true, Sandy thought, and when he read the next paragraph, he knew his intuition was correct.

The murdered woman has been identified as Sally Smith Fleming, the gallery's assistant manager for four years, who had remained after the usual closing hours to meet a client from New York, who has not been identified. Mr. Martindale told the police that he received a telephone call from the client the day before and had asked his wife, Helena, who co-manages the gallery, to stay late and meet with him. Mrs. Martindale had apparently passed on the assignment to Ms. Fleming. Police have been unable to locate Mrs. Martindale to speak with her about the incident.

Sandy nearly choked on his iced tea. The woman wasn't Martindale's wife? He broke out in a sweat and had to mop his face with his napkin. Feeling dizzy, he pressed the cold tea glass to his forehead and tried to think. He had come within minutes of murdering the wrong woman.

And Helena Martindale was still alive.

CHAPTER

19

Sandy sat in the San Francisco restaurant, Postrio, and looked across the table at Mike Bernini. "So," Sandy said, "what do you think?"

"I think it's interesting," Bernini said.

"That's all? *Interesting?*"

"Well, I haven't looked around; I mean, I don't know what else is available in the industry."

"Mike, the industry is in a state of shock at the moment, because of the phyloxera business. You're working at one of the few vineyards that's ahead of the game on that point. As I understood things, your principal difficulty has been your relationship with Larsen."

"That's right," Bernini replied, "but how do I know I won't have a similar relationship with you?"

"For a start, I don't approach the business of winemaking as chemistry; I believe it's an art and that you're an artist."

"I'd want a free hand," Bernini said.

121

"I'm not going to give you a free hand, and neither is anybody else. I'm not unknowledgeable about wine, and if I own a vineyard I'm going to want the product to meet my expectations in terms of both quality and marketability. If you and I disagree as to what direction the winemaking should take, I'm going to make the final decision. What I can promise you is that I will respect your abilities and give you every opportunity to meet the requirements I set. If I want a big wine, I'll expect you to make a big wine and not a thin one, but my requirements are not going to be either impossible or unreasonable."

Bernini looked uncertain.

Sandy leaned forward on his elbows. "Mike, I want you to go home and think about what you want to do with the rest of your life. If you want to be in the construction business or the computer business or some other business, then go do it. But if you decide you want to make wine, then I'm offering you the opportunity of a lifetime. I have an expanding business in New York and London to run, and I'm not going to have the time to look over your shoulder while you do your work. My intention—and I'm perfectly willing to put this in writing—is to work with you to define a set of parameters for what we want to do and what we think is possible to do, and then let you get on with it. I think that, together, you and I can build a great winery that the world will admire, and in so doing, we can both make enough money to keep us in the style to which we'd like to become accustomed."

"All right, I'll think about it," Bernini said.

"I'm going to want an answer next week," Sandy said. "If I'm going to buy this vineyard without you, then the negotiations are going to be very different. But if you want to do this—*really* want to do it—then just say so and we'll get your lawyer and my bankers together and work out a deal that's right for both of us." Sandy glanced at his watch. He had already paid the check, and he had only another five minutes to spare. He stood up and offered Bernini his hand.

Bernini got up and shook hands. "I'll call you next week, Sandy," he said.

Sandy left the restaurant. Parked at the curb was a Lincoln Town Car with his name on a card in the window; the driver was leaning against the car, smoking a cigarette.

"I'm Mr. Kinsolving," he said to the man, then got into the back seat. "Let's go."

The driver got into the car and drove away from the restaurant.

Sandy could see the driver's eyes in the rearview mirror. "So?" he asked.

"I guess you thought you got lucky, didn't you?"

Sandy didn't say anything.

Martindale chuckled. "I can just see the scene; you arrive at the gallery, and there's all this mess, and you think God has saved you from this awful fate."

"What the hell happened?"

"I don't know, for sure; I think perhaps Helena asked Sally to meet the customer, and she just got unlucky. They've arrested the guy, you know."

"No, I didn't know; I don't read the San Francisco papers every day."

"Black kid, eighteen or nineteen; walked in and popped her, then took the cash and the gun. They found the gun on him when he got busted in a dope deal. Pity it wasn't Helena, huh?"

Sandy remained quiet. He felt trapped, and he resisted the temptation to bolt from the car. Martindale was driving aimlessly around the city.

"You're awfully quiet, Sandy."

"I don't have anything to say, really. What's next in your plans?"

"Oh, my plans haven't changed; they've just become more difficult. Helena has moved in with Saul Winner."

"Winner? Is that the painter she's been seeing?"

"Yes."

"I've seen his work at the Modern, in New York."

"Oh, yes; Saul is a very important artist. He lives in one of those big old houses on Nob Hill, and he even has some security. It's going to take some time for me to work out just how your job should be done. Can you come to San Francisco on a notice of, say, a day or two?"

"I don't know. Maybe."

"Well, then, I'll just work something out, find a time when she's regularly away from Winner's house, and when I have it all together, I'll call you."

"I'm not going to be at your beck and call, you son of a bitch," Sandy said.

Martindale stopped the car, then turned in his seat and stared at Sandy. "You'd better understand this right now," he said. "This is going to happen when *I* say it's going to happen, or you're going to suffer some terrible consequences. Do you understand me?"

Sandy gritted his teeth. "I understand you."

"I hope so," Martindale said. "You see, you're in this position because you care what happens to you. I, on the other hand, don't give a damn what happens to me, not at the moment. That gives me a very large advantage in dealing with you."

Sandy didn't reply, but he knew Peter Martindale was

right: he cared desperately what happened to him, and it was the only reason he was playing Martindale's game.

Martindale drove Sandy to the Ritz-Carlton and deposited him under the portico. Sandy watched him drive away. He experienced an urge to chase the car down and strangle the man to death, but he knew he was in no position to do that. He could only wait and hope for a way out.

CHAPTER

20

Sandy picked up Cara Mason at her East Sixty-third Street town house for their Saturday night dinner date, and Cara asked him in for a drink. She led him past two offices to an upstairs living room, where a tall blonde woman waited for them.

"Sandy," Cara said, "I'd like you to meet my partner, Thea Morgenstern."

"How do you do," Sandy said, shaking the attractive woman's hand.

"Thea and I share the house as well as the business," Cara said.

Thea Morgenstern spoke up. "I'm sort of the house mother here; I have to meet all of Cara's dates to be sure I approve."

"Thea—" Cara began.

"And do you approve?" Sandy asked.

"Sweetheart," she said, pouring a Scotch, "with the kind of design job you've given her, I'd approve of the hunchback of Notre Dame."

"Thea!" Cara exclaimed, with comic shock. "Sandy, I apologize for my partner. She's far too interested in money."

"I have a great deal of respect for money, myself," Sandy said, laughing.

"I've seen Cara's sketches of your job," Thea said, "and I think you're going to be delighted."

"That's more than I've seen," Sandy said.

"And you won't just yet," Cara broke in. "Not until I'm ready, and that will be next week sometime."

"You're going to love it," Thea said. "So masculine, and yet, I think any woman would be very happy in it." She arched an eyebrow at Cara, who blushed.

"Sounds perfect," Sandy said. "What else are you girls—excuse me—ladies—"

"Women," Thea said.

"What else are you women working on?"

"Well, there's Cara's South Carolina job," Thea said.

"You're doing something in South Carolina?" Sandy asked. "I didn't know you ranged so far afield."

Cara looked uncomfortable. "A town house in Charleston, but don't worry, it won't interfere in the least with your project."

"I'm so glad," Sandy said, smiling to put her at ease. "And Thea, what are you working on?"

"Oh, all my stuff is so dull, compared to Cara's," she said. "I mean, making over a wine shop is something more interesting than anything I'm working on."

"We haven't gotten into the wine shop," Cara said, "so lay off, Thea."

"We should do that soon," Sandy said. "It's going to entail a trip to London."

"Take her away," Thea said.

"Not just yet," Cara exclaimed. "Thea would sell me into white slavery for a job, Sandy, and I think I'd better get you out of here before she embarrasses me further."

"Ready when you are," Sandy said. "Thea, a pleasure to meet you; I'm going to be keeping your partner very busy for a while."

"You do that, Sandy," Thea replied, shaking his hand again. "Do what you will with her."

"Thea!" Cara grabbed her handbag and led Sandy out of the house. In the car, she laughed. "Thea's something of a character, as you can see."

"I liked her," Sandy said. "Have you known her long?"

"Since we were children. We grew up together."

"In San Francisco?"

"Yep. Where are you taking me for dinner?"

"Cafe des Artistes. I know you've probably been a hundred times, but I do love the place."

"Actually, I've never been there."

"You amaze me; it's one of New York's landmarks."

"Well, I guess I've led a sheltered life," Cara said.

"That, my lady, is coming to an end," Sandy proclaimed.

They were seated in a good corner of the old restaurant, and Cara handed him her menu.

"I place myself in your hands," she said.

"You're a smart woman," Sandy replied. "Let's start with a pair of Champagne *fraise des bois*," he said to the waiter.

"Mmmm," she said when she had had her first sip. "It's like strawberry champagne."

"Just a little dash of wild strawberry liqueur at the bottom," Sandy said.

"And what are we going to have for dinner?"

"We'll start with the table of charcuterie behind you there."

"It all looks wonderful."

"And then, for a change of pace, I think we'll have the bourride."

"What's bourride?"

"A sort of fish stew, with lots of garlic."

"I love garlic."

"As long as we both have it, we're all right."

"And what will we drink with the bourride?"

"Something special, something I sent over this afternoon: a bottle of very old white burgundy, a Le Montrachet, '55."

"That, I've heard about," she said, "but I've never had it."

The wine arrived as she spoke, and after the ritual of tasting, a glass of golden liquid stood before each of them. Cara tasted hers.

"I've never tasted anything remotely like it," she said. "I didn't even know white wines lived that long."

"If they're very lovingly cared for," Sandy said. "This one has been in the same spot in the same cellar for about twenty years. In fact, I bought the wine with the cellar."

"You buy cellars?"

"I own several. I'm always looking for more storage space for wines, and I prefer cellars to warehouses. I'll give you a tour one of these days."

"A tour of cellars," she said, sipping her Le Montrachet. "No one has ever been so romantic."

"There's nothing more romantic than good wine growing old in a deep, dank cellar."

"I'll take your word for it."

They sat, sated, amid the ruins of an assortment of desserts, sipping another white wine.

"And what is this one?" she asked. "It tastes like honey."

"It's a Chateau Coutet, 1961; a very great white Bordeaux."

"It's the perfect ending to the evening," she said.

"No, it isn't," he replied. "There are other appetites yet to be satisfied."

She gazed across the table at him. "Yes," she said.

Sandy beckoned the waiter. "Check!" he called.

CHAPTER

21

When Sandy woke, his first sensation was of pain, then of numbness; his left shoulder hurt, and the fingers on that hand were numb. He opened his eyes and his vision was filled with a tangle of auburn hair. The top of Cara Mason's head was a lovely sight, he thought.

He experimented with moving his shoulder to see if he could get the blood flowing in his fingers, but when he moved, she moaned and snuggled closer. She lifted her head and opened an amazingly green eye.

"Yes?" she asked hoarsely.

"It's just that my arm is asleep," he said.

"Oh," she said. "Just a moment." She climbed on top of him, then rolled off on the other side. Now her head was on his right shoulder. "Better?"

"Much. But I still have a problem."

"What's that?"

"I have to go to the bathroom."

"You don't really want to be in bed with me, do you?" she asked, digging him in the ribs.

"I very much want to be in bed with you," he groaned, "but—"

"All right, I'll let you go to the bathroom, if you'll come right back."

"I promise."

She rolled off his arm and put a pillow over her head.

Sandy ran to the bathroom and ran back. He dove under the covers and pulled her close to him again.

"That was quick," she said.

"It doesn't take long."

Her hand snaked under the covers and felt for him. "That's not all that doesn't take long," she said, giggling.

"You're right," he said. "Now, what are you going to do with it?"

Cara rolled on top of him and sat up, holding him firmly in both hands. "Well, let's see," she mused, running a finger along the length of him. "Ooo, that got a response, didn't it?"

"It did," he panted.

"Well, let's see if it will fit in here." She lifted her buttocks, then slowly sat down on him.

"It fits," he breathed.

"I'll bet I can make it smaller," she said, moving slowly up and down. "Not right away, I hope, but eventually." She moved faster.

Sandy sat up and put his arms around her. "That's it," he said. "Make it smaller. Eventually." He kissed her, tugging at her lips with his teeth, playing with her tongue. "Oh, my!" he said suddenly, "It's about to get smaller!" He fell back onto the bed, arching his back, matching her strokes.

Cara gave a short, sharp yell, quivered for a moment and fell forward onto his chest. "My God!" she panted. "That worked wonderfully, didn't it?"

"Wonderfully," he managed to say while trying to let his breathing return to normal.

They lay locked together for another five minutes, he stroking her hair, she kissing his chest and neck.

"This is wonderful," Sandy said at last.

"No, it's better than wonderful," she said. "I just can't think of the word right now."

"Has it been a long time?" he asked.

"Long time," she replied. "Forever."

"Why?"

"You weren't around."

He laughed. "You must have had other offers."

"They weren't you. You seem to be perfect, Sandy Kinsolving. Is there something terribly wrong with you that I don't know about?"

"Probably, but I never know what a woman thinks of as terribly wrong. What do women want, anyway?"

"This," she said, snuggling closer.

"That's all?"

"That's it, mostly."

"Funny, that's what men want, too."

"I'm hungry," she said.

"Me, too."

"My turn to cook," she said, raising her head and looking at him. She laughed. "Your hair is funny."

"So is yours," Sandy replied.

She clapped both hands to her head and leapt from bed, running toward Joan's bathroom.

Sandy got up, brushed his hair, slipped into a robe and found one for her. He looked around the room. It was oddly bare, but he was very glad that he had removed Joan's things a few days before. He left the robe on the bed for Cara and went to his own bathroom. He shaved and showered, and as he dried himself he caught the aroma of bacon frying. He found his slippers, splashed on some cologne and headed for the kitchen.

Halfway there, he remembered the papers. He walked to the front foyer, reaching it just as the elevator doors opened. His son was standing in the car, holding the Sunday *New York Times*.

"Morning, Dad," Angus said, stepping from the elevator.

"Ah, morning, Angus," Sandy replied, gulping.

"Something wrong?"

Sandy shook his head.

"You look funny."

"Funny?"

"You look guilty, like I'd caught you at something." He sniffed the air. "Uh, oh," he groaned. "You got lucky didn't you?"

"I don't know that I'd put it quite . . . Yes, I got lucky. Would you like to meet her?"

"I don't guess you're up for tennis this morning, then?"

"Probably not."

"Maybe it would be better if I met her another time," Angus said, grinning.

"You're a good son," Sandy said.

Angus handed him the newspaper. "Have a nice Sunday." He pressed the elevator button.

"Thank you, kiddo. We'll talk tomorrow?"

"You bet." The elevator doors slid open, Angus stepped aboard, still grinning. "Congratulations," he said as the doors closed.

Sandy laughed and padded toward the kitchen. The table was set for two, and Cara had found a plastic rose somewhere and put it in a little vase. There was a pitcher of orange juice on the table, and she was struggling with a champagne cork. He took the bottle from her and opened it. "A Buck's Fizz?" he asked.

"A what?"

"Champagne and orange juice."

"That's a mimosa."

"In London, it's a Buck's Fizz; I like it better. You just missed meeting my son."

Her face registered shock. "Like this?"

"He figured out the situation and very kindly excused himself."

"Obviously a well-brought-up young man."

"Certainly."

They dove into breakfast silently, exchanging only glances.

"What are you doing for lunch?" he asked finally.

"I haven't even finished breakfast," she protested.

"This will take a little planning; I need an answer."

"I'm all yours—*if* I can go home and change."

"You're on. What are you doing for dinner? You won't have to change."

"Oh, all right."

"And breakfast? It's part of the package."

"If I'm late for work, you'll just delay getting your sketches," she said.

"I can live with that." He put down his fork. "Let me make a couple of phone calls."

CHAPTER

22

The light twin aircraft set down gently; they had
left Teterboro something over an hour before.

"Where *are* we?" Cara demanded. She was
blindfolded.

"You'll have to guess," Sandy said.

The airplane taxied to a stop before the little terminal, and the pilot cut the engines.

"We'll meet you here at ten tomorrow morning," he
said to the pilot, and the man nodded. Sandy took their
two bags in one hand and Cara's arm in the other.

"Can't I see where we are?"

"Not yet." He led her to the little car, an old MGB
convertible, stowed their bags and helped her into the
front seat. When they were away from the airport he
took off her blindfold.

She looked around. "So, where is this?"

"You don't recognize it?"

"This is an eastern place; I'm a westerner."

"It's called Martha's Vineyard."

"I know *about* Martha's Vineyard," she said. "Where are we going now?"

"To Edgartown,"he replied. "I think you'll like it.

He stopped the car in front of the house, a spic-and-span, two-story Victorian with a widow's walk, painted white with green shutters.

"It's gorgeous," she said. "A bed and breakfast?"

"It's mine," Sandy replied. "I bought it fifteen years ago." He got their bags, led her up the front walk, and opened the front door with his key.

She stepped into the foyer and looked around at the old furniture and nearly bare walls. "You never got around to fixing it up, huh?"

"I fixed up everything but the interior," he said. "I put a roof on it, replaced a lot of rotten wood, painted it, rewired and replumbed it. But you're right, the furnishings leave a lot to be desired. I was hoping maybe you could make some suggestions."

"Oh, boy, could I make some suggestions!"

"But don't worry about that now. Come on; I'll give you a quick tour, and then we've got someplace to go."

"I thought we were there."

"Sort of." He showed her the house's three bedrooms, his little study, and the kitchen. She seemed entranced with the place.

"How much time do you spend here?"

"Not as much as I've wanted to. Joan never liked the island, said there were too many tourists. She was right, of course, but the tourists mean there are some good restaurants and galleries, so I don't mind them."

"Good point," she said. "Besides, I'm a tourist."

"Okay, get into your swimsuit, and bring some jeans."

"What now?"

"Stop asking questions, and do as you're told."

"Yessir," she said, saluting smartly.

The little sloop cut through the water like a sharp knife, parting the small seas, heeling to the breeze. They sat up to windward, their feet on the leeward seat, while Cara helmed the yacht parallel with the beach.

"Head in there," Sandy said, pointing to an indentation in the shoreline. He went forward and got the anchor ready, then, with hand signals, conned her to their anchorage. When he was sure the anchor had dug in he came aft to a waiting beer. "Very impressive," he said. "You know how to make a boat go to windward."

"I grew up on San Francisco Bay," she said. "It comes with the territory, if you're my father's daughter. Ready for some lunch?"

"Sure am." He set up the little cockpit table, and watched her arrange lunch on it.

"So," she said, "how did you make all this happen on the spur of the moment?"

"Pretty simple," he said. "I called Teterboro and ordered up the air charter, then I called Seth Hotchkiss at the filling station and asked him to put the battery in the car and leave it at the airport, and I asked him to pick up some lunch and leave it in the fridge. Easy when you know how."

"Your talents never fail to amaze me," she said, kissing him. "I must remember to lay a big tip on the doorman at the Ritz-Carlton the next time I'm in San Francisco."

"You think he was matchmaking?" he asked.

She shrugged. "Who knows?"

"I'll always be grateful to him, in any case."

She clinked her beer can against his. "To doormen," she said. "And matchmakers."

They sat on the deck at the Edgartown Yacht Club and sipped brandy. The sun was well down, and the stars shone in their millions.

"It's all so perfect," Cara said, sipping her cognac.

"It is now," Sandy replied. "It's as though some great piece of a puzzle fell into place."

She laid her head on his shoulder. "That's a lovely thing to say."

"Cara, don't you think you could give my little design job a lot more attention if you were living in the place?" He held his breath. This was precipitous, and he wasn't sure how she'd react.

She sat up and looked at him. "You're offering me the apartment? Are you moving?"

He laughed. "A little slow on the uptake, aren't you? I'm not going anywhere."

"Oh," she said, and her shoulders sagged.

"'Oh'? What kind of answer is that?" He hadn't really expected her to accept, but still, he was stung with disappointment.

"It's not an answer, it's a stall," she said. "I'm stalling so I can think for a minute."

"Take your time."

She did. She gazed out over the water at the moored yachts, bobbing at their moorings, and her face was inexpressibly sad. Finally she turned to him. "Please take this in the best possible way. After what's happened to us this week, your idea is perfectly logical; it's just that I can't."

"Give me your reasons," he said.

"I can't do that, either," she replied. "Not as fully as I would like."

"Some impediment?"

She nodded. "That's fair to say."

"Another man?"

She shrugged. "Sort of."

"Sort of a man?" Sandy asked.

"It's all the answer I can give you right now, Sandy. My life is in something of a muddle, and I have some straightening out to do before I can give you the answer you want." She put her hand on his. "Believe me when I tell you, I'd like nothing better than to go back to Sixty-third Street, pack up, and move in with you."

"If it's what you want, then do it," Sandy said.

"It wouldn't be fair to you, to both of us, really. I know this is hard to take, but you're just going to have to trust me. When I'm on my feet—in more ways than one—I'll tell you, and we can start from there. Will you wait until I tell you that?"

"How long?"

"I honestly don't know. There's no easy solution, but now that I have a motive to sort it out, I'll move faster. I hope you don't think that's too mysterious."

"It's pretty mysterious, all right, but I'll trust your judgment."

"Thank you, Sandy," she said, then kissed him.

He kissed her back. "There's no impediment to going back to the house and going to bed with each other, is there?"

She smiled and kissed him again. "None whatever."

The following morning they met the airplane and

flew back toward New York, each silent and sad, lost to the other. When he dropped her off at Sixty-third Street, she kissed him passionately.

"Thank you, thank you," she said.

"Not at all."

"Can I show you some sketches on Wednesday?"

"Come to the office," he said, handing her his card.

"I'd rather come to the apartment," she said. "After all, it's what I'm designing."

He nodded.

"Seven o'clock?"

He nodded again, and she was gone.

CHAPTER

23

On Monday afternoon Sandy met with Sam Warren at the Mayfair Trust.

"Larsen's lawyer called this morning," Warren said. "He's come down to ten million, five. The lawyer took credit for talking him into being sensible, but he says ten million five is the least he'll take."

"We haven't even made an offer yet," Sandy said.

"True. I think the lawyer, when he looked at the deal, saw that Larsen was way out of the ballpark and talked him around. I also choose to ignore the bold talk about nothing less than ten million, five. We should just make our offer as if he'd said nothing."

"We still have to make a deal with Mike Bernini, before we can make our offer," Sandy said. "And I haven't heard from him."

"What's with the guy?" Warren asked. "You saw him, what do you think?"

"He didn't seem all that interested," Sandy replied. "I thought he'd jump at a new deal, but he didn't."

"Maybe he's a better negotiator than we think."

Sandy shrugged. "Maybe he just doesn't know what he wants."

"Lots of people are like that. Do you want me to put together an offer to him, just as a starting point, to get things moving?"

"No; if he doesn't want it, then I don't want him. I'm not going to beg the guy to come aboard."

The phone rang, and Warren picked it up. He listened for a moment, then handed the receiver to Sandy. "It's your office."

Sandy took the phone. "Hello?"

"A couple of calls, Sandy," his secretary said. "Mike Bernini called; I know you were expecting to hear from him."

"Thanks, Becky," he said, scribbling the number.

"There was one other call; somebody named Bart. He wouldn't leave a last name." She gave him the number.

"Any idea who he is?" Sandy asked. "Doesn't ring a bell."

"He said you'd know."

"Thanks, Becky." He hung up, grinning. "Bernini called," he said to Warren. "You mind if I call him from here?"

"Go right ahead; I'm dying to know what he has to say."

Sandy called the number and asked for Bernini.

"Sandy?" Mike Bernini asked.

"Yes, Mike."

"I'm glad you called back so quickly. First, I want to explain something; I know I didn't give you the reaction you wanted last week, and there was a good reason. My wife has been wanting to leave the valley. I wasn't happy at work, and that added to her doubts about staying in Napa, but we've talked it over, and I want to stay on if you buy out Larsen."

"That's terrific, Mike; I'm delighted to hear it."

"Everything depends on your offer, of course."

"Do you have a lawyer who can deal for you?"

"Yes."

"Have him call Sam Warren at the Mayfair Trust." He gave him the number. "Ask him to call first thing tomorrow morning, and we'll have the offer ready. They can work out the details."

"Great, Sandy; I hope we can come to terms."

"I hope so, too, Mike; I think we can really make something of this property. Everything depends on Larsen being reasonable, though; any offer I make you will be contingent on Larsen and I agreeing on a price and other terms."

"I hope it works. If it's any help to you, I think Larsen wants to sell badly."

"Thanks, I'll keep that in mind. We'll talk later in the week." Sandy hung up. "That's a load off my mind," he said to Warren.

"I'll put something together before five o'clock for your approval."

"Good. Sam, I've been admiring the pictures in your offices."

"Thank you, Sandy; we're very proud of them."

"Do you buy at auction?"

"No, we've bought everything in the place from a San Francisco dealer named Peter Martindale."

Sandy froze.

"He specializes in nineteenth-century English painting. I'll give you his number, if you like; next time you're out there go by his gallery. You're redoing your apartment, aren't you?"

"Yes, but I've pretty much decided on going with American painters."

"Well, if you change your mind, let me know."

Not bloody likely, Sandy thought.

Sandy left the bank and walked into Central Park, looking for a phone. He found one at the zoo, then dialed the number Martindale had left.

"Well, hello, Sandy," Martindale said. "How are you?"

"What do you want?" Sandy asked.

"I want you in San Francisco on Thursday; take the earliest plane you can get."

"Why?"

"Because I've worked it out. I'll pick you up at the Ritz at five o'clock in the Lincoln and brief you; then I have to get out of town."

"Thursday?"

"Don't disappoint me, my friend; the consequences would be devastating. And don't worry, it's going to be a snap; much easier than what *I* had to do." He hung up.

Sandy hung up, swearing. He walked around the zoo slowly, gazing blankly at the animals, feeling desperately sorry for himself. He had to find a way out of this, he thought. Every time he seemed to get his life in order, there was Martindale on the phone again.

He went back to his office. "Becky," he said to his secretary, "get me on a Thursday morning flight for San Francisco."

"Sure thing. A Cara Mason called; asked that you get back to her this afternoon."

He went to his desk and rang her number.

"Hi, Sandy," she said. "I'm afraid something's come up; do you think you could possibly wait until Monday for your sketches?"

"What's the problem?" he asked, trying to mask his disappointment.

"It's the Charleston job; I have to go to South Carolina tomorrow, and I won't get back until Sunday. I promise I'll have the sketches ready on Monday evening, though. Can we go over them at seven, then have dinner?"

At least she wanted to have dinner. "Sure," he said. "Monday evening at seven."

"Thank you so much for understanding," she said. "And I want to tell you again what a wonderful time I had over the weekend. I'll remember it always."

He felt a little better. "I'm glad. Have a good trip to Charleston, and I'll see you Monday evening."

"I'll look forward to it," she said.

Sandy hung up. Seven days until he could see her again. And he had something awful to do before then. If he could just get through the week, then maybe it would all be behind him when he saw her on Monday. He hadn't told her he was going to San Francisco; he didn't want anybody to know but his secretary. He'd have to arrange a meeting with Bernini or Larsen, something to legitimize the trip.

CHAPTER

24

Sandy sat in the Four Seasons Grill, across from his son, and sipped a good burgundy.

"So," Angus said, "there's a lady in your life."

"There is," Sandy said, "although she's just barely in."

"You haven't nailed her down, then?"

"Tell you the truth, she doesn't seem nail-downable, at least right away. She says she's got some sorting out to do in her own life before she's ready for any sort of commitment."

"You don't have a thing to worry about," Angus said. "How could she resist you? You're handsome, charming, and *rich*!"

"You're right, of course," Sandy replied.

Angus grinned. "I'm rich, too!" he crowed.

Sandy lifted his glass. "To being rich," he toasted.

"I'll drink to that," Angus said.

"How about you? Anything happening in the woman department?"

Angus blushed. "Funny you should ask. There's a girl in my class that I've seen a lot of lately."

"Why haven't I met her?" Sandy asked, wounded.

"When I say 'see a lot of,' I mean mostly studying. And when I say 'in my class,' I mean she's finishing at the same time. She's a surgical resident, actually."

Sandy started. "When do you finish?"

"On Friday."

Sandy had forgotten. "Good God! Is there some sort of graduation ceremony, or something? I've got to be in San Francisco on Friday."

"Relax, Dad, there's no ceremony to feel guilty about missing. We just finish work, pick up a certificate and we're out of there."

"Whew!" Sandy sighed.

"What takes you to San Francisco?"

"I'm buying a vineyard—at least, I *hope* I'm buying it. Negotiations are underway."

"That sounds exciting."

"It really is. It's something I've wanted ever since I got interested in wine. I've always thought of wine as the perfect partnership between God and man—God provides the right soil and climate and weather; man supplies the agricultural and winemaking skills, and above all, the drinking. God is generous; he doesn't ask for any of the wine."

Angus laughed and looked at the liquid in his glass. "I don't think I'll ever drink wine again without thinking of that."

"To change the subject, have you done anything about that business idea of yours?"

"Not yet. I wonder if I'm going off half-cocked; the idea doesn't seem quite so great as it did at first."

"It sounded like a good idea to me; it ought to be more fun than just practicing cardiology."

"Maybe you're right; in any case I think I'll take a couple of weeks off, first."

Sandy had a good thought. He took out his checkbook, wrote a very large check and handed it to Angus.

"Jesus!" Angus said, shocked. "What's this for?"

"I want you to do something for me."

"What?"

"You were going to take your grandfather's and your mother's ashes to Scotland, weren't you?"

"Yes. I'd planned to go next week."

"I want you to keep going."

"Keep going where?"

"Anywhere you want to go. Take your girl with you; see Europe, see the world. I don't want you back in this city until September, at the very earliest."

Angus gazed at the ceiling. "You know, I did sort of have this fantasy about picking up a Porsche at the factory and touring a bit."

"Great idea! Do it!"

"Three months?"

"Make it four!"

"Four months?"

"Listen, Angus, I know you; you're like me. You'll start this new business, and you'll give it your life for years. This is the first time since you were twelve that you don't have to be anywhere on Monday—not at school, not at college, not at med school, not at the hospital. For the first time ever, you're your own man. Take some time, travel, enjoy yourself. It'll be a long time before you'll feel this free again."

Angus looked at him. "There's a Porsche dealership a few blocks from here, isn't there?"

"I believe there is."

"Dad, I don't know anything about money; can I afford a Porsche?"

"Yes, you can."

"Let's get out of here," Angus said.

The two walked up Park Avenue together.

"By the way," Sandy said, "when you get back I want you to go and see a man named Sam Warren at the Mayfair Trust."

"What's that?"

"It's a private bank, a very good one. As your trustee, I've had them invest your trust fund, and I want you to sit down with Sam and talk about your plans." He handed Angus the banker's card. "You should talk with him briefly before you leave, open a checking account, and make some arrangements for credit abroad."

"Good idea," Angus said. "Dad, what sort of income can I expect from my trust?"

"Sam can give you a better idea, but I should think something on the order of seven hundred thousand to a million a year."

"That much?"

"Believe me, it isn't as much as it sounds. You're going to get hit hard by taxes, you know. I suggest you sit down with Sam and work out some sort of budget, so much put into your checking account each month, enough to cover your basic expenses. Sam will give you good business advice, too." He laughed. "I don't know why I'm give you fatherly advice about money; you've always been as tight with a buck as anybody I've ever known. I think you get it from your grandfather."

"Maybe I do; seems to come naturally."

"By the way, I'd like to invest in your business idea; I think it will do very well, indeed."

"Maybe I can work you in," Angus said, grinning.

They reached the car dealership, and spent an hour choosing a car and placing an order for European delivery. Then Angus said he wanted to drive a car, and Sandy excused himself.

"One last thing," Sandy said to his son. "While you're gone I want to be the only person who knows how to get in touch with you—except for Sam Warren, of course."

"Why?" Angus asked.

"Never mind why. Send all the postcards you like, but don't give anybody else an itinerary but Sam and me. Give me your word."

"This seems very mysterious to me, Dad."

"Trust me."

"Okay, you have my word; nobody knows my whereabouts but you and Sam Warren. And Maggie, of course; the girl I told you about."

"Angus, Maggie is going to be with you."

"You really think she'll come?"

"If she won't accept an offer like that, then you've chosen the wrong girl; keep looking."

"I'll tell her you said that."

"Good." Sandy hugged his son, an uncommon gesture of affection between the two of them, then he left the car dealer's and walked back toward his office.

Step one. He'd put his son out of reach of Peter Martindale. Step two was next.

CHAPTER

25

Sandy stood under the portico at the Ritz-Carlton and watched the Lincoln come to a stop. Martindale gave him a little wave; he was wearing a chauffeur's cap and dark glasses. Sandy got in.

"How are you, Sandy?" Martindale asked cheerfully as they drove away.

"I'm here; what's going on, Peter?"

"We're going to take a little drive," Martindale replied, "and then all will be revealed. Cheer up, your obligation is nearly at an end."

Sandy rested his head against the bolster and closed his eyes for a moment. He didn't want anything revealed; he wanted to be free of this maniac, free of any debt to him. Am I ungrateful? he asked himself. After all, Martindale had a great deal to do with where

I am today. No, he didn't, he thought, contradicting himself. Jock had done it all in his will. All but Joan's inheritance, he remembered reluctantly.

"Here we are," Martindale said.

Sandy opened his eyes. They were turning into the parking garage of a tall office building. Martindale was collecting a ticket from a machine, and the barrier was lifting. He drove down an incline, and the sunlight disappeared. It was like every other parking garage, dimly lit, lots of reinforced concrete.

"Pay attention," Martindale said. "Right, then left, then down a level, making a one-hundred-and-eighty-degree turn, then left again. Please note the elevators on your right."

"Why are we here, Peter?"

"Patience, Sandy, patience. Now, watch." Martindale stopped at a barrier, took a plastic card from his pocket and inserted it into a box mounted on a steel post. The barrier rose, and Martindale drove into a separate parking lot and pulled into a parking space. "A carpark within a carpark, you see," he said, "reserved for members of the law firm, Winthrop and Keyes, and their clients. It rises automatically when a car departs."

"I see," Sandy said. "Why do I care?"

"One more thing to note," Martindale said, "and then I'll tell you. Look over there." He pointed.

"The telephone booth?" Sandy said.

"Correct; the firm has generously supplied an old-fashioned telephone booth for the convenience of its people. You don't see actual telephone booths much any more."

"What of it?"

"It's very conveniently located. Tomorrow afternoon at two-thirty, Sandy, my wife will attend a deposition at Winthrop and Keyes. Helena has, you see, filed for divorce. She will arrive on time—she *always* arrives on time—in a red Mercedes 500SL convertible, a shiny new one, bought for her with my hard-earned money. The car wears a vanity license plate—DEALER, it says. She will stop at the entrance to the private carpark, give her name to the receptionist upstairs, be admitted, and park her car. She will proceed to the elevators, ride upstairs, and give her sworn testimony. When she is finished, probably in less than an hour, she will return to her car and drive away. Is that clear?"

"Yes."

"But she will not drive away, for you will be waiting in the telephone booth I have just shown you. You will arrive here between two forty-five and three o'clock. If you leave the door of the booth ajar, the light inside will not go on; if someone other than Helena comes along, you will be talking on the telephone; if someone seems to be waiting for the telephone, you call out that you will be a long while on the phone, and he will go away. You will see Helena as she enters her car. You will check to see that no one is about, then you will leave the telephone booth. Here, take this." He handed something wrapped in a handkerchief over the seat to Sandy.

Sandy took it and unwrapped the handkerchief. It was a short-barreled pistol, and Sandy had been to enough movies to know that the extension of the barrel was a silencer. "Where on earth did you get this?" he demanded. "It's illegal, isn't it?"

Martindale laughed. "Sandy, really; it's not necessary or advisable for you to know. Of course, it's illegal," Martindale said. "It's a thirty-eight; two in the head should do it. Take her handbag, keep any cash, then dump the bag in the waste receptacle over there," he said, pointing to a trash can, "where it will surely be found, thus establishing a motive of robbery." Martindale handed a key to Sandy. "Then, get into this car, which will be parked here, put on the cap and dark glasses and drive out of the lot. Drive slowly, cautiously. Drive the car to my gallery. There is a carpark across the street; park it there, leave the key in the glove box, and lock the car with the button on the door handle, here." He pointed to his left, then he looked back and smiled broadly at Sandy. "Then go and sin no more."

"Where will you be?" Sandy asked.

"In Tucson, where I will have gone to an opening of an artist I represent. I will take part in the deposition by telephone, then attend the opening, thus establishing, beyond doubt, my presence in another city."

Sandy was silent.

"Is this simple enough for you, Sandy?"

"How will I know it's your wife?" Sandy asked. "Last time, I thought the other woman was Helena."

"By her bright blonde hair," Martindale said, "and by the car, which I have described."

"The other woman had bright blonde hair," Sandy said.

"The other woman is, tragically, dead," Martindale replied. "Incidentally, don't touch the gun for any reason; wear gloves and some sort of coat when you fire it, and discard both as soon as possible. Certain residues are left on clothing when a gun is fired."

"I see," Sandy said.

"Is everything perfectly clear?" Martindale asked.

"Yes."

"Repeat your instructions as I've told you."

Sandy repeated what he was to do.

"Perfect. You really are a quick study, Sandy."

"And when this is done, Peter, it's over."

"Absolutely. When it's done, you and I will never again see each other, or even speak. Unless, of course, we happen to be seated next to each other on an airplane." He chuckled.

"Make sure that never happens," Sandy said.

"Don't worry, I will. Now, Sandy, I want you to get out of the car, take the elevator up to the lobby, and leave the building. You can get a cab back to the Ritz-Carlton; I have business upstairs."

Sandy rewrapped the pistol and put it into his coat pocket. He got out of the car and left Martindale sitting there.

Back on the street, he decided to walk to the Ritz-Carlton. The weight of the gun in his pocket was a constant distraction. When he reached his room he put the pistol in a drawer, under his underwear, then sat for a long time, staring out the window at the San Francisco skyline, wondering how he had come to this.

CHAPTER

When Sandy woke the following morning, he found that a fax had been slid under his door; he opened it and read the message from Sam Warren, that he and Mike Bernini's lawyer had concluded negotiations on a contract and that Larsen had come down to nine million even on his selling price for the vineyard. He telephoned Warren.

"Hello, Sandy," the lawyer said. "I trust you got my fax."

"I did, Sam, and I'm delighted," Sandy replied. "I know you recommended eight million eight as a maximum price, but I'm inclined to give Larsen the nine million. What do you think?"

"I think you're right; it's not worth quibbling about such a small percentage of the purchase price. What I'll do is agree to the price, but insist on a purchase of assets, instead of the corporate stock. They've been resisting that, but I think we're buying that sort of freedom from previous liability with the extra two hundred thousand."

"Sounds good. When do you think we can close?"

"It'll take a few weeks; we have to do our own inventory of the stock and take a few other precautions, but we'll get a sales agreement signed almost immediately, I should think. Are you happy with the deal I worked out with Bernini's lawyer?"

"Extremely. I think he'll be worth every penny. I thought I might take him to lunch today and celebrate."

"Let me call Larsen's lawyer and get the final agreement first," Sam said. "He should be in his office in another half hour."

"Call me back, then," Sandy said. He hung up and ordered breakfast, but when it came, he wasn't as hungry as he had thought. His elation over being so near agreement with Larsen was mixed with a deep dread of what the day held, and he left half the ham and eggs on the plate.

Warren called back inside an hour. "They've agreed," he crowed. "The deal's done. I'm faxing him documents, and Larsen will sign today and fax them back, then they'll FedEx the originals, and we'll have them by Monday. I'll have copies hand delivered to your lawyer."

"Thank you so much, Sam, for handling all this so expeditiously," Sandy said.

"It's what we do," Warren replied, then said goodbye and hung up.

Sandy called his office in New York and got his secretary on the line. "There's a case of Lafite Rothschild nineteen forty-five in the number one cellar," he said.

"Please send a stockman down for it, then put a big red ribbon on it and send it directly over to Sam Warren at the Mayfair Trust."

"Did we get the vineyard?" she asked.

"We did."

"I'm so happy for you, Sandy," she said. "I'll get the wine right over to Mr. Warren."

Sandy thanked her, then hung up and called Mike Bernini and invited him to lunch in the Ritz-Carlton's restaurant. He made the table reservation, then showered, shaved, and got dressed. He had some shopping to do before lunch. He left the hotel and, visiting several inexpensive shops, bought pretty much the same items he had thrown away not long before—a reversible raincoat, a tweed hat, and thin leather driving gloves. He left them in his hotel room and was in the restaurant in time to meet Mike Bernini.

He had a convivial lunch with Bernini, and they split a bottle of good champagne. Sandy tried to stop glancing at his watch, but he was unable to, nor was he able to hide his nervousness.

"Sandy," Bernini said, "are you feeling well? Is it too hot in here for you?"

Sandy dabbed at his forehead with his napkin. "I think I may be getting some sort of bug," he said. "Maybe I'll take a little nap after lunch."

"Good idea; take care of yourself," Bernini said.

At two o'clock Sandy shook Bernini's hand and said his good-byes. He went to his room, retrieved his clothing purchases and got the pistol from the safe in the closet.

At 2:45 Sandy arrived at the office building, wearing

the raincoat, plaid side out, the cap and sunglasses. The pistol banged against his thigh as he walked down the ramp into the garage. He avoided the elevators and continued down one level, following the route of the day before.

He stooped to pass under the barrier and, as he walked into the law firm's private parking area, he saw the red Mercedes 500SL with its distinctive license plate, DEALER. He went straight to the telephone booth and sat down, leaving the door ajar. He found he was sweating profusely.

He sat sideways in the booth, watching the lights above the elevator doors. He was too far away to read the numbers, so he walked quickly to the elevators and saw where the forty-first number was, then he returned to the booth and sat, waiting.

It will all be over soon, he kept telling himself, trying not to think about what he was about to do. He unwrapped the pistol and put it back into his raincoat pocket, making sure he could extract it quickly when needed.

I am not this kind of man, he kept telling himself, then he would think about his son and his business and his new vineyard, all of which he might lose if he didn't do this. His mind raced from one thing to another; he saw Cara's beautiful face, felt her auburn head on his shoulder, kissed her lips. Then he was firing the silenced pistol through the glass of the Mercedes, and blood was everywhere. He was covered in blood and glass, and there was blonde hair all over the front seat of the car.

He jerked back to reality. He saw the elevator door close and watched as the lights above it illuminated, one by one. He saw the forty-first light go on and stay on for a few seconds, then the order of the lights reversed. The car was coming down.

He hoped it would stop for other passengers, that other people would be present, preventing him from doing this awful thing, but the car ran smoothly, and nothing stopped it before its garage destination. He held his breath as the doors opened; maybe it would be somebody else. But a blonde woman in a red dress stepped from the car and walked purposefully toward the law firm's private parking area. She was attractive, he thought, though she wore more make-up than he liked on a woman. She walked toward the red Mercedes, stopped behind it, and opened the trunk.

Sandy opened the door of the telephone booth as quietly as he could and stepped out, pulling the pistol from his raincoat pocket and holding it slightly behind him, so that if she turned she would not see it. He walked quietly to within a few steps of her. This time there must be no mistake about who she was. His throat was dry and he swallowed hard. "Excuse me, ma'am," he said, nearly choking.

She spun around, startled. "Yes?" she said. Then she looked at him, seeming confused. "Sandy?" she asked.

He knew her? Oh, God, he thought. Can I do this? He thumbed back the hammer on the pistol.

"Sandy?" she repeated. "What on earth are you doing here?"

He narrowed his eyes. She was familiar, but he couldn't place her. New York, he thought, but where? Some cocktail party? Was she a friend of Joan's?

"Sandy, say something," she said. "What's wrong? You're frightening me."

The voice conflicted with the face, but suddenly, he knew.

"Cara?" he asked, struggling to maintain his composure. Then he looked down and saw a small pistol in her hand, and it was pointed at his chest.

CHAPTER

27

They sat in the Mercedes convertible, both breathing hard. Cara's gun was in her lap; Sandy had surreptitiously returned the silenced pistol to his raincoat pocket.

"Sandy, what are you doing here?" she demanded.

"I'm buying a vineyard; I was in a lawyer's office upstairs signing a purchase agreement," he half-lied. "Your turn."

"I really don't want you involved in this," she said, shaking her head.

"You told me you were going to Charleston," he said. "Why are you here, and what is it you don't want me involved in?"

"Charleston was just a cover," she replied.

"A cover for what?"

"A cover to keep anyone from knowing that I was coming to San Francisco. Only Thea, my partner, knew."

"I don't understand," he said.

"I don't want you involved," she repeated.

"I got involved last weekend at Edgartown; I remain involved. Please tell me what's going on; maybe I can help."

She was silent for a moment, then sighed and spoke. "I've lied to you," she said."

"I'm sure you must have had a good reason," he replied. "Now tell me the truth."

"It's a long story."

"I've got all the time in the world."

Her shoulders sagged. "All right. My name isn't Cara Mason, it's Helena Martindale. Cara is a family nickname, and Mason is my mother's maiden name."

"Go on."

"I haven't been living in New York for a year; I came to New York on the plane with you; I was in trouble, and Thea offered to hide me."

"Tell me about the trouble."

"I'm . . . I *was* married to an Englishman named Peter Martindale. We lived here, in San Francisco, where he runs an art gallery. We were married for a little over two years, and I came to learn that he was . . . a little strange. I told him I wanted a divorce, and he didn't take it well."

"He didn't want the divorce?"

"No. Not because he was in love with me—he never was, I think. The money for the gallery came out of my inheritance, and he wanted more."

"And you wouldn't give it to him?"

"No. He'd used up nearly half my funds setting up the gallery. I had a lien on the pictures he'd bought, but as he sold them, he never repaid the money I'd loaned him. When I told him I planned to divorce him, he tried to make it up between us. I stayed with him for a while, then I moved in with a friend and filed for divorce. This was about seven months ago."

"Were you having an affair?" Sandy asked.

"No, no. He's a painter named Saul Winner; Saul is in his sixties and has a nineteen-year-old boy for a lover. I moved into his house temporarily, but I continued to go to the gallery, to keep an eye on my investment. Peter got stranger and stranger, and one night a couple of weeks ago, he asked me to meet a client from New York at the gallery, late, while he was in Los Angeles. I wanted to use the opportunity to be in the gallery while he was away so that I could go over the books with our bookkeeper, Sally, to see just how much he'd taken in since he started the gallery. It was a lot, I think, but before I could get the whole picture, I got a call from Saul, who was having a big spat with his boyfriend. I had to meet him in a bar and listen to him cry in his beer for over an hour, and when I came back to the gallery, the street was full of police cars and an ambulance. Sally had been murdered. I thought Peter might have had something to do with it—that maybe *I* was the intended victim. I ran. I drove to Saul's house, got my clothes, then checked into the Ritz-Carlton under the name of Cara Mason. I called Thea, and she said, 'Come to New York; be my partner.' It was a lifeline, and I grabbed it. You were in the car from the hotel and on my plane." She turned and looked at him. "I was about to grab at you, too, but I felt I had to settle things with Peter first."

"And did you?"

"Yes. We agreed on a property settlement; Peter got to keep all the money I'd loaned him for the gallery and the apartment. I got my freedom. I was upstairs signing the final papers a few minutes ago. I'm now a free woman."

"I'm glad to hear it," Sandy said. "Why the gun?"

"I haven't changed my will, yet. I think Peter may be capable of killing me for what's left of my money."

Sandy sat and thought. So Martindale had lied to him about everything. Helena hadn't been having an affair with Saul Winner, she hadn't been trying to take half the gallery—in fact, she'd given it all to him. And he *still* wanted her dead. Jesus Christ.

"Where is Peter now?" Sandy asked.

"In Tucson; he called from there while I was in the lawyer's office."

"Is it your lawyer who's upstairs, or Peter's?"

"Both. Different lawyers in the firm represent each of us."

"Here's what I want you to do: I want you to go back upstairs and make a new will right this minute, or at least, revoke the old one. Make sure that the lawyer lets Peter know immediately that it's been done; that should remove any possible motive for murder." He dug his hotel key out of his pocket. "Where have you been staying?"

"At Saul's house."

"Don't go back there, even to get your clothes, and don't call Saul. Who owns this car?"

"I do; it's registered in my name."

"Do you know of somewhere you could store it for a while? Someplace where Peter won't find it?"

She thought for a moment. "I have some friends who are out of the country for a while, and I have a key to their house; there's a big garage."

"Good." He took the small pistol from her hand. "Where did you get this?"

"It was my father's."

"Do you have a permit for it?"

"No."

"I'll get rid of it; you certainly can't take it to New York with you on the plane."

She shook her head, took the pistol, and put it into the glove compartment. "It was my father's, and I don't want to lose it. I'll just leave it in the car."

"All right; call a cab from the house, then pick up enough new clothes and things to last you a couple of days." He handed her his key. "This is to my suite at the Ritz-Carlton; go there and wait for me, and don't answer the telephone."

"What are you going to do?"

"I'm going to help you disappear," Sandy said. "And by the way, I'm going to keep calling you Cara; I've sort of gotten used to it."

She smiled. "I'd like that; it's what my parents always called me."

He reached over and kissed her. "Go on back to your lawyer's office; I'll see you at the Ritz as soon as I can get there." He got out of the car, and walked her to the elevator.

When she was on her way up, he went back to Martindale's Lincoln, put on the chauffeur's cap and the dark glasses, and drove out of the garage. He found his way to the gallery and parked at the lot across the street, as he had been instructed. He put the cap and sunglasses on the front seat, put the ignition key in the glove compartment and started to get out of the car, then he stopped. Leaving the car door open, he got out and looked around the garage. It was empty of people. He walked around the garage, looking for a soft surface, and he found it in a stack of cardboard boxes that had been broken down flat and left for pickup next to a garbage can. He took the pistol from his raincoat pocket, looked around to be sure he was still alone, then fired two quick shots into the cardboard boxes. He was surprised at how quiet the weapon was.

Walking back to the car, he dug out the handkerchief the pistol had been wrapped in, rewrapped it, and tucked it under the driver's seat. Then he locked the car and walked out to the street, looking for a wastebasket. He found one and got rid of his new raincoat and cap, then hailed a cab.

On the ride to the hotel, he went over his plan carefully.

CHAPTER

28

Sandy got to the hotel first, quickly checked his messages and returned Sam Warren's call on one of his two lines.

"Hi, Sam; what's happened?"

"The sales agreement has been faxed to me, and I'm faxing it to you; we'll have the original on Monday."

"Great news! Sam, do you by any chance know the name of a law firm in this building in San Francisco?" He gave the address.

"Yes, we do some business now and then with Carter and Ellis; they're in that building."

"What's the name of a lawyer there?"

"I usually deal with Terry Ellis, why?"

"Oh, it's nothing."

"You need a lawyer out there?"

"No, Sam; it's for a kind of practical joke."

"You want me to call Terry for you?"

"No, really, I just needed a name."

"Whatever you say. By the way, a case of quite spectacular wine arrived in my office today. I don't know how to thank you."

"*I'm* thanking *you*, Sam, and I want you to enjoy every bottle."

The other phone line rang.

"Got a call coming in; better run; see you Monday." Sandy punched the button on the other line. "Hello?"

"It's Bart."

"Yes?"

"How did it go?"

"I've satisfied all my obligations to you," Sandy replied.

"Did you leave the building without hindrance?"

"I did. The package we discussed is in the trunk of the red car."

There was a brief silence, then, "And where is the car?"

"It's rather wet."

"*What?*"

"You heard me."

"I told you to leave the package in the garage; I wanted it to be found."

"You told me no such thing, so I improvised. It's taken a dunking; and you won't be seeing it again. Nobody will."

"That wasn't part of the deal."

"This is *my* end of the deal; I handled it as I saw fit. Don't worry, no one is ever going to be able to connect you with this transaction."

"But you can't prove to me that the package is in the car, can you?"

Sandy allowed himself a chuckle. "I guess you're just going to have to take my word for it, Bart."

"You're enjoying this, aren't you, Sandy?"

"I confess I am."

"So there's no chance I'll ever see the package again?"

"Not unless you're a superb swimmer."

"Then we're done."

"That's exactly it, Bart; we're done. Don't ever try to contact me again; don't phone, don't write, don't tap on my window. Because if you do, I promise you I'll terminate the relationship in the most prejudicial manner, and the hell with everything else. Do you understand me clearly?"

"I believe I do."

"Good. Now you can go fuck yourself." Sandy hung up the phone, and he was trembling. His next thought was to make sure that he and Cara didn't run into Peter Martindale at an airport. He found the yellow pages and looked through the *a*'s, then dialed a number.

"Hayward Air Charters," a woman answered.

"I'd like to charter an airplane," he said.

"I'll connect you with Pete Harris."

"Pete Harris," a man's voice said.

"I'd like to charter a jet for a trip to New York, something that will get me there nonstop."

"When would you like to leave?"

Sandy glanced at his watch; just after four. "Around six o'clock," he replied.

"How many people?"

"Two."

"I've got a Hawker one-two-five that should do nicely; it's twelve hundred dollars an hour, including fuel. Way we do it is we take the clock time for the east-

bound trip, double it, and add an hour for the head-
winds on the trip back."

"How long will the trip take?"

"About four and a half hours."

"Fine."

"Your name?"

"Kinsolving." He gave the man a credit card number.

"Can we send a limo for you? It's included in the
service."

"Thank you, yes; at the Ritz-Carlton in San Francisco
at six."

"Got it, Mr. Kinsolving; our man will see you at six."

"By the way," Sandy said, "could you arrange a very
good dinner and some champagne for the flight?"

Sandy hung up, suddenly tired. He stretched out on
the bed and closed his eyes.

He woke with a start as the door to the suite opened.
He sat up and saw Cara walk in, carrying a suitcase.
The blonde hair was auburn again. He embraced her. "I
like your hair better this way," he said.

"It's pretty much my natural color, now. The wig is
in my handbag."

"I can't tell you how glad I am to see you," he
breathed.

"I'm going to need some clothes," she said.

"No, you won't; we're leaving the hotel at six for New
York. I've chartered an airplane from Hayward, south of
Oakland, so that we can avoid the major airports."

"Good thinking," she said.

"Did you see anyone you know?"

"I'm afraid I saw Saul. I had to go back to his place
to retrieve some things, but he can keep a secret. He's

been told to say that I took my bag with me when I went to the meeting at the law firm, and he doesn't know where I went from there."

"Sounds good." He glanced at his watch. "I'm afraid we don't have time to do what I'd planned to do when you got here."

She laughed. "Well, we can always join the mile-high club."

It was nearly five A.M. when they arrived at Sandy's apartment, tired, happy, and still laughing about the effort required to make love in a corporate jet.

CHAPTER

29

Sandy woke up shortly before noon, rested and happy. He crept out of bed, made muffins, coffee, and orange juice for two, then tucked the Saturday *Times* under his arm and took the tray into the bedroom, where Cara was still sound asleep. He set the tray on the bed and kissed her on an ear.

"Mmmmm," she murmured, turning over and putting her arms around his neck. "What a lovely way to be wakened."

"What's your schedule for the coming week?" he asked.

She sat up and accepted a glass of orange juice. "Well, I have a dinner meeting with my most important client on Monday evening, and after that—"

"Is he also your only client?" Sandy asked.

"I'm afraid so. Thea couldn't believe it when I corraled him before even arriving in New York."

"I'm afraid your only client is going to be leaving town on Tuesday," he said.

She looked at him narrowly. "You have something better to do?"

"Yes, I'm going to London."

Her face fell. "For how long?"

He smiled. "How long do you want to stay?"

She smiled. "I'm going, too?"

"I want to get you out of the country for a while, and I have a perfect business excuse: I have to show you the London shop, so that you can design the New York store to resemble it."

"Not just a dirty weekend, but a dirty business trip," she said. "I love it."

He climbed into bed beside her, laughing, and picked up the *Times*. "Also, I want you to meet my son, Angus."

"Is he in London?"

"He will be in a couple of days; he's flying to Prestwick, in Scotland, on Monday, to run a family errand, then he's coming to London. His new girlfriend will be with him; I haven't met her yet."

"I'll be on my best behavior," she said.

"Only in public, I hope."

"Only in public. Where are we staying?"

"I have a little flat over the shop, but there's no service, so I think we'll stay at the Connaught, which is just down the street. Also, I don't think I'm quite ready to introduce you to the London staff as . . . what you are. You'll just be the designer, and they'll think I'm staying in the flat."

"I hear the Connaught is very good."

"I think it will meet your standards. That reminds me, I'd better go and fax them now." He went into the study, switched on his computer, wrote a letter to the manager of the Connaught, and faxed it from the computer. He was on the way back to the bedroom when the house phone rang. He picked it up.

"Hello?"

"Mr. Kinsolving, Detective Duvivier is here to see you," the lobby man said.

Oh, no, Sandy groaned to himself. It had been so long since he had heard from the detective, he thought he had been forgotten. "Ask him to wait ten minutes, then send him up."

"Yes, sir."

Sandy hung up the phone and went to the bedroom. "I'm going to lock you in here for a few minutes, and I don't want you to suddenly appear naked in the living room," he said, "though ordinarily I wouldn't mind."

"What's up?"

"A visitor, and I can't brush him off."

She picked up the paper. "I'll be quiet as a mouse."

"Good." He went to his dressing room and got into some casual clothes, and he was waiting for Duvivier at the elevator when it arrived.

"I'm very sorry to disturb you on a Saturday," the detective said.

"That's quite all right," Sandy replied. "Please come into the study." Shortly they were settled. "Would you like some coffee?"

"Thank you, no," Duvivier said, sitting on the edge of the sofa."

"What's up, then?"

"I wanted you to know right away that we've made an arrest in the matter of your wife's murder."

Sandy froze for just a moment before he could bring himself to speak. "I'm glad to hear it; who is he?"

"His name is Thomas Wills," Duvivier said.

Sandy sat up straight. "You mean our building's janitor?"

"That's correct."

"That's impossible; Thomas wouldn't harm a fly, let alone an occupant of this building."

"Actually, he has a record of violent crime," Duvivier said.

"I don't believe it. I told you at our first meeting that every employee of this building has his background checked."

"His conviction wouldn't have showed up, unless he had been fingerprinted," Duvivier said. "You see, he has been living for some years under an assumed identity. His real name is Morris Wilkes."

Sandy slumped. "How long ago did this criminal activity take place?"

"Nearly twenty years ago. Wills served seven years for voluntary manslaughter."

"What does that mean?"

"He killed another man in a barroom brawl, was charged with murder, then pled to manslaughter for a reduced sentence. Some time after his release, he changed his name, picked up a new social security number and driver's license, and got a job in your building."

Sandy shook his head. "I'm sorry, I just don't buy it. Where is he being held?"

"At the Nineteenth Precinct, at the moment."

"What evidence do you have?"

Duvivier counted off on his fingers. "First, motive—money; he knew about the jewelry in the safe; second, opportunity—he had complete access to the scene, had his own keys; third, physical evidence—his fingerprints on the doorjamb of the storage room and on several places in the room. Finally, no alibi."

"If you had all that, why didn't you arrest him immediately?"

"We didn't know about his background. All the interviews we conducted agreed with your assessment of the man, but then we got a tip from a good source about his real identity."

"Is there anything else you have to tell me about this?" Sandy asked.

"No, sir."

"Then I'll have to ask you to excuse me, detective; I have some work to do."

"Of course."

Sandy walked him to the door, shook his hand and put him into the elevator. Then he went straight to his study, got his phone book and called his lawyer.

"Jim Barwick," a sleepy voice said.

"Jim, it's Sandy Kinsolving; I'm sorry to disturb you on a Saturday."

"That's all right, Sandy; if it's about your sales agreement, Sam Warren expects to have it on Monday morning. I've already read the fax, and it looks good to me."

"No, it's something else. An employee of our co-op, whose name is Thomas Wills, has been arrested for the murder of my wife."

"Excellent!" Barwick said. "I'm delighted to hear it."

"No, it's not excellent; he didn't do it."

"You know that for a fact?"

"No, not exactly," Sandy said, "but if you knew the man, you'd know he couldn't possibly have done it. He's one of our most trusted employees in the building."

"Sandy, the police know what they're doing," the lawyer said. "They don't arrest people for murder precipitously."

"Of course they do, Jim; they do it all the time."

"All right, Sandy, what can I do to help?"

"I know you don't handle criminal cases, Jim, but I expect you know somebody who does, and I want you to get the man a lawyer. Send the bills to me."

"How much do you want to spend?"

"I want him to have excellent representation; it doesn't have to be F. Lee Bailey."

"I know a young guy, Murray Hirsch."

"Is he very good?"

"He is; he used to be an assistant district attorney. He's only been in private practice for around five years, but he's very smart, and I think he'd do a good job."

"Fine."

"Do you know where—what's his name?"

"Thomas Wills. The police told me he assumed that name after serving time for voluntary manslaughter many years ago. His real name is, apparently, Morris Wilkes. He's at the Nineteenth Precinct, but I don't know which name he's being held under."

"I'll get right on it, Sandy."

Sandy said good-bye and hung up. He walked slowly back into the bedroom, where Cara was buried in the *Times*.

She looked up at him. "What's wrong? You look awful."

He sank onto the bed. "They've arrested one of the building's employees for Joan's murder," he said.

"That's wonderful!" she exclaimed.

"No," he said, "it's not wonderful."

CHAPTER

30

Sandy sat on a bench in the Nineteenth Precinct and waited. He'd have much rather spent Sunday morning in bed with Cara, but he felt an obligation to be here.

A young man wearing sweatclothes and carrying a legal pad under his arm walked into the precinct house. He looked to be in his late twenties and very fit; he was carrying the latest in graphite squash racquets. He walked over toward Sandy's bench. "Mr. Kinsolving?" he asked, choosing the only person in the room who could possibly be Sandy.

"Yes," Sandy said, standing up.

"I'm Murray Hirsch." The two men shook hands. "Let's sit down here for a moment, before we see Mr. Wills."

Sandy sat back down. "How is Thomas?"

"Somewhat distressed," Hirsch replied. "That's understandable."

"Under the circumstances," Sandy agreed.

"I saw him yesterday for more than an hour."

"And?"

"He's very nearly convinced me that he's innocent."

"As he most certainly is," Sandy said emphatically. "We've all known Thomas for a long time, and he's not the sort to kill anybody."

"I've told him that you and the other occupants of the building feel that way," Hirsch said, "but we're going to have to deal in reality here."

"Explain the reality to me," Sandy said.

"The reality is that the police have enough evidence to get Mr. Wills indicted for the murder of your wife and the battery of the chauffeur. But, if Mr. Wills decides that he doesn't want to plead, that he wants to go to trial, then I think I have a pretty good chance of getting him off."

"Only a pretty good chance?" Sandy asked.

"Mr. Kinsolving, a criminal trial—especially one involving a black servant accused of murdering a popular socialite—is a fluid thing. Tides run one way, then another, and a conviction or an acquittal will depend a lot on the jurors we get and a dozen other factors that I can only partially control."

"I'm perfectly willing to testify on Thomas's behalf," Sandy said.

"That could be very helpful, if we get that far," Hirsch replied. "What I'd like to do is to try and get the charges dropped before the matter comes to trial."

"And how will you do that?"

"Mr. Kinsolving, you say that the other occupants of your building all support Mr. Wills. Have you actually talked to them about it?"

"Well, no," Sandy admitted, "but I have no doubt that they will."

"The first thing to do is to write a letter to the district attorney, resoundingly supporting the innocence of Mr. Wills, and get every occupant and employee of the building to sign it. Do you think you can do that?"

"Yes, I think I can."

"Good. What we want to do is to put as much pressure as possible on the D.A. to drop charges. I know a couple of people at the newspapers, and I think I can get some space for him there along the lines of, 'High-class co-op residents, the rich and famous,' as it were, 'support innocence of old retainer. Husband of murdered socialite agrees, says man is innocent.' You get my drift?"

Sandy got it all too well; he was going to have to get this letter signed before stories like that appeared in the papers. The other occupants would shrink from that kind of publicity. "If you think that's the way to go," Sandy said.

"I do. This way, if it works, will also save you some major money. I understand you're footing my fee."

"That's right; and now that you mentioned it, what is your fee?"

"If I can get the charges dropped prior to trial, twenty-five thousands dollars; if we have to go trial, fifty thousand. Appeals, we can discuss later; I hope they won't be necessary."

"Agreed. Can you get Thomas released on bail?"

"Are you willing to put up bail?"

"Of course; what is it likely to be?"

"A hundred thousand, or so; that's if I can demonstrate your support, show roots in the community, steady employment, etcetera."

"You may say for publication that the widower of the murdered woman is putting up bail, and I will state, as president of the co-op board, that Thomas still has his job."

"That will be a big help. There'll be a bail hearing tomorrow, and I'll put all that before the judge. Now, shall we go and see Mr. Wills?"

"First, I think there's something you ought to know," Sandy said.

"What's that?"

"From the very beginning, I mean since my wife was murdered, I've had the impression that the investigating detective, Duvivier, thinks that I may have had something to do with the murder of my wife."

Hirsch's eyebrows shot up. "I've read the clippings; as I understand it, you were talking on a car phone at the time of the murder and that was verified by a number of witnesses."

"I think Duvivier thinks I hired someone to kill her."

"Why?"

"As I say, it's only an impression, but he knows that I benefitted from my wife's will. He also knows that at the time she was murdered I thought I had practically been left out of her father's will. He died a few days before she did."

"I see," Hirsch said. "So you think Duvivier believes Wills to be innocent and that he's arrested the man just to put pressure on you?"

"Something like that; I think it's a possibility."

"Mr. Kinsolving, speaking within the bounds of client-attorney privilege, did you have anything to do with your wife's murder?"

"Absolutely not," Sandy replied firmly.

"Then I take it you are not willing to confess to her

murder in order to get Thomas Wills released on bail or even acquitted at trial?"

"Of course not; I want to help Thomas simply because I believe he is incapable of murdering anybody."

"Good. I'll let the D.A. know about Duvivier's suspicions. Now, let's go and see Mr. Wills."

Sandy stood up as Thomas Wills walked into the little room where he and Murray Hirsch were allowed to meet him.

"Thomas," Sandy said, extending his hand, "I want you to know that I don't believe for a moment that you killed my wife, and neither does anybody else in the building."

Wills shook his hand and sat down heavily. He was trembling.

"I appreciate that, Mr. Kinsolving," he said, "but that policeman that talks funny says he's going to put me away."

"That's Duvivier," Sandy said to Hirsch. "He's Haitian by birth and has an accent."

"I've heard about him," Hirsch said. "He has a reputation of being very intuitive about cases, so his superiors and the D.A. will listen to him, but nobody's going to trial with just his intuition. He's going to have to present solid evidence, and I believe I can knock down just about anything he's got."

"You see, Thomas," Sandy said. "Everything's going to be all right, so don't you worry. Mr. Hirsch is going to try to get you out on bail tomorrow, and then you can come right back to work."

"You think all those folks in the building are going to want me back?" Wills asked.

"They certainly will, when they hear what I have to say," Sandy replied. "Is there anything I can do for you? Any family you'd like me to contact?"

"No sir, I don't have no family."

Hirsch spoke up. "Just about the only real problem I've got at the moment is substantiating Mr. Wills's story about where he was when the murder occurred," the lawyer said. "He lives alone, and he has told the police he spent the evening reading his bible and watching television. I'll have an investigator canvas his building to see if we can get some backup. Incidentally, expenses of that sort are additional to my fee."

"That's fine," Sandy said. "Thomas, I want you to relax and not worry. We'll try and have you out of here tomorrow."

"I can't stay in jail, Mr. Kinsolving," the man said. "I been in jail before, and it does something bad to me. I can't stand it again." His hands were still trembling.

Sandy put a hand on his shoulder. "I won't let them keep you in jail, Thomas," he said. "I'll get you out." It was the very least he could do, he thought. He couldn't let the man pay for his own mistake.

CHAPTER

31

Sandy rapped sharply on the desk with a paper-weight, calling the meeting to order. Some three-quarters of the building's occupants were seated around the living room of his apartment, some of them on the floor. The building's entire staff, excepting one man who was minding the main entrance, was lined up against a wall.

"Thank you all for coming on short notice," Sandy said to the room. "I don't think we've had an extraordinary meeting of the residents in many years, but we have something very important before us this evening. As many of you already know, Thomas Wills, our custodian, has been arrested and charged with the murder of my wife, Joan."

There was a buzz around the room while those who knew confirmed this for those who did not.

"Now," Sandy continued, "I don't think that any of us here could possibly believe that of Thomas. He has been our loyal employee for nineteen years, doing whatever we've asked of him, cheerfully and well. I don't think there's a violent bone in his body. So what I hope you each will do is to add your signature to mine on the following letter, addressed to the district attorney." Sandy read aloud:

Dear Sir,

We, the residents of Fifteen-fifteen Fifth Avenue, and the employers of Thomas Wills, wish to express our disbelief that Mr. Wills could have had anything to do with the crime with which he is charged. We have known Mr. Wills for many years and have always found him to be a gentle, honest, and religious man, the sort who would not harm anyone. We urgently request that Mr. Wills be granted reasonable bail, and we pledge that he will be welcome to resume his duties in our building.

Sandy looked out into the room at blank faces. No one said anything.

"Well?" Sandy asked.

An elderly man on one of the sofas raised his hand.

"Martin?"

"Sandy," the man said, "I feel pretty much the same way you do about Thomas, but I think that before I sign such a letter I'd like to know the evidence against him."

"The police have told me that their evidence consists of, one, the fact that Thomas had a key to the basement, and thus, access; two, that Thomas's fingerprints were found on the doorjamb of my storage room; and three, that Thomas served prison time more than twenty years ago for killing another man in a barroom brawl." He paused and let that sink in. "Now, of course, Thomas had a key to the basement; he spent a lot of time there; also of course, his fingerprints would have legitimately been on the doorjamb of my storage room and, probably, on yours as well. God knows he's been in and out of that room a hundred times, carrying things for us. Finally, the news of his previous conviction came as a surprise to me, but the lawyer I have engaged to represent him says that, in all likelihood, Thomas acted in self-defense, but was inadequately represented at his trial. Certainly, in all the years he has worked for us, Thomas's behavior has always been law abiding, not to mention kind and gentle. He is a pillar of his church." Sandy stopped and waited again.

A middle-aged woman raised her hand.

"Mrs. Jacobson?" Sandy said.

"Mr. Kinsolving," she said, "I've lived in the building for only three years, a shorter time than you and the others. I've had little or no contact with Mr. Wills, but I wonder if we're going to be comfortable with having a man in the building who has been charged with murder?"

It was time to bully these people, Sandy thought. "Mrs. Jacobson, if you have even the slightest doubt of Thomas's innocence in this matter, then you should not sign this letter. I would like to say, though, that I am the injured party here; it was my wife who was brutally murdered, and my driver who was attacked. And I will not entertain for one moment the possibility that Thomas Wills harmed either of them. Now, I think we all know what the problem is; those of you who feel comfortable doing so may sign the letter along with me. As to the others, I thank you for your kind attention."

Sandy stood at the desk and glared at his audience, practically daring them not to sign. Then one by one, each of those present, including the recalcitrant Mrs. Jacobson, signed the letter and went home.

Sandy was in his office early on Monday morning. As soon as his secretary came in he gave her the residents' letter and asked her to messenger it to Murray Hirsch. That done, he called his travel agent and asked her to arrange air passage to London for himself and Cara, then faxed the Connaught for reservations for Angus and his girl. Then he called Sam Warren.

"Sam, I'm going to be out of the country, in London, for a week or so. Is there anything we can't handle by fax and phone during that time?"

"Nothing, Sandy. We won't have the closing documents on the vineyard until the end of next week at the earliest."

"Did my son, Angus, come to see you about an account?"

"He did, and I've opened one for him. I've also arranged for a Platinum American Express card for him, which will be FedExed to him in London, and I've alerted our European network of associate banks, in the event he needs any assistance while he's traveling."

"Perfect. You can reach me at the London shop from tomorrow." He gave the banker the phone and fax numbers.

"Have a good trip," Warren said.

Sandy hung up and turned to business. He worked steadily through the morning, approving buys of wine in France, California, Australia, and Chile, answering correspondence and talking with employees. Shortly after eleven o'clock he received a phone call from Murray Hirsch.

"Yes, Murray, how did the bail hearing go? Did you receive the letter in time?"

"Mr. Kinsolving, are you sitting down?"

"Yes."

"Thomas Wills hanged himself in his cell late last night."

Sandy's heart nearly failed. "How is that possible?" he asked weakly.

"It's possible, believe me; happens all the time. I feel a little responsible myself. Knowing the distress he was in I should have asked for a suicide watch on his cell."

"I don't see how you could have anticipated this," Sandy said. "You certainly aren't to blame." He knew exactly who was to blame. He himself was. No, he reminded himself, Peter Martindale was to blame.

"There's something else," Hirsch said, "good news, of a kind."

"What do you mean, 'good news'?"

"Thomas was guilty of your wife's murder."

"*What?*"

"He left a note in his cell, confessing to the murder, taking full responsibility."

"Why the hell would he have done that?" Sandy demanded.

"A guilty conscience, I presume. God knows, *I* thought he was innocent, and I know you did."

"Oh, Jesus, how could this have happened?" Sandy asked aloud.

"Mr. Kinsolving, I assure you, this happens regularly. Some people in jail are hardened criminals; others just can't face the guilt associated with their acts."

Sandy took a few deep breaths. "What do we do now?" he asked helplessly.

"There's not much we can do, actually," Hirsch replied. "Mr. Wills had no family; apparently, his church was his family. I suppose I should get in touch with his pastor and ask him to make arrangements for claiming the body and effecting interment."

"Yes," Sandy said wearily, "I suppose that's the thing to do. I'm leaving the country on business tomorrow, and I'd appreciate it if you would handle whatever needs to be done."

"I'll be glad to do that," Hirsch said. "And Mr. Kinsolving, there will be no fee for my representation of Mr. Wills."

"Thank you, Murray. Please tell his pastor that I'll pay the costs involved, and, " he thought for a moment, "and tell him that I'll be making a twenty-five-thousand-dollar donation to the church in Thomas's memory."

"That's very kind of you, Mr. Kinsolving."

"Please get in touch with my banker and tell him to whom the check should go." He gave Hirsch Sam Warren's number."

"I'll do that, Mr. Kinsolving. I'm sorry this has turned out the way it has."

"Thank you, Murray." Sandy hung up and slumped over his desk. Would this never end? Would Peter Martindale's insane behavior keep having repercussions in his life and in those of other innocent people? He sat there, immobile, for the remainder of the morning.

CHAPTER

32

Alain Duvivier waited on the hard bench outside his captain's office. Shortly, a sharp rap on the glass above his head told him that the captain would see him now. He got up, walked into the office and took the offered chair, which was also very hard.

Captain Morello, a short, balding man of sixty, looked at him balefully. "Well, I hear you cleared a homicide this morning, huh, Al?"

Duvivier shrank inside his suit. "In a manner of speaking, sir."

"Saved us and the taxpayers a lot of time and trouble, huh?"

Duvivier said nothing.

"Only now I hear things," Morello said. "I hear things up and down the halls of this building."

"Sir?"

"I hear that . . . " he shuffled papers on his desk until he found the name, "Thomas Wills, aka Morris Wilkes, didn't do it. Or, at least, *you* don't think he did it."

Duvivier closed his mouth.

"I hear you think the victim's husband offed her, or rather, had her offed. I hear you arrested Wills just to put pressure on the husband. Is this just an idle rumor, Al? Talk to me."

"I had enough evidence for an arrest," Duvivier said quietly.

"Speak up, Al, I can't hear you," Morrello said.

"I had evidence," Duvivier repeated.

"Good, good; always nice to have evidence. Tell me, do you think Wills offed the woman?"

Duvivier shrugged. "I have some doubts."

"How serious are those doubts?" Morrello asked.

Duvivier squared his shoulders. "All right, captain, you're right; I think the husband did it, and I arrested Wills to put pressure on him. I think Kinsolving is, mostly, a decent man, and I thought that if he thought an innocent man might go to prison for his crime, he might talk to me."

"So now an innocent man is dead," Morello said.

"Yes, sir," Duvivier replied, tired of being quiet.

"Only he's *not* innocent; he left a note, confessing; is that right?"

"That's right, sir."

"So now we're marking this one down as cleared, is that right?"

"Yes, sir, I suppose so."

"Well, I'm not supposing," Morrello said. "I'm marking it down as cleared. Do you know what that means?"

"It doesn't mean that I still can't go after Kinsolving," Duvivier said.

"Of course it does. It means just that very thing."
Morello stood up and started pacing. "Just look at the position you've put the department in, Al. You've arrested a man you believe to be innocent in order to put pressure on the guilty party. Only, the innocent man surprises you and confesses, then offs himself. Do you see the position?"

"I'm not sure I do, sir."

"Well, let me explain it to you. Now, in the unlikely event that you're ever able to make a case against the husband, and you arrest him and send him to trial, his lawyer is going to say to the jury, 'My client didn't do this murder, another man has already confessed to it, felt so guilty about it that he offed himself.' You getting my drift, Al?"

"Yes, sir."

"I don't think you are; not fully, anyway. Let's take it a step further. You do your job, you get the goods on the husband, what are the papers saying about the department? They're saying we drove an innocent man to suicide, and what's more, if the last guy was innocent, maybe the husband is innocent, too. You see what an impossible position that is for the department? What you've done is, you've made it a practical impossibility to *ever* arrest the husband or anybody else for this murder."

"Captain—"

"You listen to me," Morello said. "From now on, until further notice, you don't arrest *anybody* for *any* murder until you come in this office and lay out your evidence for me. Do you understand?"

"Yes, sir; I understand."

"Good, now get out of here."

Duvivier trudged up the stairs to Kinsolving's office over the wine store. He didn't want to be here, but this was his last attempt at some sort of absolution.

Kinsolving looked up from his desk. "Yes? What do you want, Detective?" His tone was cold, angry.

"I take it, sir, you've heard the news about Thomas Wills."

"I have."

"I wanted to tell you personally how sorry I am," Duvivier said. He shifted his weight to the other foot; Kinsolving had not asked him to sit down.

"Why are you sorry?" Kinsolving demanded. "You got a confession, didn't you?"

"Well, yes, in a way."

"Then what are you sorry about?" Kinsolving seemed to be getting angrier.

"Well, it was just the circumstances—"

"Tell me, Detective, did you really believe that man was guilty of murdering my wife?"

"I . . . I wasn't sure," Duvivier replied. "I did have evidence."

"You didn't believe it for a moment, did you? How could anybody talk to that man for even five minutes and believe that he did it?"

"Mr. Kinsolving, I realize you're upset."

"I'm *extremely* upset. And I want you to get out of my office, Detective; I want you to leave and not contact me again, unless you've found my wife's murderer. Is that clear?"

"I understand, sir."

"Good. Now get out."

Duvivier hit the sidewalk more depressed than he had ever been in his life. He walked aimlessly east, toward the park. Maybe he should just find a nice quiet place and hang himself, like Thomas Wills. Central Park had trees. He walked toward the park, sick in his heart.

CHAPTER

33

The 747 landed at Heathrow just after 9:00 P.M.; Sandy and Cara were met by the Connaught's representative as they left customs, and in a moment they were ensconced in the back seat of a very large limousine.

"I feel very regal," she said, laughing. She peered out the windows at the passing landscape, still lighted by the waning sun. "I can't believe it's still light," she said.

"London is a lot farther north than New York," Sandy explained. "New York is actually on about the same latitude as Lisbon; being closer to the north pole, London has much longer days in summer, and, unfortunately, much shorter ones in winter. Is this the first time you've been to England?"

"It is," she replied. "I've been to Rome and Paris, but

never here. When Peter went to London on buying trips, I had to stay behind and run the gallery."

"I'll make sure you see everything," Sandy said.

It was after ten when the car pulled up in front of the hotel. The night porter was there to help them with their bags and, shortly, they were unpacking in a corner suite.

"It's not like a hotel, somehow," Cara said, looking around.

"No, it's more like being a guest at a friend's country house," Sandy replied. "That's one of the things I love about it."

"But you usually stay in the flat over your shop," she said.

"That's right, but only since I bought the shop. This used to be my resting place, and I still use the bar and the restaurants frequently."

"They did seem to know you," she said.

"Are you sleepy?" he asked.

"Nope."

"That's normal with travel to the east. It's only about five-thirty in the afternoon in New York, after all, and we're still running on New York time. The thing to do when traveling east is to stay up as late as possible, get as tired as possible, then get a good night's sleep. That defeats at least half of jet lag."

"What do you suggest?" she asked.

"Anabel's," he replied.

They left the hotel and walked down the street toward Berkeley Square, Cara pausing to look into every shop window along the way. In the square they walked slowly past the tall plane trees in the little park and came to a stop before an awning leading to a basement.

"What's this?" she asked.

"This is Anabel's," he said.

"A restaurant?"

"A club and a restaurant." He led her down the stairs.

"Good evening, Mr. Kinsolving," the doorman said as they entered.

"Good evening," Sandy replied. He didn't come here all that often, and it always amazed him that they remembered his name. He signed the register, and they went down a hallway into a kind of sitting room, with a fireplace and a small bar.

"It's lovely," Cara said. "I especially like the pictures."

"The man who owns the place, Mark Birley, is the son of a well-known English painter, so I guess good pictures are in his genes. Let's keep going."

They moved through a pair of swinging doors, and a short, gray-haired man in a tuxedo approached them.

"Good evening, Louis," Sandy said.

"Good evening, sir. Two?"

"Yes." Louis *never* remembered his name, Sandy reflected.

The restaurant was dark and intimately lit; at the far end was a small dance floor. Music wafted softly through the room. They were shown to a table along the wall and given menus.

"What would you like for dinner?" he asked.

"What are you going to have?"

"Scrambled eggs and smoked salmon," he replied.

"I'll have the same," she said. "It's the first meal you ever gave me."

"Seems like a long time ago," Sandy mused.

"So much has happened."

More than you know, he thought. He ordered their eggs and a bottle of Krug, just to keep this meal the same as their first together.

They walked up the hill toward the Connaught, and Sandy steered Cara past the hotel and into Mount Street.

"Where are we going?" she asked. "I'm getting sleepy."

"Just a few steps. I want you to see it at night." He stopped before the shop. "This is it," he said. "What do you think?"

She peered through the darkened windows. "This is what? Oh! The shop!"

"That's right."

"It's lovely; I can see why you'd want the New York shop to look the same. I'll give you your first design tip; let me design some lighting for inside that you can leave on until past midnight."

"That will use a lot of electricity," he said.

"It'll be cheap advertising, though. Every time some stranger walks past the place at night, he'll look inside, and you'll win a new customer."

"Good advice," Sandy said. "I'm anxious for you to see the inside."

"How about right now," she said. "Do you have a key?"

"I do." He unlocked the door and let them inside, then went to disarm the security system and switch on the lights. When he returned she was standing in the middle of the shop, turning slowly.

"It's absolutely wonderful," she said. "Who made it look this way?"

"I don't think anybody remembers," Sandy said.

"The shop has been here since the late eighteenth century, and it somehow just came to look this way."

"With no designer?" she asked. "Sort of diminishes my trade, doesn't it?"

"There's an old story," Sandy said, "about an American tourist in Oxford who wanders into the courtyard of one of the colleges, I forget which one, and he is confronted by the most beautiful lawn he has ever seen, smooth, perfect, and weed free. Having spent years trying to get his own lawn in shape, he approaches an elderly gardener and asks, 'Tell me, how do you get your grass to look like this?'

"'Well,' the old fellow says, 'First you prepare the ground, then you plant the seed, and then you roll it and cut it and roll it and cut it . . . for about three hundred years.'"

She burst out laughing. "So time is the best designer."

He took her in his arms and kissed her. "I'm sure you run a close second," he said.

They walked back to the hotel, collected their key from the night porter, and took the lift upstairs.

"Mmmm, linen sheets," she said, snuggling into bed. "My grandmother used to have linen sheets on all the beds in her house. That was when people could afford to hire someone to iron them, I suppose."

"I'm afraid you're right," Sandy said, climbing into bed beside her. "In the case of the Connaught, all the laundry is sent to the Savoy Laundry, which is a kind of Victorian institution, in a London suburb, with a great deal of equipment that has been there for decades. When you send out some laundry you'll see what a wonderful job they do."

She wriggled across the bed and put her head on his shoulder. "This is nice," she said. "I'm going to sleep well here."

Soon she was breathing deeply, but Sandy continued to stare at the ceiling. Whenever he closed his eyes he saw Thomas Wills, swinging by the neck in his jail cell.

34

Sandy left while Cara was still dressing and walked to the shop, so that she could present herself at a later hour. It was a little soon after Joan's death, he thought, for the staff of the London operation to conclude that he was seeing another woman.

As he was about to open the shop's door, a man across the street caught his eye, for no other reason than that he was wearing a bowler hat. The English had given up the bowler reluctantly, Sandy reflected, but still, he hadn't seen one for at least ten years. He entered the shop, greeting staff as he went, then headed upstairs to his office.

Maeve O'Brien, the office manager and secretary, greeted him warmly. "Did you have a good flight, Mr. Kinsolving?"

"Yes, thank you, Maeve."

"All of us here are so sorry about your double tragedy. We hope you're feeling better now."

"Yes, I am, and thank everyone for me, will you? By the way, a Miss Cara Mason from New York will be calling at the shop this morning. She's an interior designer here to see how she can make the New York shop look more like this one. Will you send her up as soon as she arrives?"

"Yes, of course, Mr. Kinsolving. I've put the monthly figures on your desk; I expect you'll want to have a look at them."

"Thank you, Maeve, I think I'll do that right now." Sandy sat down at his desk and began going over the computer printouts.

A minute later, Maeve was back. "Mr. Kinsolving, I'm sorry to disturb you, but there's a gentleman here to see you, a Mr. Jeremy Morris."

"Do I know him?"

"I don't think so, sir, but he's been here a number of times during your absence." She lowered her voice. "He's a little peculiar, sir."

"Oh, all right, send him in." Sandy sat back and waited for the man, then rose and extended his hand as he entered.

"Jeremy Morris, sir," the man said, shaking hands, "and it's very pleased I am to make your acquaintance."

It was the man in the bowler hat Sandy had seen across the street a moment before, and his accent was all over the place—a little cockney, a little south London, even an occasional attempt at upper-class pronunciation. He was wearing a worn MacIntosh and a small, waxed moustache. Along with his slicked-down hair, Sandy thought he looked like something out of an Agatha Christie novel.

"Please sit down, Mr. Morris," Sandy said. Where the hell had he heard that name? "Are you a lover of wine?"

"Well, mostly I take a little beer with my supper, if you know what I mean, sir; I've never acquired an especial fondness for the grape."

"That's too bad," Sandy said. "Now what can I do for you?"

"I've been eagerly awaiting your return from America," Morris said. "Having spoken with, but not actually made the acquaintance of your late wife."

"Oh?" Where the *hell* did he know that name from? "My wife?"

"Yes, yes," Morris said.

"In what connection?"

"Well, the late Mrs. Kinsolving had the occasion to employ my services a short while ago, you see." He looked around at the office door, then pushed it shut. "I hope you don't mind; I wish to be discreet."

Sandy suddenly remembered where he'd heard the name; it had been on a compliments slip. "Go on, Mr. Morris."

Morris fished in an inside pocket and came up with an envelope; he handed it to Sandy. "For your perusal, sir," he said.

Sandy didn't need to look at the pictures, but he made a show of doing so, nonchalantly. When he had done so, he tossed them onto the desk. "Well?"

"Well, sir, I thought perhaps you'd wish to have the opportunity to purchase these snaps before—"

"I was under the distinct impression that my wife had already purchased them—and the negatives," Sandy said.

Morris managed an obsequious smile. "Well, sir, you know how these things go; you and I are both men of the world, are we not?"

"Not the same world," Sandy said.

"Be that as it may, sir, I thought that, from what I've

read in the New York newspapers, you might like to keep these snaps away from the eyes of the New York police department, and I'm here to be of service."

"Why should I wish to keep these from the New York police?" Sandy asked.

"Well, sir, given the circumstances of your late wife's demise, I thought perhaps it might be in your interests to keep these rather on the quiet side, if you know what I mean."

"I'm afraid I don't have the slightest idea what you mean," Sandy said.

"Must I be blunt, sir?"

"Please do."

"Well, to be quite candid, sir, I've read that you stood to inherit quite a large amount in the event of your wife's untimely death."

"So?"

"I don't wish to give offense, sir, but surely you can see that these photographs might very well plant in the mind of the New York police that you might have had some motive . . . "

Sandy took a pad from his desk drawer and began writing on it. "Mr. Morris, if you feel you have some relevant information in the matter of my wife's death, then you should immediately contact a Detective Duvivier of the Nineteenth Precinct. I'll give you his number." He held the slip of paper out for Morris to take.

"*Sir?*"

"Mr. Morris, when did you last read the New York newspapers?"

"Well, I—"

"Perhaps you should read yesterday's *New York Times*. There you will learn that my wife's murderer confessed to the crime over the weekend."

Morris looked momentarily flummoxed, but then he recovered himself. "Well, I'm so very pleased to hear that, sir; I'm sure it's a great load off your mind. However, there's the matter of the newspapers on *this* side of the water, you see."

"I beg your pardon?"

"I'm very much afraid that our newspapers, especially those of the tabloid size, take a very much greater interest in one's personal habits than do your American ones."

Uh oh, Sandy thought.

"Not in *your* personal habits, sir, but they do take a very deep interest in the, shall we say, *extracurricular* activities of the nobility."

"The nobility?" Sandy was playing for time now.

"Peers of the realm," Morris said. "As in the Earl of Kensington and his wife, the countess." He indicated the photographs on Sandy's desk. "I'm not quite sure as yet who the other lady in question might be, but if the photos were published, then I'm sure we'd hear her name in no time at all." He smiled. "If you see my point, sir."

There was a rap on the door, and Maeve stuck her head in. "Excuse me, Mr. Kinsolving, but your next appointment is here."

"I'll be another minute, Maeve," Sandy replied. "Would you please introduce Miss Mason to the downstairs staff? I'll be down in a moment."

Maeve departed, and Sandy turned back to the private detective. "What is it you want, Mr. Morris?"

"Well, sir, that sort of thing," he indicated the photographs again, "would likely bring around ten thousand pounds sterling from the appropriate publication, at the very least. I mean, involving a countess and all."

"Ten thousand pounds?" Sandy asked.

"Oh, at the very least," Morris replied. "And then there's the earl, of course; he might be willing to go a good deal more to keep the countess's countenance out of the tabs."

"Exactly what is your proposition, Mr. Morris?"

"Well, I'm not a greedy man, sir, and I certainly don't want to go about causing a lot of trouble for members of the aristocracy, not to mention yourself and your business, so I'd happily accept a consideration of ten thousand pounds sterling, in cash of course, in return for all the negatives and prints." His face suddenly went from obsequious to serious. "And not a farthing less, sir."

Sandy's shoulders slumped. "You told my wife that was what you were selling," he said.

"Well, sir, let's just call that an oversight, shall we? This time, you'll have everything, and you have my word on it."

Sandy glanced at his watch. "I can't manage it until later today."

Morris laid a card on the desk. "Why you just take your time, sir. You can deliver the sum to my premises no later than close of business today. That's 5:00 P.M. After that, there'd still be time to make the morning editions, you see."

"All right," Sandy said, defeated.

"Nothing larger than a twenty quid note," Morris said, rising. "I dislike larger bills."

Sandy nodded, and Morris left his office.

"I'll see myself out, sir," the man said. "And I do hope I'll see you by five."

Sandy sat for a while, massaging his temples.

CHAPTER

35

S andy got out of the cab in front of the Garrick Club, paid the cabbie, and walked inside. A doorman in a small oak and glass booth saw him coming, looked him up and down, decided he wasn't a member.

"Yes, sir? May I help you?"

"My name is Kinsolving; I'm meeting Sir John Drummond," Sandy said.

"Yes, sir; upstairs, in the bar."

Sandy climbed the stairs of the grand old club, past portraits and busts, mostly of ancient actors, and on the next floor found his man. Sir John Drummond was resting most of his two hundred and fifty pounds against the bar, a glass of something in his hand.

"Sandy," Drummond cried, clapping him soundly on the back. "How good to see you. What are you having?"

"I think I'd better have a single malt, Johnny," he said.

Drummond blinked, then ordered the drink. He was impeccably dressed in a pinstriped suit from a fine tailor, a heavy gold watch chain arcing across his middle from vest pocket to vest pocket. "If you need whisky at lunchtime, let's leave the bar and go straight to a table," he said. "More privacy." He grabbed both his drink and Sandy's and led the way downstairs.

Sandy had met John Drummond more than ten years before, at a dinner party, and they had made a habit of seeing each other regularly when Sandy was in London. Drummond was a retired barrister, but he had always had his fingers in a number of British pies. Sandy had never known anyone who knew so many people in so many walks of life so very well.

Downstairs, they took a table in a corner of the high-ceilinged dining room, its tobacco-stained walls holding still more portraits of old actors and scenes from old West End productions. It was only half past twelve, and the room was uncrowded, since most of the members came to lunch at one or later. Sandy had been here many times, always with Sir John. Drummond handed him a menu, and a waitress quickly appeared to take their order. When she had gone, Drummond turned to him. "Sorry to hear about Jock and Joan. A shock to lose them both within so short a time."

"Yes, thank you, Johnny. The worst is over, I'm glad to say."

"Then tell me how I can help you, my boy."

"You're the only person I know to whom I could go for advice in a case like this," Sandy said.

"A case like what?" Drummond demanded.

"I'm being blackmailed, Johnny."

Drummond's heavy eyebrows shot upward. "Details?"

"Well—"

Drummond held up a cautionary hand. "No names, if you please; I don't like to know more than I have to about these things."

"Short and simple. Joan put a London private detective on me, and he got photographs of me in bed with a lady . . . or two."

"Or two?"

"I'm afraid so. One of them rather well known about town. The detective is threatening to go to the tabloids with the photos unless I pay him ten thousand pounds before five o'clock today. Joan had apparently already paid him, but he kept copies."

"Mmmm," Drummond grumbled.

"I'd pay him the money and be done with him, Johnny, but I simply don't think that would be the end of it."

"Quite right, my dear fellow," Drummond said. He waved over a waitress, and they placed their orders, then Sir John stood. "Will you excuse me for a moment? Call of nature."

"Of course."

Drummond got up and left the table.

Sandy sipped his drink and glanced idly around the room, which was slowly filling with barristers, actors, journalists, and government officials.

Drummond returned just as the first course arrived. "Well, done any sailing lately?" he asked, digging into some smoked mackerel pâté.

"Only once this season, at Edgartown."

"You must come down to Cowes this summer, my boy; do some racing with us."

"I'd love that. This is a short trip, but maybe later in the summer."

"Come to Cowes for a week, first week in August, bring a girl; I'll put you up."

"Sounds wonderful; can I let you know next week?"

"Surely."

"I'm buying a vineyard in California, and I have to get that sewed up and organized before I can make a commitment for August."

"Quite right."

"I'll send you some bottles, when we have our first vintage."

"Look forward to trying the vino."

The main course arrived, and the two men began eating. Drummond had still said nothing about Sandy's problem. They finished, declined dessert, ordered coffee.

Drummond tossed his down, hauled a gold watch from his vest pocket and regarded it glumly. "Got to run, my boy. Look forward to hearing from you next week." The two men rose and shook hands. "Go and have a pee," Drummond said, "to give me time to get out, then meet an acquaintance of mine, who's waiting for you in a taxi outside; he's aware of the gist of the problem; you tell him anything else he needs to know. Stop by your bank and cash a check for five hundred quid; give it to the fellow when the problem's been satisfactorily solved."

"Thank you, Johnny," Sandy said gratefully. "I'll be in touch." They parted at the dining room door; Drummond went toward the street, and Sandy found the men's room down the back hall.

When he emerged from the club into the sunlight, a taxi was waiting at the curb, and a hand motioned him inside.

Sandy got into the cab. A hefty man in a tweed suit and a trilby hat stuck out his hand. "Good day," he said.

Sandy shook his hand. "I'm—"

"Names are unnecessary, sir," the man said quietly. He reached forward and closed the glass partition separating them from the driver. "Now, sir, who is this private copper?"

Sandy handed him Morris's card, and the man grimaced. "Know the bugger well," he said. He opened the partition again and gave the driver Morris's address in the London suburb of Clapham.

"Oh," Sandy said to the driver, "I'd like to stop for a moment at Cadogan Place and Sloane Street." He sat back as the cab pulled into traffic. He and the other man made small talk about the weather and sports until the cab stopped in front of Sandy's bank. He went inside, cashed a check for five hundred pounds, returned to the cab and the journey resumed.

"Wait for us," the man said to the driver.

They got out of the cab in front of a small grocery. Sandy looked upstairs and saw, painted on the window, "J. Morris, Private Enquiries."

"You go up first," the man said to Sandy. "There's a woman who works there; tell Morris to get rid of her, and when I see her leave I'll come up. Show him some money, but don't give it to him."

Sandy nodded, found the stairs and walked up a flight and rapped on an opaque glass door.

"Come in," a woman's voice sang.

Sandy opened the door and found a plump, motherly woman, sitting behind a small desk, knitting.

"He's waiting for you, luv," she nodded toward an open door, then went back to her knitting.

Sandy walked into the rear office. Morris was sitting behind an impressive desk, refilling a lighter with fluid.

"Ah, Mr. Kinsolving," Morris said, beaming. He got up, went to the door and looked around. "All alone, are we?"

"See that we are," Sandy said, nodding toward the secretary.

"Mavis," Morris said to the woman, "Go down to Woolsey's and get me some pipe tobacco, will you? Take half an hour to do it."

The woman put down her knitting and left the office. Morris returned, sat behind his desk, and began stuffing a pipe with tobacco.

"Let's see the negatives," Sandy said.

"Well, sir, let's see the money," Morris replied, beaming at him. "If you would be so kind."

Sandy produced an envelope with the five hundred pounds he had gotten from his bank, flashed the bills at Morris, and returned them quickly to his pocket.

Morris stood up. Both sides of his office were occupied with storage cabinets and files. He went to a drawer, took out an envelope, and spread the prints and some negatives on his desk. "There you are," he said, "all the remaining goods."

"Glad to hear it, Jerry," a voice said from behind Sandy. "And where are the rest?"

Morris's face fell. "What are *you* doing here?" he demanded.

Sir John Drummond's acquaintance walked into the room, seemingly unconcerned with Morris. He walked around the desk slowly, looking at the ceiling, then stopped. "Ah, there we are," he said, pointing at a small camera fixed to a corner above the molding.

"You're not the law anymore, my friend," Morris said. "You have no business here."

The former policeman was walking along one side of the room, looking into cabinets. "Where are the real negatives, Jerry?" he asked.

Morris looked at Sandy. "Is he with you?"

"He is," Sandy said. "If I were you, I'd give him the negatives."

The ex-cop was fiddling with a panel, and suddenly, it came open. "Ah ha ha!" he crowed. "Look what we have here!"

Sandy stood up and looked into the little closet. A video cassette recorder was running silently, and the walls were lined with videotapes.

"Jerry, I won't ask you again," the ex-cop said.

"That's the lot, damn you," Morris said, gesturing at the photographs on the desk.

The ex-cop shook his head. He picked up the can of lighter fluid on the desk, walked to the video closet, removed the cassette from the recorder and began spraying the fluid over the tape and all the other equipment inside.

"Goddamit, you stop that!" Morris cried. "I'll have the police on you."

"I'm sure the boys would love viewing those tapes," the ex-cop said. "Why don't you phone them?"

Morris stood, fuming, behind his desk, but he did nothing for a moment. Then he went to another file drawer, extracted another envelope, and tossed it onto his desk.

The ex-cop turned to Sandy. "See if that's what we're looking for, will you?"

Sandy shook out the contents of the envelope. He held the negatives up to the light, then scooped all the prints and negatives into the envelope. "That's it," he said.

"Is it everything, Jerry?" the ex-cop said to Morris. "Absolutely everything?"

"It's everything!" Morris cried. "I swear it."

"Uh oh," the ex-cop said. He picked up the lighter from the desk, flicked it and tossed it into the closet. There was a muffled noise, then the closet burst into flame.

"Last chance, Jerry," the ex-cop said.

Morris, whose eyes were very nearly bugging out of his head, ran to yet another filing cabinet, grabbed yet another envelope, and tossed it at Sandy.

Sandy caught it, inspected the contents, then took all the negatives and prints and tossed them into the flames. "I think we're done here," he said to the ex-cop.

"Good; we'll be running along then, shall we? Jerry, you can get your fire extinguisher out now. And if this gentleman ever hears from you again, or hears from someone who heard from you, I'll be back, and next time, I'll toss *you* in there," he indicated the flaming closet, "before I light the match."

Sandy and his companion walked down the stairs.

"You take the cab, sir; I'll get another one," the ex-cop said.

Sandy took the cash envelope from his pocket and pressed it into the man's hand. "I can't thank you enough," he said.

The two men shook hands and parted.

CHAPTER

36

At precisely eight-thirty they were seated at a corner table on the street side of the Connaught Restaurant, a spacious room with candlelight reflecting from polished mahogany paneling and tables set with snow-white cloths and gleaming silver and crystal. Half an hour earlier Sandy had met Angus's girlfriend, whose name was Maggie Fox, and Angus had met Cara. Any early awkwardness had passed after a bottle of Veuve Cliquot '66, and by the time the first course arrived they were the best of friends. Sandy, ever the good host, had ordered for all of them.

"It's beautiful," Maggie said as a small plate was set before her. "What is it?"

"Two versions of the same dish," Sandy said, pleased that she had asked. "Croustade d'oef de caille—one called Maintenon, the other Christian Dior.

Maintenon is quail's eggs in a little pastry boat covered in a cold white sauce and sprinkled with Beluga caviar; Christian Dior is the same, but on a bed of duxelles of mushrooms and covered with hollandaise sauce. There's no polite way to eat them, just gobble them up."

Maggie did just that. She was tiny, not much more than five feet, of slender build, with large eyes, perfect teeth, and short hair as thick as fur. "Oh, God," she murmured. "I've never had anything like it."

Cara and Angus had similar remarks to utter, but Sandy was concentrating on pleasing Maggie. "Which do you like best?" he asked.

"I can't decide," she sighed.

"No one I know has ever been able to make that decision," Sandy said.

"And what's the wine?" she asked, sipping from the glass of white.

"A Puligny Montrachet, Les Combettes, '70," he replied.

"It goes beautifully with the quail's eggs."

"Thank you," he said, beaming at her.

The main course was Noisettes d'Agneau Edward VII, little filets of lamb on fried bread, and a slice of pate with a brown sauce.

"This is perfectly wonderful," Maggie said. "And the wine?"

"A red Bordeaux, or as the English like to call it, a claret. This one is a Chateau Palmer '78, one of my favorites."

"The perfect accompaniment," she said, raising her glass to him.

"Thank God you're not a vegetarian and a teetotaler," Sandy said. "I'd have to deny you my son."

She laughed aloud. "What a relief!" she crowed. "Anyway, I don't think a surgeon can be a vegetarian. It's not appropriate, somehow."

"I see your point. Will you practice general surgery?"

"Certainly not. I plan to lead a civilized life, and that doesn't include getting up in the middle of the night to perform emergency appendectomies. In the fall I'm entering a residency for plastic surgery, specializing in the face. You see, when I was a little girl I was something of a tomboy, and I broke my nose falling out of a tree. It was repaired by the most marvelous surgeon, and my fate was set, as well as my nose."

"He did a fine job," Sandy said.

"How kind you are."

"Where do you come from?" he asked.

"From a small town in Georgia called Delano."

"I didn't detect an accent."

"That's because I went to Harvard for my undergraduate work and med school and then to New York for my internship and residency. I've been in Yankeeland so long my accent has gotten scrambled; when I get a little drunker, it may reemerge."

Sandy was in love with her before dessert came.

Dessert was crème brûlée, with a crust so thick you had to rap on it with the back of a spoon to break through, and with raspberries mixed in. Sandy was just beginning his when he looked up and saw Peter Martindale walk into the restaurant. Sandy watched, frozen, as Martindale and another man were shown to a table in the far opposite corner of the room.

"Something wrong, Sandy?" Cara asked, looking at him oddly. Her back was to the room.

"No, no, I was just entranced by this dessert."

"Me, too," she said, smiling at him. They had hardly exchanged a word the whole evening, he had been so preoccupied with pleasing Maggie.

Sandy raised a hand and summoned the maitre d'. "Mr. Chevalier," he said in a low voice, "someone I would rather not speak to has just come into the restaurant; he's sitting in the far corner. I would be very grateful if you would move that screen by the door a couple of feet so as to block his view of us."

"Of course, Mr. Kinsolving," the man said, and a moment later the adjustment had been made.

Sandy breathed easier, and he resisted the impulse to bolt from the restaurant. When they had finished dessert he suggested they have coffee in his suite. On their way out Sandy made sure to keep the screen between Cara and Martindale. After all, the art dealer believed his ex-wife dead, and Sandy didn't want to give him too great a shock.

As they waited for the lift, Sandy sidestepped to the front desk. "Is there a Mr. Peter Martindale registered here?" he asked, then prayed as the young woman flipped through the register.

"No, sir," she said.

"Thank you," he replied, then got onto the elevator with his party.

In the suite, they ordered coffee, then shared a bottle of port. Maggie, as she had promised, became more southern as she drank, and, Sandy thought, even more charming. He hoped the hell his son had the good sense to hold onto this young woman.

"How long will you be in town?" he asked his son.

"We're leaving for Stuttgart tomorrow, to pick up the car."

"And then?"

"France. Maggie wants to visit the wine country, so we're driving to Beaune for our first night."

"Would you like me to set up a tour of a vineyard or two for you?"

"Dad, that would be wonderful."

"It certainly would," Maggie chimed in. "It will probably be a bore for Angus, since he's grown up around wine, but I'm really excited about it."

"You get better and better," Sandy said.

Sandy lay in bed and stared at the ceiling, as Cara slept soundly beside him. This business with Peter Martindale was becoming too complicated. Tomorrow he was going to have to tell Cara everything. In effect, he would be trusting her with his future. He hoped he knew her well enough for that.

CHAPTER

37

They were in the middle of breakfast before Sandy plucked up enough courage to begin talking.

"I have some things to tell you," he said.

She looked up from her eggs. "I'm all ears."

"This is going to be difficult for both of us, and I hope you'll hear me out before you start making judgments about me."

"I'll do my best," she said.

"I'm . . . acquainted with your ex-husband," he began.

Her eyebrows went up. "You know Peter? Why on earth didn't you tell me?"

"We met on an airplane—God, it seems like a year ago, but it was only in May."

"Oh," she said, relieved, "is that all?"

"I'm afraid not," he replied. "There's a great deal more."

"Tell me; I'll try not to interrupt."

He began with the movie on the airplane, with his drunken spilling of his life story, then went on to Peter's sly suggestion.

"He really proposed that?" she asked, shocked.

"Yes."

"He's even crazier than I thought."

"Probably." Sandy resumed his story, took her through the reading of Jock's will and his meeting with Joan.

"Oh, God, Sandy, I'm so sorry about Mr. Bailley's will," Cara said.

"Don't be sorry, just listen." He struggled on, telling her of his meeting in the park with Peter, then, before she could interrupt him, went on to his reconsideration of the plan and his message to Peter, canceling their pact.

Cara had put her fork down now and was pale. "Sandy, you did the right thing. Peter would have gone through with it."

"Peter did go through with it," Sandy said.

Cara's mouth dropped open. "Are you telling me that Peter murdered your wife?"

"I am."

"Didn't you go to the police?"

"Don't you understand? I couldn't do that; Peter would have implicated me, and I'd be in jail, now, awaiting trial for conspiracy to murder."

"But you backed out of the bargain!"

"Of course I did, but Peter would have denied that. You know him; don't you think he could have convinced the police that I was his accomplice?"

She nodded. "Yes, you're right; he could have convinced them. So how did you keep your part of the bargain?"

"I—"

"Wait a minute," she said, and she stood up, looking frightened. "Is that what you were doing in that garage in San Francisco? You were there to murder *me*?"

"Cara, please sit down and listen."

Slowly, she sat down, never taking her eyes off him, remaining on the edge of her seat.

"I was there to warn Helena Martindale that her husband intended to kill her. I had no idea you and she were the same person. I had no intention of killing her or you." This was not quite true, he remembered. He had, after all, contemplated doing just that, but he could never let Cara know he'd even considered it, or they would be finished.

She sat, obviously thinking hard. "Now I'm beginning to get it," she said. "You told Peter that you'd done it, didn't you? You told him I was dead."

"In the circumstances, it seemed the best thing to do. I needed some time without pressure from Peter to figure out what to do about all this, and I did the right thing, because he bought it. He thinks that your body is in the trunk of your car and that your car is at the bottom of San Francisco Bay."

She slumped against the back of her chair, dumbfounded.

He gave her a moment, then went on. "So, as long as Peter thinks you're dead you're safe from him; do you understand that?"

She tried to speak and failed, so she nodded.

"I mean, it's not a permanent solution to the problem; one way or another, sooner or later, he'll find out you're alive. I brought you to London to keep that from happening for a while longer." He looked at her closely. "Are you all right?"

She nodded. "I'm just running through it in my

mind—who knows I'm alive that might inadvertently let Peter know? I don't think there's anybody. Saul Winner won't say anything—not on purpose, anyway, and Thea certainly won't, but that won't keep me from running into some mutual acquaintance on the street in New York who might mention it to Peter."

He was relieved that she was analyzing the problem. "I confess I actually thought of finding some way to kill Peter, but he was way ahead of me. He told me he'd written his own account of what happened to Joan, implicating me, and deposited it in his lawyer's safe."

Cara managed a wry laugh. "Well, Sandy, it was sweet of you to think of murdering my ex-husband, but it would be exactly like Peter to actually do what he said he did—the letter with the lawyer, so please put the idea out of your mind."

"I wish I could," Sandy said ruefully. "I have fantasies about strangling him with my bare hands or booting him off the Golden Gate Bridge."

She laughed again. "Believe me, I've had the same fantasies."

"There's something else you should know," Sandy said.

"Oh, God, not something else!"

"I'm afraid so. Peter is in London. In fact, he was in the restaurant downstairs last night when we were having dinner. He just walked in with another man and sat down."

Cara was alarmed. "Did he—"

"No, he didn't see us. I had the maitre d' move a screen to block his view, and he's not staying in the hotel."

"Thank heaven for small favors," she said, relaxing again.

"But I'm inclined to think that if Peter is in London,

we should be back in New York. How much more do you have to do in the shop to have what you need for the New York designs?"

"I've taken photographs and made sketches," she said. "That's really all I need."

"Then maybe we'd better forgo your sightseeing on this trip and head home. There's a flight early this afternoon."

"Then let's go. I suppose it would be too much of a coincidence for Peter to be on the same flight."

"I think that's stretching it, even for Peter."

"I'd better start packing," she said.

"I'll call my travel agent and let the hotel know we're checking out."

They both stood up to begin their tasks, then they stopped and looked at each other. Sandy held out his arms and she came to him, hugged him. He was relieved to know that, after hearing his story, she still wanted to be in his arms.

"You know," she said, "I'm glad all this is out in the open. I felt so alone before, fighting Peter all by myself; I'm glad to have some help."

Sandy felt the same way.

38

They left the Connaught in a limousine, in plenty of time for their flight. Traffic was lighter than Sandy had expected, and the drive to the airport was shorter than usual. At the airport, they went through security, then were checked into first class, and Sandy never stopped looking around the terminal.

They settled into a corner of the first-class lounge, since they were early for their flight, and nibbled on sandwiches. Sandy arranged himself facing the door. If they were going to run into Peter Martindale, he wanted to see him first.

Their flight was called on time, and they took the short walk to the gate. Aboard the aircraft, Sandy put their carry-on luggage into an overhead bin and chose two seats that allowed them to view the other passengers in the compartment. First class was under-populated on that day, he thought; only four other passengers shared the compartment with them. Sandy ordered Buck's Fizzes, and they sipped the drinks while the business and tourist classes boarded. To Sandy's relief, no other passengers entered the first-class compartment.

Exactly on time, the aircraft pushed back from the boarding chute and began to taxi toward the runway. Then, abruptly, the big jet made a one-hundred-and-eighty-degree turn and started back the way it had come.

"Ladies and gentlemen," a voice said. "This is your captain speaking. We've been directed to return to the boarding gate to pick up a passenger. We anticipate only a short delay, and we should be in the air inside half an hour. We apologize for any inconvenience."

Sandy stiffened. He thought they'd gotten away clean, but now they were headed back. He had no doubt, somehow, who the new passenger would be. The aircraft trundled along the tarmac for a while, then came to rest at a boarding gate. The engines were never turned off. The usual noises of the boarding chute being attached came through the hull of the airplane, then receded.

Sandy braced himself. Then, to his surprise, not one but half a dozen passengers entered first class, and none of them was Peter Martindale. Instead, they were six Arabic-looking men in an odd assortment of suits, a couple of them cheap and ill-fitting, others sharply tailored. Sandy thought he recognized one of them, a balding, heavyset man with a thick moustache, but he could not place the face. The men took their seats, the airplane was pushed back again, and soon, as the captain had promised, they were in the air, flying west.

The stewardess was handing out menus and entertainment programs when Sandy turned to Cara. "Does the man in the front row look familiar to you? The one with the moustache?"

Cara shook her head. "Probably some Middle Eastern politician. With our luck, there's probably a bomb on board, too."

Sandy laughed. "With our luck," he echoed.

"You know," Cara said, perusing the program in her hand, "I've never seen *Strangers on a Train*. In the circumstances, maybe I should."

"Thank God we have individual screens," Sandy said, rolling his eyes. "I'm watching *Singin' in the Rain*." He placed his film order, adjusted his headset, and reclined his seat to a comfortable angle. Somewhere during the Hollywood party scene, he fell sound asleep.

When he awoke, lunch was being served, and the Arab party was making a good deal of noise, talking loudly and drinking a lot of champagne. So much for Muslim rules against alcohol, Sandy thought.

When they had finished lunch, Cara got her briefcase down from the overhead storage compartment and set it on her table. "This seems like a good time to do a little business," she said. "It's long overdue, in fact."

"What's up?" Sandy asked.

"You haven't seen the sketches for your apartment." One by one, she showed him nicely executed drawings of her designs for each room of his home.

"I love them," he said. "I love them all. Don't change a thing, unless there's something extra you want. After all, I want you to feel as much at home there as I do."

She smiled at him. "I'm glad you like them. In fact, I think I unconsciously projected my own tastes into these designs. I wonder why?" She showed him photographs of upholstered furniture she was recommending, and he approved them all. "I didn't bring fabric samples," she said. "We can go over those when we get home."

Sandy shook his head. "Don't bother showing them to me. Choose the fabrics you like and order the furniture."

"All my clients should be as easy as you," she said.

"Nobody is as easy as I am," he replied, "and you don't have any other clients. That's the way I want to keep it, too."

The pilot made up lost time, and they arrived at Kennedy on schedule. Their luggage came up quickly, and they were soon through customs, but not quite as quickly as the party of Arabs from first class, who had apparently received VIP treatment from the officials. Sandy, pushing a luggage cart and with Cara on his arm, emerged into the arrivals area just behind the group of men, and he was unprepared for the reception that met them. Flashbulbs were going off, and ahead of the Arab party he could see a phalanx of newsmen standing impatiently behind a rope held by a pair of policemen, shouting questions at the Arabs.

The next part of their reception seemed to happen in slow motion. A dark-skinned man among the reporters, wearing a trench coat and carrying a camera, suddenly dropped the camera and produced some sort of automatic weapon from under his coat. By the purest chance, Sandy happened to be looking directly at him as this occurred, and he knew immediately what would happen next. He let go of the luggage cart, turned toward Cara and knocked her down with his body, falling on top of her.

As they fell, gunfire erupted in the terminal, followed immediately by loud screams and general chaos. Sandy did not look around him; he kept his head down and Cara's face in his chest. No more than ten seconds later, the firing stopped, but not the yelling. Sandy waited another ten seconds before raising his head.

The first thing he noticed was that his left forearm was covered in blood, and after a second's thought, he decided it was not his. Many people were on the floor, and only a few were beginning to get up. The two uniformed policemen, pistols drawn, were standing over a huddled figure, kicking him and screaming at him. The armed photographer, Sandy assumed. Other policemen were running into the terminal from outside.

Sandy got to his knees and looked down at Cara. "Are you all right?" he asked.

"I nearly smothered, I think, but I'm all right. What happened?" She got up onto an elbow and looked at the Arab party. "Oh, dear God," she half-whispered.

Sandy helped her to her feet and put his arms around her.

"Sandy! You're hurt!" Cara yelled. "Your arm!"

"It's not my blood," he said. "I'm all right." He looked down and saw whose blood it was. The familiar-looking Arab from first class lay at his feet, his chest a mass of blood, part of his head shot away.

Suddenly, a man in civilian clothes flashing a badge was in their faces, shouting, "You two! Over there! Into that office, now!"

Sandy hustled Cara toward the room, grateful to get-away from all the screaming and blood.

CHAPTER

39

"A re you people all right?" the policeman asked, closing the office door behind them and shoving the luggage cart into a corner. He indicated Sandy's bloody arm. "Do you need a doctor?"

Sandy shook his head. "It's not my blood."

"I expect it belongs to the gentleman out there," the cop said, showing them to chairs and pulling up one for himself. "Let me see your passports, please."

Sandy had both passports in an inside coat pocket, and he handed them over.

"Mr. Kinsolving," the cop said, reading from the document, "were you traveling with those men out there?"

"No," Sandy said. "We were about to take off from Heathrow, but we turned around and went back for that party. Who are they?"

"The leader, the one without the face, is called Said. He's high up in one of the Palestinian organizations; the others are aides or bodyguards."

"Armed bodyguards?"

"Their weapons were taken from them in London."

"Why wasn't security better?" Sandy asked.

The cop sighed. "We were told that they'd missed their plane in London and that they'd be on the next one, an hour later."

"A breakdown of communication, I guess," Sandy replied.

The cop nodded. "What did you see as you came out of customs?"

Cara spoke up. "I didn't see anything; the first thing I knew, Mr. Kinsolving had pushed me down and was lying on top of me."

"What is your relationship with Mr. Kinsolving?" the cop asked.

Sandy broke in. "We're business associates. We had been to London to photograph a shop I own there, in preparation for redesigning my New York shop to resemble it."

"What business are you in?" the detective asked.

"The wine business."

"Do you have a business card?"

Sandy produced one.

"And what did you see that made you push the lady to the floor, Mr. Kinsolving?"

"I saw a photographer drop his camera and take a weapon from under his coat."

"And when did the shooting start?"

"As we were falling, I think. It happened very quickly."

"You have very good reactions, Mr. Kinsolving. Are you sure you didn't know Said?"

"I did not. I thought he looked familiar, but I suppose I must have seen his picture in the papers."

"Did you know the photographer?"

"No. Officer, if I had had the slightest inkling that what happened was about to happen, I would not have been standing directly behind Mr. Said, I can promise you."

"I need both your home addresses," the cop said.

"Here's my address," Sandy said, handing him a personal card. "You can reach the lady through me. Do you need us any longer?"

"No. Thanks for your cooperation. If you'll wait a few minutes I'll send you home in a patrol car."

Sandy had no wish to arrive at his apartment house in a police car. "Thank you, but there should be a car waiting for us outside, if we can get out there."

The detective rose, went to the door and brought in a uniformed officer. "Take these people through the cordon and find their car for them; if the car's not there, find them a cab." He shook hands with both Sandy and Cara and helped Sandy turn the luggage cart around.

Sandy followed the policeman through the chaos that still prevailed in the terminal. The paramedics had arrived, and bodies were being loaded onto stretchers.

"How many were killed?" Sandy asked the cop.

"Said and three of his party," he replied. "Another guy was hit pretty bad, and one of the bodyguards wasn't hurt. The shooter isn't expected to live."

Outside the terminal ambulances had traffic snarled. To Sandy's surprise, a uniformed driver was still standing at the curb, holding a sign with Sandy's name on it. The driver loaded their luggage into the trunk, and they piled into the car. The cop had a word with a colleague about letting their car through, but another twenty minutes passed before they were able to drive away.

"I'll tell you something," Cara said when they were headed for the Triborough Bridge. "I've led an exciting life since I met you."

Sandy laughed aloud. "That's as close to gunfire as I ever hope to be."

In another three-quarters of an hour they were in Sandy's apartment, unpacking.

"Tomorrow, let's send for the rest of your things at Thea's," he said, tossing aside his laundry.

"There's not much still there," Cara said. "I came to New York with only two bags and a briefcase."

Sandy hung up some suits and turned to his second bag. He opened it and began removing clean shirts.

"Look," Cara said, pointing at the end of the suitcase. Sandy bent over and looked. A neat hole punctured the leather. He moved aside some clothes and looked at the inside of the case. "Good God," he said, holding up a shoe.

"I don't believe it," Cara said.

The bullet had penetrated the case and was now visible protruding from the shoe, apparently stopped by the cedar tree inside. Sandy plucked it out and held it up between thumb and forefinger. It was only slightly deformed.

"Was it an expensive shoe?" Cara asked.

"Don't ask."

"Somehow, I feel awfully lucky," she said, slipping

her arms around his waist. "To be alive, of course, but to be here with you, too."

"Me, too," Sandy replied. "Let's hope our luck holds."

Somehow he had the feeling that, with their picture all over the papers, it wouldn't hold long.

CHAPTER

40

The ringing woke Sandy early; he glanced at the bedside clock as he reached for the phone. A quarter to seven.

"Hello?"

"Dad?"

"Angus, where are you?"

"I'm in Beaune. Are you all right?"

"Of course I'm all right. Why wouldn't I be?"

"You're all over the *Herald Tribune* this morning," he said. "You and Cara."

"What?"

"Your picture at the airport; you're standing right behind that Arab guy."

"Oh." After all, there had been a lot of photographers there. "Yeah, it got a little too exciting there for a minute."

"I'm glad you weren't hurt. The article doesn't mention you by name, but I couldn't see you in the second photograph."

"We ducked when the shooting started. Did you pick up your car in Stuttgart?"

"Oh, yeah, and we had a great tour of the Porsche factory, too. Maggie says hello. She had one hell of a hangover the morning after our dinner. Come to that, so did I."

"Did you call M'sieur Calvet?"

"Yes, and our tour is today. Maggie is champing at the bit."

"Take a lesson from that girl; get interested in wine."

"It looks as though I may have to."

"I thought Maggie was terrific; so did Cara."

"Maggie liked you both, too, and I think Cara is a knockout."

"Where're you headed after today?"

"Looks like it's to Bordeaux; more wine country."

"Good news. Keep me posted on your whereabouts, okay? Call in every few days."

"From Bordeaux we plan to drive through the south of France to Rome, taking our time."

"Good. Try the Hotel Hassler in Rome; it's a lot like the Connaught."

"We will."

"How's the car running?"

"Just great; it's a real pleasure to drive. Well, I'd better get going."

"Glad you called. Keep in touch."

Sandy got out of bed and went to the front door for the *Times*. Spread across the bottom of the front page were three photographs of the Said shooting, in sequence. In the first, he and Cara could be seen clearly, he apparently looking toward the photographer/shooter. In the second, their heads were nearly out of sight behind the luggage cart, as Said was struck by gunfire, and in the third, they were nowhere to be seen. He took the paper into the bedroom, where Cara was struggling to sit up in bed. "Have a look at this," he said.

Cara blinked at the sight of the photographs, then read rapidly through the story. "I'm glad they didn't mention our names," she said.

"The cop must not have given them out."

"It's a hell of a way to get on the front page, isn't it?" she said.

"A hell of a way."

"Do you think this will make the San Francisco papers?"

"Maybe. Let's cross that bridge when it collapses under us."

"Whatever you say. How about some breakfast?"

"Please."

Cara got into a dressing gown and headed for the kitchen. Sandy shaved, showered and got dressed, then went into the kitchen.

Cara was dishing up eggs and bacon. "I think I'll get our furniture orders in this morning," she said, "then this afternoon, I'll come to your shop and do some measuring, if that's all right."

"That's fine."

"I'm going to have to use Thea's resources to find the right cabinet maker for the shop fixtures," she said. "I think we may have to go to somebody with some theatrical set design experience, to get the right look. It's going to need some distressing, to keep it from looking too new."

"Whatever you say."

"What are you going to do about Peter?"

"I don't know yet; it's going to take some thought."

"Yes, it is."

"Maybe the best thing is just to do nothing; maybe he'll cool off and stay away," he said.

"Maybe, but I'm not going to count on it," Cara replied.

Sandy hit the work hard as soon as he got to the office. He'd been neglecting the business, what with everything else he'd had to contend with over the past weeks, and it needed attention. He called in the shop manager, Ed Klein.

"Ed, you've done a fine job managing the shop," Sandy said. "Now I want you to take a larger role in the whole business, both London and New York."

"I'd like that very much, Sandy," Klein said.

"I'm buying a vineyard, too; that's still hush-hush, until we close the deal, and I'd like you to start thinking of ways we can merchandize our own wines through the shops and mail order."

"That's going to be very exciting," Klein said.

"I'm giving you a twenty percent raise, and I'd like to pick somebody from downstairs to begin stepping into the shop manager's position. Have we got somebody who can do it, or do we have to go outside?"

"Mark Hammond will be perfect," Klein said.

"He's only been here a year or so; are you sure?"

"He works like a beaver; he knows the operation better than anybody else down there."

"I'll take your word for it."

"What's my new job called?"

"How about vice-president and general manager?"

"I like it."

"Something else; now that we're independent from Bailley and Son, I'd like you to put together an employee benefits package—health insurance, profit sharing, life insurance; whatever you think we need to create some loyalty to the company. I want our people to feel secure, and I want their loyalty. Structure it, cost it, and make a recommendation."

"I'll get right on it."

"I want you to spend at least half your time with Mark, until you're sure he has the shop in hand; the rest you can spend on whatever else we come up with." He shook hands with Ed, then turned to looking over that week's ad in the *Times*.

The phone rang; Sandy picked it up. "Hello?"

"You take a very nice picture," he said. "So does Helena."

Anger welled up in Sandy. "You son of a bitch. I told you never to call me again."

"You lied to me, Sandy."

"You deserved to be lied to. You haven't done anything but lie to me since I met you. You lied about your wife, certainly; you can't be trusted."

"You wound me."

"If I hear from you again, I will."

"Threats, now?"

"Promises. Listen to me very carefully: back off; give it up; let go. Lead your life; let us lead ours. You'll be a happier man, believe me."

"I create my own happiness."

"Don't be self-destructive. You got what you wanted from her. Be happy with what you have."

"Sandy, Sandy; you just don't get it, do you?"

"Get what?"

There was a click, and the connection was broken.

Get what? What did the man want? What would make him go away? Sandy hung up the phone and sat, at a loss about what to do next.

CHAPTER

41

Alain Duvivier sat at his desk, just outside the captain's office, and allowed himself to be watched. This was part of his punishment for screwing up on the Kinsolving murder investigation, to sit and be looked at by the captain through the glass partition of his office. He felt like an ill-behaved child who had been moved to the front row of the classroom, so the teacher could keep an eye on him.

He was working two murders on the East Side—a shopkeeper robbed and shot to death, and a bar owner who'd suffered the same fate. He thought the same perpetrator was responsible for both, and since his bailiwick was the East Side and the robber/murderer was probably from somewhere else, he was depending on favors from detectives in other precincts. His best chance was some word from another detective's snitch from Harlem or the Bronx, somebody flashing too much money, somebody who carried a .44 Magnum pistol, which was what the perpetrator had used. There was no useful physical evidence and no witnesses, either.

A patrolman from the front desk downstairs walked over with a red, white, and blue envelope. "FedEx for you, Al," the man said, tossing the envelope on his desk.

Duvivier wasn't expecting such a delivery; he picked it up and looked at the sender's address. A Thomas Williams, with an address in Los Angeles. Peculiar. He ripped open the envelope and shook out its contents. A smaller envelope fell out, then a small sheet of paper. He picked up the paper.

"He paid me to do it," the message said. It seemed to have been typed with an electric typewriter. And if it was anonymous, the return name and address would be fiction.

Duvivier dropped the sheet of paper onto his desk, aware that fingerprints might get to be a factor in this delivery. He picked up the smaller envelope by its edges, used a letter opener to cut the flap, and shook out the contents. Two keys fell onto the blotter.

"What the hell?" he asked himself aloud. He sat and looked at the keys for a minute or so, trying to remember if keys came into some case he'd worked. He couldn't remember any such case. He took a small fingerprint kit from his bottom drawer and dusted the letter, front and back. The only fingerprints that showed up corresponded to where he had held the paper. He dusted the keys, too, on both sides, but no prints appeared. He wiped off the black powder from the three items, then returned the kit to its drawer.

"Something, Al?" Leary asked from the next desk.

"I don't know," Duvivier replied. "Take a look at this." He handed over the letter and the keys. "It was sent from Los Angeles . . . " He consulted the Federal Express form. "Yesterday. Has any case we've worked lately had anything to do with Los Angeles?"

Leary thought for a moment. "There was a tourist murdered last month at that hotel on Madison; he was from L.A., but it wasn't our case. Is the envelope addressed to you specifically?"

Duvivier looked at the envelope. "Yes. And there were no prints on either the letter or the keys."

Leary held up the two keys. "Both copies; one looks like a Yale, the other, I'm not sure. Outside and inside doors of an apartment house, maybe? Like a brownstone?"

"That's certainly common enough," Duvivier said. "Could be. But what case?"

Duvivier took the keys back, took a magnifying glass from his desk and examined them both. "Third Avenue," it says. "Stamped right here." He pointed with a pencil.

"That the locksmith?"

Duvivier had a look in the yellow pages. "Third Avenue Locks and Safes," he said. "The number looks like in the eighties. Want to take a drive?"

"What else have we got to do?" Leary said, taking his coat from the back of the chair and slipping it on.

On the drive over to Third Avenue, Duvivier tried to stop thinking about the keys, to just let his mind wander. He sometimes made a mental connection this way, but it wasn't working today.

"Here's the shop," Leary said.

They double-parked, put down the visor with the department identification, to keep from getting ticketed, and went into the shop.

A man got up from a workbench and walked to the counter. "Help you?"

Leary showed him his badge, and Duvivier put the keys onto the countertop. "You make these?" Leary asked.

The man picked up both keys and held them up to the light.

"One of 'em's a Yale, isn't it?" Leary asked.

"They both are, and I made 'em," the man replied.

"Got any idea who for? You have any records?"

"I have excellent records," the man said. "Whenever I do the locks for a house or a building, I keep good records. But these are off-the-street stuff. You know, some lady comes in, wants an extra set for the maid? That kind of stuff I don't keep records on; I'd get writer's cramp."

"Got any idea what the keys might be for? I mean, like the outside and inside doors for a brownstone?"

"That kind of thing, I guess," the man said. "Typical door lock keys, as opposed to car keys or padlock keys. That's about all I can tell you."

"Thanks," Duvivier said, and the two detectives left the shop. Back in the car, Duvivier rested his head against the seat back, then sat up straight. "Head over to Fifth Avenue," he said.

"Huh?"

"Fifth Avenue."

"You had a thought?"

"I've had a thought."

Leary parked the car, and the two men got out. "I follow your thinking," he said.

"It's a long shot, but worth a try," Duvivier replied. They crossed the street, and Duvivier led the way down the steps. He tried the first key; it went into the lock, but wouldn't turn. He extracted it and tried the other key. It worked. He opened the door. "Come on," he said.

They walked half a dozen steps to the storeroom. Duvivier inserted the key into the lock and turned it. "Yes!" he said.

"They're Kinsolving's then," Leary said.

"Yes, and he gave them to someone who's now in Los Angeles. Come on, let's get out of here."

Back in the car, Duvivier asked, "Do we have a photograph of Alexander Kinsolving?"

"No reason why we should," Leary said, "and there wouldn't be anything on record, since he doesn't have a record."

"Where could we find a recent photograph, do you think?"

Leary thought about it. "Remember, Kinsolving took his wine business out of the Bailley company?"

"Yes."

"Maybe there was an announcement about it somewhere?"

Duvivier grinned. "The *Wall Street Journal*," he said. "Let's go to the public library at Fifth and Forty-second."

When Duvivier left the library he was still grinning, and he had an envelope under his arm.

Leary laughed aloud. "We're such terrific fucking detectives," he said. "They couldn't do no better on *N.Y.P.D. Blue*."

Duvivier took the photostat of the newspaper article from the envelope and placed it on the locksmith's counter. "Have you ever seen this man before?" he asked, then he held his breath.

The locksmith held the stat up to the light and thought about it for a minute. "Yeah," he said, "I think I have. Hang on just a minute, will you?"

Duvivier and Leary changed glances.

"It's not enough to hang him," Leary said.

"No," Duvivier replied, "but it might be enough to crack him, if he thinks we know where the keys came from."

The locksmith came back from his desk with a newspaper. "Yeah," he said, "I thought I'd seen him before." He tapped the front page of yesterday's *New York Daily News*.

Duvivier and Leary looked at the newspaper and saw Sandy Kinsolving at the airport, walking behind an Arab, then falling behind a luggage cart.

"Has this man ever been in your shop?" he asked the locksmith.

The locksmith shrugged. "Lots of people come in this shop," he said. "Who knows?"

Duvivier sighed.

CHAPTER

42

In the early afternoon Sandy sat in Sam Warren's conference room at the Mayfair Trust and listened to the phone conversation between Sam, his lawyer, and Larsen and his lawyers in San Francisco, as they worked through minute changes to the sales documents for the vineyard. Simultaneously, he went through the list of assets of the vineyard and through the appraiser's report, asking questions and looking for anomalies. At four o'clock Sandy affixed his signature to each of the documents, and their representative in San Francisco, having ascertained that Larsen had signed, presented the seller with a cashier's check for nine million dollars.

At last, Sandy had his vineyard. He walked back to the wine shop slowly, enjoying the summer afternoon and contemplating the changes and improvements he would make. There was an owner's house; Cara could furnish and decorate that. There was the change of name; Cara could design the labeling. He would gradually sell off the wines made under Larsen, and in the autumn, his first vintage would come in, the first wines bearing the name Kinsolving Vineyards. He was a happy man.

He was less happy when, back at the shop, his secretary intercepted him on the way to his office.

"Mr. Kinsolving, that Detective Duvivier and another policemen are waiting in your office; I didn't know what else to do with them."

"Thanks, that's fine," Sandy replied, gritting his teeth. He walked into his office and Duvivier and his partner, Leary, stood up from the sofa. "Afternoon, gentlemen," Sandy said, taking a seat at his desk. "Have you found my wife's killer?"

Duvivier walked toward the desk. "We're making real progress," he said, placing a pair of keys on the desktop.

Sandy looked at the keys; he knew exactly what they fitted and that they could have come from only one place. "Keys?" he asked.

"The keys to your building's basement and your storeroom," Duvivier said, then stopped.

"Whose keys?" Sandy asked.

"The killer's keys," Duvivier replied.

"You've arrested him?" He hoped to God not.

"Not exactly," Leary said.

"You're pursuing him, then?"

"Not exactly," Duvivier replied.

"Detective, please explain *exactly* what is going on here," Sandy said, with a note of irritation in his voice.

"We thought you might like to tell us," Duvivier replied.

"Tell you what?"

"How the killer got the keys."

"Why do you think I know that?"

"I believe you took your keys to the Third Avenue Locksmiths and had them duplicated, then gave the duplicates to the killer," Duvivier said.

"Then you're a fool," Sandy replied, "and you're wasting both your time and mine."

"We took your photograph to the shop and showed it to the locksmith," Duvivier said. "What do you think he said?"

"Detective, don't ask me questions to which I obviously do not have the answer."

"All right, Mr. Kinsolving, the locksmith said he had seen your face before. In his shop."

There was nothing to do but bluff, Sandy knew. They hadn't arrested him yet, so there was a chance that *they* were bluffing, too. "So what?" he replied.

"So now we can place you at the locksmith's," Duvivier said.

"Get to the point, Detective. What is all this supposed to mean?"

"Have you ever been into the Third Avenue Locksmith's?"

"Not that I recall," Sandy replied. "What if I have been? Would that have some meaning in my wife's death?"

"It would if you had your keys duplicated and gave them to a hired murderer," Duvivier replied.

"I didn't do that," Sandy said. "Where did you get the keys?" He knew, but he thought he ought to ask, for appearances sake.

"They were given to us by the murderer."

"You've arrested him, then?"

"He says you paid him to kill your wife."

"Then he's lying; I had absolutely nothing to do with my wife's death," Sandy replied. "But you haven't answered my question: Have you arrested somebody in the matter of my wife's murder?"

"It's you who must answer the questions, Mr. Kinsolving," Duvivier said.

Sandy stood up. "You're very wrong about that. I don't know what the hell you're doing here, but I told you that I didn't want to hear from you again, unless you'd found my wife's killer, do you recall that?"

"I do."

"Have you arrested my wife's killer?"

"Not yet."

"Then get out of my office, and if you have anything else to say to me, say it to my lawyer, Mr. Murray Hirsch. Is that clear?"

Duvivier said nothing.

"Detective," Sandy said, growing angry now, "are you here to arrest me?"

"No, sir."

"Then I bid you good day." He walked to his office door, opened it, and stood, waiting for them to leave.

The two detectives exchanged a glance, then reluctantly left the office.

On the street, Leary turned to Duvivier. "You didn't really expect that to work, did you?"

"It was worth a shot," Duvivier replied.

"Do you still think he was involved?"

"I'm certain of it."

"I wish I was as certain as you," Leary said.

Duvivier looked at his partner. "You're not with me on this, then?"

Leary shook his head. "Al, I'm sorry, but I don't read

minds like you; I just go with the evidence, you know?"

Duvivier nodded.

"I mean, I respect your ability to sniff out perps; I've seen you do it before, but I've seen you wrong before, too."

Duvivier nodded. "Sometimes I am wrong."

"You think this might be one of those times?"

Duvivier shook his head. "No. This time I'm right."

"You remember what you said to me the first night we worked this case? You said you thought he did it, but we weren't going to be able to prove it?"

"I remember."

"Al, I think that's where we're at."

"Maybe so. Unless we hear more from the guy who sent the keys."

"You mean if the guy walks in and confesses? Because that's the only way he's going to break this for us. If we don't have him, we don't have Kinsolving; it's as simple as that."

Duvivier nodded.

Sandy sat at his desk. He was becoming very weary of Peter Martindale. Still, maybe this development was positive. The keys and the jewelry were the only physical evidence that could connect Martindale to the murder, and he had given up both of those. After all, Martindale couldn't implicate him beyond doubt unless he gave himself up, and somehow, he couldn't see Peter Martindale sending himself to prison. He had played things correctly with Duvivier, he was sure of that.

The only thing he wasn't sure of was Peter Martindale, and all he could do was wait for Martindale to make the next move.

CHAPTER

43

Sandy and Cara sat in first class, sipping a glass of wine before lunch, bound for the West Coast. He spread out the Wall Street Journal and showed her the announcement of his acquiring the vineyard.

"Oh, it's the Larsen Vineyard?" she asked. "I didn't know which one."

"Are you familiar with it?" he asked.

"Oh, I've seen it on wine lists, I guess." She looked away.

"Cara, is there some other reason you're familiar with the Larsen Vineyard?"

She sighed. "Yes. Peter sold Mr. Larsen some pictures last year."

"I remember some pictures from the inventory. Peter's everywhere, isn't he?"

"It seems that way sometimes."

"Cara, let's talk about Peter; I don't really know much about him. What sort of a man is he?"

"Handsome, charming, witty, very clever. Dishonest in his business dealings, if he thinks he can get away with it."

"Is that all?"

"Obsessive," she replied.

"About what?"

"Pictures, the gallery, his apartment, his cars, and—"

"Yes?"

"Me. When I first met him I found it flattering, but by the time we'd been married a few months I found it very . . . confining."

"How did his obsessiveness with you manifest itself?"

"Jealousy, mainly; it infuriated him if I spent any time with another man, if even I talked with another man for too long at a party. Peter is excellent at scenes; he can speak a few words that will embarrass and annoy everybody, yet hardly cause a ruffle in a crowd. Words are his way; I mean, he's not the sort to haul off and slug another man. Peter is something of a coward, physically."

"That's interesting."

"How?"

"Well, it doesn't sound as though he's one for confrontation. If he ever tries that, I'll know he's bluffing."

"Either that, or he'll have some advantage you're not aware of. Peter is brave only when he knows he's safe."

"And yet, he could . . . do what he did to Joan and Albert."

"An old man and a woman? Yes, that's Peter's style."

"Still, it took some sort of courage for him to do that."

"The courage of a bully," Cara said. "He'd have no problem harming someone weaker than he, and he'd certainly not mind hurting a woman."

"Did he ever hurt you?"

She sighed. "Yes, just once. We had come home after a party, one where he'd thought I'd paid too much attention to another man. He hit me, knocked me down, actually. I was near the fireplace; I got up, picked up a poker from the hearth, and advanced on him. He wilted very quickly. I told him if he ever struck me again I'd kill him in his sleep. He never did."

"You're a brave woman."

She laughed. "Braver than Peter, anyway."

"Change of subject: I'd like you to do the design work for the Kinsolving Vineyards—labels, letterheads, signs, the owner's house, of course. Anything that comes up."

"I'd be delighted. I'm sure I'll get some ideas when I see the place."

"We'll be there before nightfall," he said. "There's no reason to go into the city; we'll drive from the airport straight to Napa."

"I would like to go into the city before we go back to New York," Cara said. "I need to see my lawyer about a trust that my father set up."

"We'll find the time," Sandy said.

From the main gate of the vineyard, a tree-lined road stretched up to a Victorian house at the end, situated on a low hill.

"I hadn't expected such a grand place," Cara said as they drove toward it.

"Frankly, neither had I," Sandy replied. "I mean, the house was in the inventory, of course, along with some furnishings, but I thought more in terms of a cottage."

When they drove up to the house, Mike Bernini was waiting for them on the front porch. Sandy introduced Cara, then Bernini gave them a quick tour before making his excuses and departing for his own home.

"It's really very nice," Cara said, wandering through the rooms. "Not as big as it looks from the highway, but roomy. There are some nice pieces here, too, things we can use." She stopped and looked at a large picture on the living room wall. "But not this, I think." She walked over to the picture and examined it closely, then lifted the frame from against the wall and looked at the back.

"You don't like this one?" Sandy asked. He consulted the inventory in his hand. "This one seems to be a John Wylie oil, a scene of the Thames."

"It's a fake," she said. "Peter sold Larsen a fake Wylie."

"It's valued here at seventy-five thousand dollars," Sandy said.

"I know it's a fake," Cara said. "The son of a bitch has done this before; I caught him at it once and made him make good. I mean, I'm no expert, but I doubt if Wylie ever painted anything as crude as this."

"Do you know an expert?" Sandy asked.

"My friend Saul Winner would give us an authoritative opinion."

"Invite him up for dinner, why don't you?"

She looked at him closely. "You have something in mind, don't you?" she asked.

"I don't know, exactly," Sandy said, "but Peter has been crowding me for too long. Maybe it's time I started crowding him."

CHAPTER

44

S andy spent his first day at his new vineyard touring the plantings, inspecting machinery, and meeting staff.

"I'm surprised at the small number of people," Sandy said. "When I read the list of employees it occurred to me that you might be understaffed."

Bernini shook his head. "I run a pretty tight ship, and Larsen was tight with a buck. The only disagreement we had about staffing was his objection to hiring very young people. He claimed they couldn't pull their weight, but it was my view that we need to build from the bottom for the long run."

"I agree with you," Sandy said. "Find us some young people. You ought to have an understudy, too; somebody who could replace you when you're too old to make wine."

"I hope that's a long way off," Bernini said, laughing.

"I hope so, too, but if you should get hit by a bus at harvest time, I'd hate not having somebody here who could make wine."

"Good point. I'll scout around. Are you comfortable in the house?"

"Yes, quite comfortable. Cara is up there now measuring and making notes. It'll be more comfortable soon. Oh, we're having our first guests this weekend."

"Do you need anything?"

"Some wine, I think."

"Shall I root around in the cellars and see what I can find?"

"Thank you."

"Larsen only had the place for eleven years and made wine for only nine. There's some older stuff that the old Italian made—the one he bought the place from. He knew what he was doing."

"Let's try a few bottles; I'll trust your judgment."

Saul Winner made a beeline for the Wylie oil. Standing there, his bag still in his hand, he laughed aloud. "The fucking charlatan," he said. "He'd never have tried this one in San Francisco; he'd have been exposed in a minute. I guess he thought Larsen was a hick, and since he was out of town, too—"

"Would you testify in court to that effect?" Sandy asked.

"In a minute; I'd love to see the bastard squirm while I discuss the points of technique that any remotely knowledgeable person would spot as deficient."

While Winner and his young companion, Nicky, were changing for dinner, Sandy called Larsen.

"Hello, Lars," he said. "How are you?"

"Very well, Sandy. Are you settling in?"

"We're very comfortable," Sandy said. "I had a question for you. You bought some pictures from a man named Peter Martindale, in San Francisco, didn't you?"

"Yes, a Wylie oil and a small landscape; I forget the other painter."

"Did you ever have them authenticated?"

"No, but Martindale gave me a certificate of authenticity."

"Oh, good; where might I find it?"

"I think it's in one of the drawers of the dining room sideboard," Larsen said.

"Did anyone ever mention to you that the Wylie might not be authentic?"

"No," Larsen said emphatically. "Do you have some reason to believe it's not?"

"Actually, I do. We have a houseguest who's an eminent painter, and he says Martindale rooked you."

"Well, I'll be damned," Larsen said. "I don't know anything about painting; I just trusted the fellow."

"What, may I ask, did you pay for it?" Sandy asked.

"Forty thousand; Martindale told me a few weeks ago that it's worth seventy-five now. Sandy, if you're convinced it's a fake, I'll be glad to reimburse you for its value, as stated in the inventory I gave you."

"Thank you, Lars, but I'd prefer it if Martindale reimbursed me. Will you join me in a lawsuit?"

"Damn right I will, and I'll share the costs, too. This really makes me angry. I'd like to knock that man's teeth down his throat."

"Please don't have any contact with Martindale," Sandy said. "Let me handle it from this end."

"Whatever you say, Sandy; tell the lawyers to send half the bills to me."

"Oh, I think we'll let Mr. Martindale foot the legal bills, Lars. I'll talk to you soon."

"I'm a closet representationalist," Saul Winner said over his third glass of cabernet. "For God's sake, don't ever quote me on that; they'd throw me out of half the museums and galleries in the country."

"Why?" Sandy asked. "I mean, lots of other modernists did representational work, especially in their early years."

"I've made sure that nobody can find something like that of mine," Winner said. "I'm on record as abhorring that sort of work, you know. Maybe in my golden years I'll shock the market by doing a landscape or two." He drank some more wine. "Are you really going to sue Peter, Sandy?"

"I am, and Larsen, to whom he sold the painting, is going to join me in the suit. Tell me, Saul, do you know somebody at the newspapers to whom we could leak the story?"

"Oh, boy, do I! I can promise you half the front page of the Sunday arts section!"

"Oh, good," Sandy said.

They were getting ready for bed when Cara spoke up. "Sandy, I don't understand; why do you want to get involved in a public brawl with Peter?"

"Because I'm sick of his threats," Sandy said. "He's said he would do all these things to me—harm my son, ruin my business, harm you. His threats carry weight, because we're not supposed to know each other—he could do these things without being suspected. When I drag him into the papers, he'll have a legitimate grudge against me, and that will neutralize at least half of his ability to hurt us. If something should happen to me or to you, he'd be the first suspect."

"It seems risky to me," she said, getting into bed. "Peter can be very vindictive.

"So can I," Sandy said.

45

As soon as New York was open for business, Sandy called Sam Warren at the Mayfair Trust.

"Sam, I need another lawyer in San Francisco. Turns out that an art dealer sold Lars Larsen a picture that turns out to be a fake. It's the one in the inventory that's valued at seventy-five thousand dollars."

"Who's the dealer?" Warren asked.

"A man named Peter Martindale."

"Jesus Christ!" Warren exploded. "He sold me most of the stuff in our offices!"

"Well, my advice is to get somebody in and have everything you bought from Martindale authenticated." A bonus, Sandy thought, if one or more of Sam's pictures should turn out to be a fake. Then there'd be suits on both coasts.

"I'll certainly do that," Warren said.

"I want a very well-known lawyer, somebody of high repute, but somebody who'll nail Martindale to the wall. It wouldn't hurt if he enjoys a bit of publicity."

"Then you want Harry Keller; 'Killer Keller' they call him in the press. He's your man. Got a pencil?"

Sandy wrote down the name, address, and phone number. "Thank you so much, Sam, and will you let me know if any of your pictures are bogus?"

"I'll get right on that," Warren said.

Sandy hung up and turned to Cara. "Ever heard of this lawyer?" he asked, handing her the slip of paper.

"Killer Keller? You bet I have; so has everybody else west of the Mississippi. Oh, and he's in the same building with my lawyer; that makes things convenient."

"Let's start making some appointments," Sandy said.

They pulled into the private parking lot of Winthrop and Keys, and Sandy parked the car. "You mind if I come along with you?" Sandy asked. "My appointment isn't for another three-quarters of an hour."

"Sure; they have a comfortable waiting room."

They took the elevator upstairs, and when Cara was announced, she said to Sandy, "Why don't you come to my meeting? You might have some ideas about this."

"If you like."

They were shown down a hallway, past a number of empty offices, then greeted by a prosperous-looking man at his office door.

"Sandy, this is Mark Winthrop," Cara said. "Mark, this is Sandy Kinsolving; I've asked Sandy to come to this meeting; he might have some ideas about this trust."

"Glad to meet you Sandy," Winthrop said. "Cara, will you two have a seat and excuse me for a minute?

My secretary and most of the office are still at lunch, so I'll have to find the file on this matter."

"Take your time," Cara said. When the lawyer had gone, Cara spoke in a low voice. "I've just remembered something. You said that Peter claimed to have left a letter incriminating you in his lawyer's safe?"

"That's what he said."

"Well, his lawyer is Keyes, and his office is just across the hall."

Sandy looked at her sharply. "Cara, we're not safe-crackers."

"We don't have to be," she said. "I went to a meeting in Keyes's office with Peter once, and I saw him open his safe."

"Surely you can't remember the combination."

"I don't have to. You know those little panels that pull out of desks that stenographers used to use to rest their pads on?"

"Yes, I think so."

"Well, Paul Keyes pulled out that panel and read the combination to the safe from a little piece of paper he had taped there."

"Still, how are you going to—" He looked up as Mark Winthrop returned.

"Got it," Winthrop said, blowing dust off the file. "It's been a while since anyone had a look at it."

Sandy stood up. "Mark, excuse me, but I've just remembered that I have to make an important call to New York. Is there somewhere I could have some privacy?"

"Sure," Winthrop said. "Pick an empty office down the hall; everybody's at lunch."

"Thank you; I'll be back shortly." Sandy left Winthrop's office and walked a few paces. Paul Keyes's name appeared on an open door. Sandy closed it behind him and went to the desk. He punched the telephone for a line and dialed his home number in New York. The answering machine picked up. He laid the phone on the desk and started looking; it took only a moment to slide out the steno panel and find the piece of paper taped to its edge. He repeated the combination several times to himself, then turned to the safe.

It was a good four feet high, an old-fashioned model with a large center knob. Sandy went to work. Nervous as he was, it took two trips back to the desk before he got the combination right. He turned the handle, and the safe door swung open.

The safe was divided into a dozen compartments, and there was no way to guess where Martindale's letter might be, so Sandy began at the top left, riffling through every file and envelope in the safe. He had spent ten minutes working his way to the bottom right of the safe when he heard voices in the hallway. People were beginning to return from lunch.

Sandy took out a batch of blue legal folders from the compartment and went through them. The very last one bore Martindale's name. Sandy opened it and found a single, sealed envelope. On it, written by hand, was the message: "To be opened in the event of my untimely death." It was signed by Peter Martindale.

The door to Paul Keyes's office opened slightly, and a man stood there, apparently talking to someone in the hallway. Sandy straightened up and stuffed the blue folder containing the envelope into his belt, buttoned his coat, and picked up the phone. "Yes, yes," he began saying. "That's all very well, but we've got to get moving on this." He pretended to listen.

Paul Keyes finished his conversation and turned to walk into his office. He stopped when he saw Sandy. "What—"

Sandy covered the phone with his hand. "I'm sorry, this must be your office," he said.

"Yes, it is," Keyes replied, looking offended.

"I'm very sorry, but Mark Winthrop sent me in here to use the phone." He glanced down and, to his horror, saw that the safe door was still open.

"It's quite all right," Keyes said, entering the room.

"I wonder if you'd be kind enough to give me just another moment's privacy," Sandy said. "I'm nearly finished."

"Oh, of course," Keyes said. He stepped back into the hall and half closed the door behind him.

"Look," Sandy said into the phone, into his answering machine, "I'm not going to be back in New York until Monday, so I'm just going to have to rely on you to handle this the best way you can." He reached out with a foot and pushed the safe door closed. "I would be very grateful if you would do that," he said, continuing his half of the supposed conversation. "Thank you so much." He hung up the phone, took a quick step to the safe, pulled up on the handle, and spun the dial. He made it back to the desk before Keyes was upon him.

"I *am* sorry for the imposition," he said to the lawyer. "I think Mark must have thought you'd be out for a while."

"Quite all right," Keyes said, holding the door open for Sandy.

Sandy left the office, and he felt Keyes's eyes on his back as he returned to Winthrop's office.

"Oh, hello," Cara said. "Turns out I didn't need your advice. The trust is revocable, and I'm revoking it. It was very simple; we needn't have come into town, after all."

"Good. All ready to go, then?"

"All ready."

Sandy extended his hand to Winthrop. "So nice to meet you," he said. "I really can't thank you enough. Ah, for handling Cara's problem so expeditiously." He took Cara's elbow and guided her out of the office.

"Did you get it?" she asked out of the corner of her mouth as they walked down the hallway toward the reception room.

"Yes, ma'am," he replied. "I certainly did."

CHAPTER

46

They got into the car. Sandy took out the legal folder, ripped open the envelope, and turned on the dome light. He read quickly.

"Jesus Christ!" he said. "He's done more than relate what happened; he's completely reversed our positions. Listen to this: 'Mr. Kinsolving then told me that if I didn't murder his wife, he would kill my wife, Helena, and see that I was blamed. It was only under the greatest duress that I acceded to his wishes. I was very frightened of Mr. Kinsolving.'"

"It doesn't surprise me," Cara said.

"He's me and I'm him. The police would have a field day with this."

"I'm glad we got hold of it," Cara said. "If Peter had accidentally died and Keyes had opened that, well, I don't know what would have happened."

"Do you suppose he made more than one copy?"

Cara looked at the document. "This is an original signature, and it's notarized. I don't think he'd have gone to that trouble twice; he'd have felt safe, knowing this was in Keyes's safe."

Sandy looked at his watch. "We're due in Keller's office."

"Let's go."

Sandy pushed in the car's cigarette lighter, waited for it to heat, then set fire to the document. He got out of the car and held the flaming paper over a steel waste basket until it was nearly consumed, then dropped it into the basket, watching it turn to ash. Then he took Cara's hand and headed for the elevators.

Harry Keller turned out to be extraordinarily handsome—thick gray hair, dark eyes, a tall, trim figure, and a gorgeously tailored blue suit. He made them comfortable, then turned to Sandy. "Tell me how I can help you, Mr. Kinsolving."

"I'll be as concise as I can," Sandy said. "An art dealer named Peter Martindale sold two pictures to a man named Lars Larsen, the owner of a vineyard I recently purchased. The pictures were part of the property I bought, and I have been reliably informed that the larger of the two, allegedly a John Wylie oil, is not genuine."

"What is the value of the painting?" Keller asked.

"Larsen paid Martindale forty thousand dollars for it, and the dealer says the picture is now worth seventy-five."

"It would be, if it were genuine," Cara said.

"Ms. Mason, do you have some expertise in this field?"

"One of my degrees is in art history, and I was mar-

ried to Peter Martindale, until recently. I worked in the
gallery with him."

"In your opinion, is Mr. Martindale of such a moral
makeup that he would perpetrate a fraud?"

"Indeed, yes."

"Would you testify to that effect in a court of law?"

"I would, if you think it would help."

The lawyer turned back to Sandy. "Mr. Kinsolving,
what would you like to do about this?"

"As the current owner of the picture, I'd like to sue
Martindale. Larsen has indicated he'd be happy to join
me in the suit."

"Mmmm. The usual procedure would be for you to
sue Larsen and Martindale, but if Larsen's willing, we
could do it that way. What would you hope to accomplish in a lawsuit?"

"I want the current value of the painting, if it were
genuine; I want Martindale to pay all of my legal bills
in the suit."

"That seems reasonable, and, assuming we can get
independent corroboration of the falsity of the painting,
I believe we could accomplish that. In fact, I think we
should be able to accomplish that in a settlement. Mr.
Martindale has his reputation to think of, after all."

"I'm not much concerned about Mr. Martindale's
reputation," Sandy said. "In fact, I think I would be per-
forming a sort of public service if this incident became
public knowledge."

Keller smiled slightly. "I suppose that in the normal
course of events, the news might get out. Have you
considered criminal fraud charges?"

"I don't want to send the man to jail. I think the spotlight
of public attention on this incident would serve to teach
him his lesson, not to mention the money it will cost him."

"Just as well," Keller said. "Unless we could establish that this is a common practice of Martindale's, the courts would rather see such a matter settled in a civil case."

"Will you represent me in this matter?" Sandy asked.

"I will be happy to. I own a number of pictures myself, and although I have never bought any from Mr. Martindale, I wouldn't like to see him get away with this. I will require a retainer of ten thousand dollars to proceed, and if we get it back from Martindale, I will, of course, refund your retainer."

"I'll have Sam Warren get you a check tomorrow," Sandy said. "How soon can we file suit?"

"I'd like to send an expert up to look at the picture and any documentation you have. Once he concurs in the painting's lack of authenticity, I'll file immediately. Shouldn't be more than a few days, I should think."

"What are our chances of achieving restitution?" Sandy asked.

"Does Mr. Martindale have any substantial assets?" the lawyer asked.

Cara spoke up. "He owns a large apartment, the gallery building, and a considerable stock of valuable pictures," she said. "I should know; I paid for most of it."

"Then our chances are very good," Keller said. "Where is the picture now?"

"In the main house at the vineyard," Sandy said, writing down the address."

"Is tomorrow too soon for my expert?"

"Not at all; we look forward to seeing him. By the way, the painter Saul Winner has said he'd be happy to testify."

"Does Mr. Winner have any axe to grind with Mr. Martindale?"

"I'm afraid so," Cara said.

"Well, let's stick to detached observers," Keller said.

"Can you ask your man to render an opinion on how good a forgery the picture is?" Cara asked. "It would be wonderful if he thought it so bad that no knowledgeable dealer could possibly mistake it for the real thing."

"A good point," Keller said, "and should we go to trial I would enjoy asking Mr. Martindale about his opinion of his own judgment. He is unlikely to want to destroy his own reputation in court, but then if he claims expertise, he makes himself out to be a con man."

Sandy and Cara laughed aloud.

"I want to be there to see that," Cara said.

Keller spoke up again. "I really do think you should consider what sort of a settlement you might accept from Martindale," he said. "He certainly won't want to go to trial."

"I'd accept what I've already told you," Sandy said, "plus a public admission that he deliberately sold a forgery, perhaps a nice ad in the San Francisco papers."

"He'd want confidentiality of the terms of a settlement," Keller said.

"I won't agree to that," Sandy replied.

Keller smiled. "You're a hard man, Mr. Kinsolving; one after my own heart."

47

Cara spread out the San Francisco Sunday papers on the bed. "This is wonderful," she said. "Listen." She read aloud. "'A bomb was detonated in the San Francisco art world last week when a lawsuit was filed against a prominent local art dealer, Peter Martindale, whose gallery specializes in nineteenth-century English paintings. The suit was brought by New York wine merchant and Napa Valley vineyard owner Alexander Kinsolving, who, when he bought the Larsen Vineyard, also acquired with the vineyard a painting, ostensibly an oil by John Wylie. The painting had been sold by Peter Martindale to the vineyard's previous owner, Lars Larsen, and, according to a certificate supplied with the picture, had been certified by Martindale as being a genuine Wylie.

"'After Kinsolving had bought the vineyard, a visitor to his property, the abstract painter, Saul Winner, saw the picture and proclaimed it a fake. Kinsolving then contacted San Francisco attorney Harry Keller who has long had the sobriquet Killer Keller, and Keller sent an independent expert, said to be an official of the San Francisco Museum, to Napa to view the painting. This expert, according to Keller, described the picture as a forgery, and not even a clever one.

"'Keller, interviewed in his office on Friday, said that his client would decline to settle out of court, unless Peter Martindale is willing to publicly admit that he deliberately sold a forgery.

"'Martindale, contacted at his gallery yesterday, said, "This gallery is in the business of dealing in fine paintings, genuine ones by eminent artists, and we would never stoop to such an action. I expect to be fully vindicated."

"'Keller, in response, said, "If Mr. Martindale wishes to have a swift opportunity to defend his reputation publicly, then my client and I will waive depositions and go straight to trial at the earliest possible moment. We have no interest in what Mr. Martindale has to say, unless it is in front of a judge and, if he likes, a jury."'"

Sandy laughed. "Keller has a way with him, doesn't he?" He held up another newspaper. "The *New York Times* has a piece, too, though a smaller one. The good news is it comes in an issue that has a feature on art galleries, so it will be widely read." The phone rang, and Sandy picked it up. "Hello?"

"Sandy? It's Saul Winner."

"Saul, you kept your promise; it's a perfect piece."

"Isn't it? Listen, a sculptor friend of mine, Martin Cage, is throwing what sounds like a very good party early this evening. Can I tempt you and Cara into town for it? I'd love to show you both off."

"Hang on." Sandy turned to Cara. "Saul wants us to go to a party this evening at Martin Cage's house. You up for it?"

"You bet I am," she replied.

"Saul, we'd love to." He wrote down the address. "See you sixish." He hung up.

"This," Cara said, "is going to be fun."

Martin Cage's house was on a low hill overlooking San Francisco Bay and the Golden Gate Bridge. Valet parkers sprinted to and from the street, disposing of the guests' cars, and waiters stood by the front door, dispensing drinks from trays. Cara took a glass of champagne and Sandy asked somebody to make him a Bloody Mary.

Saul Winner grabbed them before they had gone a dozen steps and stepped between them, hooking their arms in his. "You're *mine* for the duration of this party," he said sweeping them through the house and onto a large rear lawn, which also served as a sculpture garden for the works of their host.

At least two hundred people were standing, drinking, and, as Saul began to work the crowd, Sandy thought he had never before met so many artists, dealers, collectors, and curators in one place. Saul was introducing Cara, to the few people she didn't already know, as "the former Helena Martindale, whose friends call her Cara." Sandy discovered very quickly that he did not like the name Martindale attached to her in any way, and he resolved to do something about it.

He was astonished at the number of people who, upon being introduced, uttered encouraging words about his lawsuit. Apparently, everybody had read the Sunday papers.

A slender young man carrying a notebook and accompanied by a photographer planted himself firmly in their path and shot Saul a look. "Saul, you must introduce me."

"Ah, Simon," Saul said. "Allow me to introduce Sandy Kinsolving and—"

"And Cara," Sandy interrupted.

"Sandy, this is Simon Teach, who, you may remember, wrote the article in this morning's paper."

"Oh, yes, Mr. Teach," Sandy said, shaking the man's soft hand. "I hung on your every word."

"Oh," Teach replied, "I should think Peter Martindale is more likely to hang, don't you?"

Cara spoke up. "From your lips to God's ear."

"Ah, yes, Cara," Teach said, pumping her hand. "I believe you were once something more than friends with the aforementioned, were you not?"

"Will you pillory me for my past errors in judgment, Mr. Teach?"

"Why no, dear lady; just getting the facts straight."

A waiter turned up at Sandy's elbow with a large Bloody Mary, and Sandy accepted it gratefully. He toasted Teach. "Your continued good health," he said.

Teach raised his own glass. "And good sources," he replied. They clinked glasses.

"Ah," Saul cried, "our host!"

Sandy looked up to see a small man with shoulder-length hair making his way toward them.

"Sandy, Cara," Saul said, "may I present Martin Cage?"

"You are very welcome," Cage said with relish, "and may you always bring with you such good news. It's about time somebody nailed the bastard."

"Many of your guests have expressed similar sentiments," Sandy said, shaking the man's hand.

"Martin," Cara said, "your work is very striking. I wish there were fewer people to block my view of it."

"On another occasion, Cara, I will bring you here alone, so that you may drink in its every nuance."

"Oh, Martin!" Saul exclaimed suddenly. "You *are* wicked!"

Sandy and Cara turned and followed his gaze up the lawn, to see Peter Martindale striding confidently toward them, resplendent in a white linen suit.

Simon Teach was very nearly jumping up and down. "Oh boy, oh boy!" he was muttering under his breath. He turned to his photographer, a young girl. "Miss this and I'll strangle you with that camera strap." The girl began clicking off shots with her machine-driven camera.

"Well, Helena!" Martindale crowed as if in triumph, "what a great surprise to see you here!" He turned and looked narrowly at Sandy. "And this must be the fabled Mr. Kinsolving. Allow me to introduce myself."

Sandy looked him in the eye. "Your reputation precedes you," he said.

Martindale reacted as if he had been spat upon. He turned his attention to Cara again. "And where did you pick up this thing?" he asked. "Down by the docks?"

With no hesitation, Cara tossed her champagne into his face.

Martindale blinked, then took a silk pocket square from his breast pocket and dabbed at his damp white suit.

"Don't worry, Peter," Cara said. "It's only champagne; it won't stain your suit."

Sandy spoke up. "This should do it." He threw his entire Bloody Mary at Martindale's head.

For a moment there was a great silence, except for the whirring of the newspaper photographer's camera. Everyone waited expectantly for Martindale's response. When it came it was disappointing.

"Another time," he sputtered, then he turned and strode back toward the house.

Everyone seemed to let out a breath at once, a tiny moan of disappointment, then the babble of conversation resumed.

Simon Teach turned to his photographer. "Go!" he said. The young woman sprinted toward the street. "If you'll forgive me," he said to the others, "I have a deadline." Then he, too, was gone.

"Martin," Saul Winner breathed, "you really know how to throw a party."

"Thank you, Saul," Cage replied, beaming.

"Well, that was certainly fun," Cara said as they left the waning party.

"I thought so."

"It was brilliant of you to order a Bloody Mary," she said. "I've never seen you drink one before. What made you do it?"

"Fate, I guess."

"While we're in town, let's pick up my car at my friends' house," she said, "then we can drop off the rental car at one of the hotels.

"Good idea. Your car is certainly classier transportation."

"Yes," she said, "it is."

"Cara," Sandy said, "we have to do something about your name."

"My name?"

"Yes. How long does it take to get married in California?"

She leaned over and kissed him on the ear. "Not long."

"Let's see how fast we can do it."

"You're on."

CHAPTER

48

Paul Keyes picked up the phone in his office. "Yes?"

"Mr. Peter Martindale to see you," the receptionist said.

"Please send him in," Keyes replied. He had always found Peter Martindale charming, had even bought some pictures from him, and he was ashamed to recall that, when he had received service of the Kinsolving lawsuit, it had crossed his mind that perhaps he should have somebody authenticate his own paintings.

"Paul, how are you?" Martindale said, smiling broadly and squeezing the lawyer's hand in both of his own.

"How are *you*, Peter, is the question," Keyes replied.

"Oh, you mean that business in the paper this morning. Nothing to it; I just didn't realize how drunk Kinsolving was."

"Good, I'm glad you're not upset."

"Not in the least. Well, I guess we should talk about our defense in this suit."

"Yes, Peter, let's do that. How do you see us proceeding?"

"Well, they'll get their expert, I suppose, and it'll be my word against his. I'll make a very good witness, you can count on that."

"I'm sure you will, Peter." Keyes evened the corners of a stack of papers and moved them from one side of his desk to the other. "Now, I have to ask you some very direct questions, Peter, and it's important that you be absolutely frank with me."

"Of course, Paul; how could I be anything else with you?"

"Remember, this all comes under the heading of client-attorney privilege, so nothing you and I say to each other can ever leave this room, not even if a court asks."

"Yes, I understand that."

"First of all, tell me how you came to have Lars Larsen as a client."

"Well, let's see; I was up in the Napa Valley for a wine tasting at a restaurant there—you know the one, it's an annual fund-raiser for some charity or other."

Keys nodded. "I think I do."

"I was tasting some of Larsen's wines, and we fell into conversation, ended up having dinner together after the event at some little steak house. Drank quite a lot of his wine, as I recall."

Keys nodded. "Go on."

"Well, Larsen insisted I be his guest for the night. Quite rightly, I suppose, since I shouldn't have driven back to the city, having put away a few, so I accepted.

At breakfast the next morning he gave me a tour of the house—lovely old Victorian place; you can see it from the highway, up a lane lined with trees."

"I've driven past there and seen it," Keyes said. "Never been up to the house, though."

"Well, it's a lovely place. Some city decorator had put him in the way of some nice pieces of furniture and carpets, and it looked really good, except for the pictures, which were all cheap reproductions. I told him I thought that a property of that quality should have better things on the walls, and I suggested the next time he came into town, we should get together and talk about it."

"And did he call you?"

"Well, I called him after a bit, and as luck would have it, he was coming to town, so I took him to dinner and then wheeled him by the gallery a bit later."

"Where'd you have dinner?"

"At the Ritz-Carlton's restaurant. I thought it would be just the sort of thing for him—rich surroundings, fine food."

"Fine wines?"

"Oh, yes. I ordered something quite special, as I recall; a LaTour '59."

"How many bottles?"

"Two, I believe. Oh, I had a driver that night; no problems about being at the wheel."

"And you went straight from dinner to the gallery?"

"Well, I believe we stopped in the bar for a cognac. Awfully nice bar at the Ritz."

"Yes, I know it well. So then, after how many cognacs?"

"Oh, only one; we had some business to discuss, after all."

"So then, after one cognac, you went to the gallery?"

"That's right. We had some lovely things at the time, and Larsen was immediately drawn to the Wylie, ah, after I'd pointed it out to him."

"And did he buy it on the spot?"

"He did, and one other, smaller picture, as well; a horse thing by a lesser-known painter, after Stubbs."

"And how much did he pay for the two pictures?"

"Forty for the Wylie, twenty-five for the smaller picture, I believe."

"Would you consider those fair prices?"

"Oh, very fair, I should say, very fair."

"Peter, how did you come by the Wylie?"

"Fellow in London I buy from now and then."

"A reputable gallery?"

"Not a gallery, as such. Fellow has a stall at the Chelsea Antiques Market, you know, in the King's Road?"

"Mmmm, yes. An honest fellow, do you think?"

"As honest as the next stallholder, I suppose."

"How much did you pay him for the picture?"

Martindale pursed his lips. "Ah, well . . . I'm not sure I recall precisely—"

"Peter, this is extremely important. It will come up in court, I promise you, and you'll have to back it up with records, receipts, canceled checks, that sort of thing."

"Oh, well, I believe it was six hundred."

"Pounds?"

"Yes, that was it, six hundred quid."

"Which is, in dollars?"

"Oh, nine hundred, give or take."

"So you made a profit of thirty-nine thousand, one hundred dollars?"

"Well, there was shipping, insurance, etcetera."

"A *very* large profit, nonetheless."

"Well, yes, a *fortunate* profit, shall we say? I mean, the stallholder didn't know it was a Wylie, did he?"

"Peter, does this stallholder, by any chance, paint?"

"Believe he does, a bit."

"Peter, if I were Harry Keller, and I telephoned a London firm of private investigators and had this fellow looked at, might I find that he has, in the past, dabbled in forgery?"

"Oh, well, lots of those fellows about, you know? Look here, Paul, it really is going to be their expert's word against mine, you know, and I do have an awfully good reputation at this sort of thing."

"I know you do, Peter, and I want you to be able to hang on to it." He picked up a document from his desk and handed it to Martindale. "This fellow is in charge of English paintings at the San Francisco Museum. Please read what he has to say."

Martindale read the document. "As I say, Paul, his word against mine."

"Peter, are you familiar with"—he referred to another document—"a Sir William Fallowfield?"

"Why, yes, I believe he's a mucketymuck at the Tate Gallery, isn't he?"

"He appears to be, if my information is correct, the world's leading authority on nineteenth- and early twentieth-century English painters."

"He might well claim to be, I suppose."

"Well, it seems that Harry Keller is planning to air freight the Kinsolving Wylie to London for Sir William's inspection. I expect they will have an opinion by the end of the week."

Martindale licked his lips and looked at his shoes. "Well, if they're able to corral that old fart, I don't suppose it would look too good for us, would it?"

"Not if he takes their position. I should point out, too, Peter, that there are more technical ways to examine the painting—the kind of paint used and its age, that sort of thing. I'm sure, being in the business for as long as you have been, you're aware of some of these procedures."

"Yes, yes." Martindale was still looking at his shoes.

"Peter, if we go to trial on this, and we make it your word against their experts' word, well, you'll not only have to testify, you'd have to undergo cross-examination by Harry Keller."

Martindale looked up at him. "I'm not afraid of that shyster," he said.

"What Keller will do—indeed, what I would do, were I representing the plaintiff—is first to refer to your own testimony about your experience and qualifications to judge a painting. Then refer to the qualifications of his own experts, including those of Sir William Fallowfield, and he'll ask how you think you stack up to them. Then he'll read you some of their opinions, and he'll ask you how you, who have already characterized yourself as expert, could possibly mistake the painting in question as an authentic Wylie. Then he'll suggest—and certainly I, myself, don't believe this—that you got Lars Larsen drunk and sold him a fake. And, Peter, I'm very much afraid that, by the time his cross-examination has ended, I will have lost my case and you, your reputation."

"What are you suggesting I do?" Martindale asked.

"Peter, do you have, say, a hundred thousand dollars in ready cash?"

Martindale shook his head. "No. Maybe twenty, and that's operating capital."

"Well, since the divorce settlement you have been debt-free, have you not?"

"Yes, well, more or less."

"Then you shouldn't have any trouble collateralizing a loan of a hundred thousand, should you?"

"I suppose not."

"Well, I think you should stop in at your bank and arrange such a loan. I'll make an offer of, say, eighty-five thousand to Keller, but I think it's likely he'll insist on a total figure of something around a hundred."

Martindale was staring at his shoes.

"Peter, it's really not so bad; after all, the profit you made on the picture will cover a large part of the settlement."

"Oh, all right," he said, finally.

"Good. I'm sure this is the way to go, in the circumstances."

"In the circumstances, I suppose so," Martindale replied. He made to get up.

"Just a moment, Peter, there's something else."

Martindale sat back down. "What else?"

"Keller and his client have insisted—and Keller has been very firm about this—that you issue a statement of admission to the press."

"Jesus Christ, Paul! I can't do that! I'd never be able to earn a living again!"

Keyes raised a cautionary hand. "Just listen. I've drafted something that I think might do the trick and still preserve your professional standing."

"Let's hear it."

Keyes read from a document on his desk. "It has come to my attention that the authenticity of a painting sold by my gallery has been questioned. It has always been my policy to stand behind each work of art that passes through my hands, and, accordingly, I have taken back the painting in question and reimbursed its owner not just the original price paid, but the appreciated value of an authentic painting by the artist. Honesty compels me to do no less, and I hold out the same offer to any other client of mine who feels he has any reason to question the authenticity of any painting I have sold.

"The Peter Martindale Gallery will continue to operate in the trustworthy and straightforward manner in which it has always conducted its sales and served its clients."

Martindale nodded. "It's good."

Keyes reversed the document for Martindale's signature. "What I would like to do is to send this document and a cashier's check for eighty-five thousand dollars to Harry Keller before the day is out, with a promise that the statement will run on your letterhead as a quarter-page ad in the Sunday arts section."

Martindale's shoulders sagged. "All right." He stood up and shook his lawyer's hand.

"Good," Keyes said. "Now let's get this thing done and put it behind us."

Martindale was on his way out the door. "Not on your fucking life," he muttered.

Paul Keyes was sure he had misunderstood his client's words.

CHAPTER

49

S andy had been making calls all morning, and the
moment he finished the phone rang.

"Hello?"

"Dad?"

"Angus! How are you?"

"I'm terrific, Dad."

"Where are you?"

"We're still in Rome."

"Are you enjoying the city?"

"I'll say we are; I've never been anyplace like it. And
I have some news."

"Did you stay at the Hassler?"

"Yes, we were lucky enough to get a suite."

"Isn't the view from the rooftop restaurant marvelous?"

"I'll let you know; we're having dinner up there
tonight."

"Maggie will love it."

"Dad, Maggie and I were married this morning."

"*What?*"

"I said we were married this morning."

"Why that's wonderful, Angus! I'd hoped you wouldn't let that girl get away, but I never thought you'd take my advice so quickly."

"Well, after traveling together for a couple of weeks, we just . . . well, we wanted to get married. An American lady who owns an English-language bookshop helped us through the formalities and was our witness. Turns out that Italy is the easiest place in Europe for a foreigner to get married."

"Well, I'm absolutely delighted for you, and I have some news of my own."

"What's that, Dad?"

"Cara and I are being married the day after tomorrow. I'm so glad you called, so we could tell you in advance."

"I don't believe it! We'll be celebrating anniversaries together! Where are you doing this?"

"Here at the vineyard. How did you know where I was?"

"Sam Warren gave me the number."

"I'm glad he did. Now look, I don't want you to interrupt your honeymoon to come all this way, do you understand?"

"Are you sure you don't mind?"

"Absolutely. We're just going to have a few friends up to the house and do it here early in the evening. I don't know many people out here, but some of Cara's friends are coming up from San Francisco. In fact, I've been on the phone all morning, making arrangements and inviting people. What are your plans after Rome?"

"We're going to do some more of Europe, then ship the Porsche back and go on east around the world. We're doing Greece, India, Bali, Australia, New Zealand, then home."

"Wonderful! Maybe we can meet you on the West Coast on your way home and you can see the vineyard."

"Maggie would love that, she really would."

"It's a date, then."

"Dad, I can't tell you how happy I am for you, the way things have worked out. I think Cara is a marvelous person, and I'm looking forward to getting to know her better."

"She feels the same about you, and we both feel the same about Maggie."

"Well, I'd better go; our dinner reservation is for right now. Have a wonderful wedding."

"And you two have a wonderful honeymoon."

Sandy hung up and turned to Cara. "Did you get that?"

"They're married?"

"This morning, in Rome."

"Perfect."

The phone rang again, and Sandy picked it up.

"Hello?"

"Sandy?"

"Yes."

"It's Harry Keller."

"How are you, Harry?"

"I'm very well, and so are you."

"Pardon?"

"This morning I received a cashier's check for eighty-five thousand dollars from Peter Martindale's lawyer, along with a signed admission." He read Martindale's statement aloud. "It's running as an ad in the Sunday arts section."

"The wording lets him off kind of easy, doesn't it?"

"Sandy, let him save a little face. When you win everything you want, don't make your opponent eat dirt; it's not good practice."

"You're right, Harry."

"I know I am. Shall I send this check to Sam Warren in New York?"

"Yes, please, and Harry, Cara and I are being married the day after tomorrow. We'd love it if you and your wife could join us here around six. We'll finish pretty early, so you can be back in town at a decent hour."

"Sounds delightful; we'd love to. Oh, by the way, you should ship the picture back to Peter Martindale's gallery."

"Not until after the wedding; I want everybody to see it."

"That'll be fine. We'll see you at the party."

Sandy hung up and told Cara the news.

"This is a pretty good day all 'round, isn't it?" she said.

"Could hardly be better."

The phone rang again.

"Hello?"

"Mr. Kinsolving? This is Simon Teach, how are you?"

"Very well, thanks."

"I'd just like to confirm a couple of reports I have from various sources. I've heard that Peter Martindale has settled your suit, is that correct?"

"He's settled it on our terms," Sandy said.

"For eighty-five thousand and a public admission of guilt?"

"That's correct."

"Good. The other report I have is that you and Mrs. . . . the lady are getting married."

"That's correct, too." What the hell, Sandy thought; why not have a little coverage? "And you're invited. The day after tomorrow at six, at what used to be the Larsen vineyard."

"May I bring my photographer?"

"If we can have copies of her shots."

"I'll arrange it. See you then."

Sandy hung up.

"Who was that?" Cara asked.

"Simon Teach."

"You invited him?"

"Why not? Do you mind?"

"Well, he's a little oily, but I suppose it will be all right."

"We'll get some photographs for our album, anyway. Sweetheart, everything finally seems to be going the way it's supposed to. Isn't it great?"

"What about Peter?"

"What about him? We've just rubbed his nose in it pretty badly. Maybe he's learned not to mess with us."

Cara looked out the window at the view over the vineyard. "I hope you're right," she said.

CHAPTER

50

Simon Teach was not without gall, a characteristic which he regarded as essential to his chosen profession, so he felt no compunction whatever about telephoning Peter Martindale.

"Peter, it's Simon, how are you?"

"You have a nerve calling me, you little weasel, after what you've written about me."

"Dear Peter, if you'd simply reread what I've written you'd see that it could have been much, much worse. Believe me, I have been very kind to you in the paper the past couple of weeks." There was a silence at the other end of the line that encouraged Simon to continue. "By the way, I thought your copy for the ad was brilliant; struck just the right tone."

"Did you?"

"Oh, yes; I don't think this nonsense is going to hurt your business in the least."

"Well, Simon, I do hope you're right. Now, I'm off to L.A., and I have to make an eleven o'clock flight this morning, so what can I do for you?"

"I don't suppose you're attending the nuptials this evening, are you?"

"Simon, please don't be arch; it's unbecoming."

"Sorry, Peter, it's just that my editor has demanded that I ask you for comment on the marriage of Sandy Kinsolving to your former wife."

"Of course, be glad to comment. Got your pencil ready?"

"I'm ready."

"Please note this exactly as I speak it."

"I won't misquote you, Peter."

"Very well, here's my quote."

Simon held the receiver away from his ear, but he could still hear the shouting clearly.

"*I wish the happy fucking couple every fucking happiness!!!*" Then the voice moderated, "Have you got that, Simon?"

"Yes, Peter, I have it."

"Good, run it without the *fucking*s, will you?"

"Of course, Peter."

"'Bye. I'm off to L.A. for a couple of days."

"What for, may I ask?"

"I'm lecturing at the Arts Alliance."

"Have a nice trip, Peter."

"Oh, I will, *believe you me*."

Shortly after 3:00 P.M. Elmer "Shorty" Barnum sat in a beatup leather chair in his tin-shed office at Santa Monica Airport and worried. Shorty ran a jack-of-all-trades air service—air taxi, basic and advanced instruction, instrument instruction—whatever anybody wanted, and things were not good. His airport rent was due, he owed his maintenance man twelve hundred bucks, and he was a payment behind on his aircraft loan. What Shorty needed to get out from under was three or four charters that week, and the phone had not been ringing. The phone rang.

"Barnum Flying Service, speak to me."

"Mr. Barnum?"

"Call me Shorty."

"Shorty, my name is Prendergast. I understand you have a very nice Beech Baron with long range tanks for rent, is that correct?"

"Depends on what your logbook looks like, and, of course, a check ride." Funny accent, not quite American; Canadian, maybe?

"No, I want you to fly the airplane."

"Then the answer is yes, I have such an airplane, and it's in top shape."

"Are you available at around eight P.M. this evening for a flight to the San Francisco area and back?"

"Yes sir, I am available."

"What is your charge for such a trip?"

"You coming back tonight?"

"Yes."

"Three-fifty an hour for me and the airplane; fifty bucks an hour for any waiting time."

"I'm paying cash."

"In that case, I can manage three twenty-five an hour, but the waiting time's the same." Shorty held his breath.

"That will be satisfactory."

"Fine. What airport are we going into? I'll need to file a flight plan."

"Why?"

"Let me explain. I normally fly under instrument

flight rules—that way, if we run into some cloud we can legally fly through it, and the air traffic controllers will give us radar separation from other aircraft. It's easier than flying under visual flight rules, which is what we'd have to do if I don't file a flight plan."

"Shorty, are you telling me that you're refusing to fly without a flight plan tonight?"

"Well, I guess I can if I have to."

"This is my party, so let's do it my way."

"I don't guess you want me to fly low over the water and then drop a bag of something on some dirt strip, do you?"

"Shorty, this is entirely legitimate, but it's also highly confidential; do I make myself understood?"

"Mr. Prendergast, I'll see you at eight this evening. Bring money."

"Fear not, Shorty."

Guests began arriving shortly after six, and Sandy and Cara greeted them on the steps of the house. There was a bar set up on the front porch, and the vineyard's wines, old and new, were prominently displayed.

It was some time after seven before the judge called for silence and began reading the marriage ceremony. Five minutes later, Sandy and Cara were man and wife, and her previous married name had been forever obliterated.

At that moment, the desk clerk on duty at the Bel-Air Hotel looked up to see Peter Martindale walk into the lobby. She was surprised to see him, since his room was at the extreme north end of the hotel—he always requested that area—and he would normally have driven his car to that end and parked near his room.

"Good evening," Martindale said.

"Good evening, Mr. Martindale. I hope you've had a good day."

"A tiring day, my dear," Martindale replied wearily. "I'm just going to have a bite from room service and curl up with the TV. Would you please hold my calls? On no account do I wish to be disturbed."

"Of course, Mr. Martindale."

A little after eight, Shorty Barnum looked up to see a tall man wearing a black raincoat and a soft felt hat standing in the doorway of his office. He was also wearing what was almost certainly a false beard and a wig that protruded from under the hat. "You Mr. Prendergast?" Shorty asked.

"I am."

"I'd like to collect my estimated bill up front, if you don't mind," Shorty said. "We can adjust the final figure when we return."

"Of course."

"Let's see, say two hours up and two back; how long on the ground?"

"An hour or so."

"Okay, say thirteen hundred up front?"

Prendergast pulled a chair up to Shorty's desk, produced an envelope and began counting out bills, mostly twenties and fifties. Shorty was now sure the beard and wig were phony. He'd been in business for a long time, but he'd never had a customer wearing a disguise.

"How about fifteen hundred up front?" Prendergast asked.

"Suit yourself," Shorty replied and reached for the stack of cash.

But Prendergast laid a hand on the cash. "First, let's talk about some other conditions of this flight, shall we?"

Shorty sat back in his chair. "Conditions?"

"Do you have a Mode S transponder in your aircraft?"

"Nope, it's Mode C."

"So your aircraft registration number won't appear on an aircraft controller's screen until you tell it to him?"

"That's right."

Prendergast got up, walked to the window and looked out at the runway. "Pretty dark on this field, isn't it?"

"Well, it ain't LAX," Shorty said.

"Shorty, when you take off, you give your tail number to the tower, don't you?"

"That's right; in fact, I give it to the ground controller before we get cleared to taxi."

"But at night, if the number were off by a digit or two, nobody in the tower would notice, would they?"

"I guess not, but why would I want to give the tower a false tail number?"

Prendergast held up the envelope. "To double your fee," he said. "Shall we make it an even three thousand?"

Shorty peered at the man. "Where we going, Mr. Prendergast?"

"To a private strip just north of San Francisco, Shorty, but I promise you, there will be nothing illegal about this flight, except of course our little fib about the tail number. And, as I mentioned before, this is a very confidential trip, and that means you'll answer no questions from anybody, and I mean *anybody*, about our trip."

"Mister, you're telling me the God's truth about this, now? I mean, I'm not looking to have the feds confiscate my airplane."

"I guarantee you, you'll have no problems with the feds or any other law enforcement agency."

Shorty decided to take a chance. "Mr. Prendergast, my fee for *an absolutely* confidential flight and VFR at night with a phony tail number is five grand, even." Shorty set his jaw and waited.

Prendergast tossed the envelope onto the desk. "Count it."

CHAPTER

51

S andy, with considerable flourish, tugged at the corner of the cloth, and it fell away to reveal the new label of the Kinsolving Vineyards. There was enthusiastic applause.

"Ladies and gentlemen," Sandy said, "from this moment this vineyard has a new name. In the autumn, after our first harvest, we will make the first wines bearing this label, which my wife designed. Cara and I are so pleased that each of you could join us for this occasion, the beginning of a new marriage and the beginning of a new tradition in the growing and making of fine Napa Valley wines."

More hearty applause. No one showed the slightest interest in driving back to San Francisco, so the party continued. Sandy whispered to Mike Bernini to bring more wine from the cellars.

Shorty Barnum finished his runup and held short of the runway. "Cessna one, two, three tango foxtrot ready for takeoff," he said to Santa Monica tower. "VFR to Oakland."

"Cessna one, two, three, tango foxtrot, cleared for takeoff," the tower responded. "After takeoff turn right to three six zero and expect vectors to the VFR corridor."

Shorty lined up on the runway center line, did a final check of the panel, and pushed the throttles gradually forward. "Tango foxtrot rolling," he replied.

The twin-engined aircraft quickly picked up speed, then lifted from the runway and rose above Santa Monica Beach. Shorty set eight thousand feet into the altitude preselect, turned the heading bug to three six zero degrees, and punched on the autopilot. He took his hands off the yoke, and the airplane began to fly itself. He glanced next to him at Prendergast, or whatever his name was. The man had removed his hat and the wig was now clamped onto his head by a headset.

"That was very good, telling them you were a Cessna," Prendergast said. "Keep up the good work."

"Sure," Shorty said, and turned his attention to looking for traffic. He did not like flying through some of the world's busiest airspace VFR, and he had on the aircraft's nav lights, its strobe lights, and its landing and taxi lights. Tonight, he wanted to be seen by everything flying. He received a vector that put him on course for Oakland, and soon he leveled off at eight thousand feet.

Prendergast glanced at his watch by the glow of the instrument panel. "Yes, yes," he said. "Looking good."

"I told the tower Oakland," Shorty said. "Thought

that would put us generally on the right heading. Now, you want to tell me where are we going?"

"A very nice little private field," Prendergast said, handing over a slip of paper. "These are the coordinates."

Shorty fed the coordinates into the Global Positioning System receiver in his panel, pressed the direct button twice, checked the heading, and looked at his chart. "We'll need to fly east of our course to get around San Francisco's Class B airspace," he said. "I want to talk to as few controllers as possible, and anyway, they'd just vector us all over hell and back if we tried to fly through their airspace."

"Good thinking, Shorty."

"GPS puts our ETA at one hour and thirty-four minutes; we've got a little tailwind."

"Very good."

"You a pilot?" Shorty asked. The guy certainly knew something about flying, but he wasn't sure how much.

Prendergast remained silent.

"I've got some music aboard," Shorty said. "What's your pleasure?"

"Please yourself," Prendergast replied, gazing out at the night. They were leaving the lights of L.A. behind, and those of Santa Barbara lay ahead.

Classical, Shorty figured. He switched on the radio and pressed the CD button, and behind his seat, the player loaded a CD into the remotely mounted player. His passengers always loved this. Vivaldi's Four Seasons flowed into their headsets. Shorty didn't know a damn thing about classical music, but a woman of his acquaintance had suggested a few selections.

Prendergast nodded slowly and held up a thumb.

He's not American, Shorty thought. He says things like "please yourself." What the hell, he was making money; what did he care if his passenger wore a false beard and didn't talk?

Sandy moved Cara around the impromptu dance floor on the broad front porch, accompanied by a small band that Saul Winner had recommended. A few yards away, Saul himself danced, with Nicky's head on his shoulder. The party was mellowing, now, and half the guests had departed for town. Soon the others would begin to say their goodnights, and he and Cara could go to bed. Sandy was looking forward to his wedding night.

Shorty consulted the GPS and spoke up. "Your airport is dead ahead, fifteen miles," he said.

Prendergast, who had been sitting as stonily still as a Buddha, came to life. "The lights are pilot operated on one-two-two-point-eight," he said. "Five keys."

Shorty dialed the frequency into the radio. "What's the name of the field?" he asked. "I want to announce our intentions to any possible traffic there."

"No announcements," Prendergast said. "There won't be any traffic."

"What's the field elevation?" Shorty asked.

"I don't know; probably about the same as Napa," Prendergast replied.

They were descending through four thousand feet over the little town now, and Shorty looked up Napa's elevation: thirty-three feet. He flipped out his speed brakes, increased his rate of descent and eased back on the throttles. Five miles later he picked up the microphone and pressed the transmit key rapidly five times.

"There!" Prendergast said, pointing ahead and slightly to their right.

Shorty looked out and picked up the runway lights. "How long is the runway?" he asked.

"Thirty-five hundred, maybe four thousand feet," Prendergast said. "You've got plenty of tarmac."

Tarmac. Another of those non-American words.

"Land to the northeast," Prendergast said. "The forecast winds at Napa were zero five zero at five knots."

"Gotcha," Shorty said, then began his final checklist. He increased his rate of descent again, and the speed brakes kept him from coming in too hot. He flipped on his landing lights and lined up with the runway. The runway numbers came into view and Shorty pulled the throttles all the way back. He made a smooth landing and applied his brakes immediately. Prendergast could be wrong about the runway length.

"Turn right onto the runup pad at the end of the runway, then do a one-eighty and cut your engines."

Shorty turned off the runway, spun the airplane around and shut everything down.

Prendergast popped the door. "I'll be back as soon as I can," he said. "Don't leave the aircraft, except to have a pee. When I get back I'll want to go immediately."

"Gotcha," Shorty said. He eased the back of his seat into a reclining position but held his head up long enough to watch Prendergast disappear into the woods not far from the end of the runway, the rays of a flashlight bobbing ahead of him.. Then he lay back and closed his eyes. Sure was peaceful out here, he thought.

All the guests had left who were leaving. Sam Warren and his wife had retired to the guest room, and Cara was taking a bath. Sandy undressed, slipped into a dressing gown and went downstairs to turn off the lights. He walked out onto the darkened front porch and took a last look at the lovely evening. There was half a moon and it cast a beautiful light over the vineyards. He was very happy to be who he was and where he was. He turned and went back into the house, not bothering to lock the front door. Mike Bernini had told him that nobody locked their doors around here.

He turned off the living room lights and headed for the stairs, blinking and feeling his way until his eyes became accustomed to the darkness. His hand found the newel post at the bottom of the stairs and a millisecond later, something heavy and firm struck the back of his neck. He managed to hold on to the newel post for another second before it got darker, and he lost consciousness.

CHAPTER

52

Sandy's dreams were awful; they spun violently in his head, and he couldn't get make them slow down. Then his eyes opened, and he wondered where he was.

His cheek lay against soft carpeting, and there was a large, dull pain in the back of his neck. He lifted his head, and the pain increased. He was on a strange staircase; he could feel the bannister next to him, but he couldn't see anything. There was no staircase in the New York apartment, so where could he be?

He had a sudden memory of dancing, so he began there and worked his way forward. He was dancing, then he was shaking hands with people. Sam Warren was there, saying good night and climbing the stairs. The stairs were in the house at the vineyard! He got to his knees. What the hell was going on? He struggled to his feet and held onto the bannister, willing his feet to climb the stairs. Why? What was the rush? What was waiting for him upstairs?

He climbed faster, his breath coming in short gasps, his neck hurting. Cara was up there somewhere. He paused at the top of the stairs to get his bearings. Their room was to his right, wasn't it? He tried shaking his head to clear it, but that made his neck hurt even more. He stumbled toward the bedroom.

The door was open and moonlight flooded the room. Had the lights been off? He looked toward the bed. Someone tall was standing there, shaking his upper body in an odd way. Then he realized that two people were standing there, and one of them was doing something to the other. "Cara!" he shouted, then moved toward them.

"Sandy, help me!"

The two figures separated and the tall one fled past him to the door. Sandy grabbed weakly at the man, and for a moment, he had hold of a raincoat sleeve, then something heavy hit him in the face, and he went down. Before he blacked out for a second time he heard, as from a great distance, Cara's scream.

Shorty Barnum was jarred awake by the shaking of the airplane. Someone was opening the rear door. "Prendergast?" he asked, blinking rapidly.

"Yes, let's go," Prendergast said, latching the rear door and falling into a seat. "Get the bloody thing started." The man was breathing hard.

Shorty checked the circuit breakers out of habit, then picked up his checklist.

"For God's sake, man, let's get out of here!" Prendergast shouted from the backseat. He sounded less American than ever.

Shorty fired up the two engines and checked the panel gauges. The engines were still warm from their flight up from L.A., and everything was in the green. If Prendergast was in such a hurry, he wouldn't bother with a runup. Shorty eased the throttles forward and taxied onto the runway. Still rolling, he pushed the throttles to wide open and let the airplane gather speed. A moment later they were rising through the darkness, and it was not until then that Shorty realized that he had not bothered to turn on the runway lights. Still, he had had plenty of visibility from his landing and taxi lights.

He got the landing gear up and trimmed for his climb. He set nine thousand feet into the altitude preselect, chose a heading that would take them east of San Francisco airspace, and switched on the autopilot. As he climbed, his attention was attracted to flashing red lights on the ground. They were on top of a car, and they were moving in the direction from which the airplane had just come. A police car or a fire truck, he thought. He couldn't hear any sirens over the engines.

When Sandy woke up his head was in Cara's lap, and a strange man was speaking to him.

"Mr. Kinsolving? Can you hear me?"

"Yes," Sandy said and tried to sit up.

"Just lie still, darling," Cara said, and he let his head fall back to the warm nest.

"Can you see me?" the man's voice asked.

Sandy struggled to focus his eyes, and after a moment, his vision was filled with the upper body and head of a young man in a tan shirt and trousers. "Yes, I can see you. What's happened?"

"You appear to have had a blow on the head," the

young man said. "I'm Deputy Wheeler of the Napa sheriff's office. An ambulance is on its way, and we'll have you at the hospital in a few minutes."

"Hospital? What for?" Sandy tried again to sit up, and this time he made it. With the deputy's help he got to his feet, but he was dizzy, and he sat down heavily on the bed, rubbing his neck.

"With a head injury it's always best to get some X-rays and have a doctor take a look at you."

"Quite right, Sandy," Sam Warren said. He stepped forward and put a hand on Sandy's shoulder. "Are you in a lot of pain?" he asked.

"I've got a hell of a headache," Sandy replied. "Cara, do you think I could have some aspirin?"

"An ice pack would be a better idea," the deputy said.

Cara left and returned with some ice cubes in a towel; she pressed them to the back of Sandy's head.

Sandy sighed. "That's better," he said. "Now tell me what's happened?"

"You've had an intruder in the house," the deputy said.

Suddenly, everything came back to him. "Cara, are you all right? I saw you struggling with a man."

"Yes, I'm all right," she replied, stroking his hair. "Don't worry about me."

"Who was he?"

"I don't know for sure, but it could have been Peter," she said.

"Peter? Here?" He tried to think. "I was downstairs on the front porch; I turned off the living room lights and . . . I don't remember anything until I was in the bedroom. He hit me, I think."

The deputy spoke up. "Looks like he hit you from

behind when you were downstairs, then again when you got up here. Mrs. Kinsolving saw that."

"Mrs. Kinsolving? What the hell did Joan have to do with this?"

"That's me, darling," Cara said, sitting beside him on the bed.

"Forgive me, I'm just getting my bearings."

"You've got some swelling on the side of your face," the deputy said. "Could somebody get some ice to put on it?"

"I'll do that," Sam said, then left the room.

"Did he try to hurt you?" Sandy asked Cara.

"Yes. He tried to strangle me with something."

"That necktie, I figure," the deputy said, pointing at the tie Sandy had been wearing earlier than evening. It was lying on the floor at the foot of the bed.

"I was lucky," Cara said. "I reached up with my arm to push him away, and my wrist was caught in the loop." She looked odd. "It's funny; he *smelled* like Peter, but he seemed to have a beard."

Shorty turned on final approach to Santa Monica Airport, and he was grateful for the runway lights rushing up at him. He hadn't had much for dinner, and he was tired, as well as hungry. He made his usual good landing, then slowed the airplane and turned off the runway toward his premises. He turned the plane and brought it to a stop, all lined up to be pushed back into the hangar. Then, before he could even cut the engines, the rear door opened, and Prendergast was out of the airplane.

Shorty turned off all the switches, then pulled back the mixture controls all the way. The engines died, and he turned off the ignition, alternator, and master switches. He was home, and he was five thousand dollars richer. That would get him out of the hole he was in.

He got out of the airplane and looked around. Prendergast had vanished, but from behind the hangar he heard a car start, then drive away. He could see parts of the access road from where he stood, and the car, he wasn't sure what kind, drove away at a leisurely pace, stopping at all the stop signs where the taxiways crossed the road.

Prendergast had sure been in a hurry to get out of the airplane, but he didn't seem to be in much of a hurry driving away. Still, Shorty was glad he'd collected the money in advance.

He pushed the airplane back into the hangar, locked up, got the five thousand dollars from his desk drawer and went home.

CHAPTER

53

Sandy woke in a bed in the little Napa hospital to find a man in his room wearing a lab jacket and looking at an X-ray against a light box.

"Good morning," Sandy said.

"Ah, you're awake," the man replied. "I'm Dr. Swift, and I want to take a look at you before we let you go home."

"Sure," Sandy said, swinging his feet over the side of the bed. An empty bed with mussed covers stood nearby.

"Your wife stayed here, too; I've already had a look at her. There was some bruising on her neck, but she's all right."

Sandy submitted to a thorough neurological examination, then waited for the doctor to speak.

"There's no fracture," he said. "You have a mild concussion, and I'd like you to spend today in bed at home.

If you feel nauseated, I want you to have your wife drive you back here at once, understand?"

"I understand," Sandy replied. He stood up, took his dressing gown from the end of the bed and slipped into it.

Cara came out of the bathroom and kissed him. "How are you feeling?" she asked.

"My neck's a little sore, but I'm not in any real pain."

"Then let's get you home; I've already paid the bill while you slept." She was wearing jeans and a sweater.

"Where did you get the clothes?" he asked as they walked down the hallway.

"I changed before I left the house."

"I feel a little strange leaving the hospital in a dressing gown," he said, getting into the car.

When they arrived at the house, the sheriff was waiting on the front porch, along with Deputy Wheeler.

"My name's Norm Ferris," he said, shaking Sandy's hand. "How are you feeling?"

"Much better," Sandy replied.

"Do you feel up to answering some questions?" the sheriff asked.

"Sure, come into the living room."

When they were all comfortable, the sheriff began. "Mrs. Kinsolving, last night you said that you thought the man who tried to strangle you was Peter. Who is Peter?"

"My ex-husband."

The sheriff nodded as if that was to be expected. "Can you be sure?"

"No, he just smelled like Peter, and he was the same size. I thought for a moment that he had a beard, but Peter doesn't have a beard."

"When did you last see Peter?"

"A few days ago in San Francisco."

"This would be Peter Martindale, then?"

"Yes."

"I read the newspaper article about the party at the sculptor's house," the sheriff said. "And I take it, Mr. Kinsolving, that you had recently brought a lawsuit against Mr. Martindale?"

"That's correct."

"Do you think Mr. Martindale is the kind of man who might become so angry about a lawsuit that he would attack your wife?"

Cara spoke up. "I think so, and I know my ex-husband much better than Sandy does."

"I telephoned Mr. Martindale's gallery this morning and was told that he is in Los Angeles, staying at the Bel-Air hotel," the sheriff said. "I tried to telephone him there, but the operator said that Mr. Martindale was not taking any calls. I've asked the L.A. police to go to the hotel and question him about his whereabouts last night."

"Good," Sandy said.

Detectives Harrow and Martinez of the LAPD knocked on the door of the room to which the front desk had directed them. A DO NOT DISTURB sign hung on the doorknob.

"Pretty fancy place," Harrow said, looking around at the lush tropical planting.

"You're right," Martinez said. "Wonder what it costs a night here?"

The door opened and a tall, slender man stood before them; he was wearing a necktie but was in his shirtsleeves. "Come in, gentlemen," he said. "The front desk said you're from the police?"

"That's correct, Mr. Martindale," Harrow said, showing his badge.

Martindale showed them to a seat. An open suitcase lay on the bed.

"You're checking out?" Harrow asked.

"Yes, I have a business appointment this morning, then I'm flying back to San Francisco. What is this about, please?"

"I'd like to ask you a few questions," Harrow said, "in connection with an investigation by the Napa County sheriff's office."

"Napa, as in wine?" Martindale asked.

"That's right. Can you tell me where you were last night, Mr. Martindale?"

"I was here, at the hotel."

"Did you have dinner in the dining room?"

"No, I came in about six-thirty from a lecture I had given; I asked the front desk not to put any calls through, then I had something from room service, watched television for most of the evening, then went to bed."

"What did you watch on television?"

"Some news on CNN and a movie, *The Bedford Incident*."

Harrow wrote down the name. "The one with Richard Widmark, about a submarine?"

"Widmark and Sidney Poitier," Martindale replied. "Excellent movie. I don't think anything less would have kept me awake. I was very tired."

"Did the room service waiter come and get the dishes after you ate?"

"I put them outside the door when I had finished."

"What time was the movie over?"

"Sometime after midnight; I'm not sure exactly what time."

"Did you speak to anyone before you went to bed?"

"I called the front desk when the movie was over to see if there had been any calls, but there hadn't been any."

Harrow nodded. "Were you in Napa County last night, Mr. Martindale?"

"No, I was here, as I've told you."

Harrow stood up. "Thanks very much for your cooperation, Mr. Martindale."

"Can you tell me what this is about?" Martindale asked.

"I'm afraid I don't have the details; you'd have to call the sheriff's office in Napa and ask them."

"Well, it's damned peculiar," Martindale said. He appeared mystified.

Harrow shook hands with the man and he and Martinez left the room. They took a few steps through a tunnel and emerged into a parking lot. "He could have left the hotel without being seen," Harrow said.

"That's right," Martinez echoed, "he could have parked his car right here."

"Kind of pushing it to get to Napa by what, ten-thirty, then back here in time to call the front desk at . . . "— he looked at his notes— "twelve-fifty, the lady said."

"I guess it could be done," Martinez said. "Maybe a private jet?"

"Damned if I'm going to tell Sheriff Ferris that," Harrow said. "The department will have us checking every charter service in town."

"Maybe Martindale had the opportunity to get up there and back, but we'd have a hell of a time proving in court that he did, unless we canvassed all the charter services and found somebody who'd testify that they flew him up there."

Harrow nodded. He put his notebook back into his pocket and started for their car.

Ferris hung up the phone. "Mr. Martindale appears to have an alibi," he said. "He was in his room at the Bel-Air last evening, had dinner there, watched a movie on TV, then went to bed."

"He could have snuck out of the Bel-Air," Cara said. "All the rooms open to the outside; you don't have to go through the lobby to get out of the hotel."

"Maybe," Ferris said. "We'll check on it, of course, but the L.A.P.D. reckons Martindale was at the Bel-Air all evening. We'll do some checking locally, too."

Everybody shook hands, and the sheriff and his deputy left.

"Let's get you to bed," Cara said.

"Do you think it really was Peter?" Sandy asked.

"I'm damned certain it was," she said. "He's covered his tracks, as usual."

CHAPTER

54

Deputy Tony Wheeler sat down at his desk in the sheriff's office and spread out a map of greater Los Angeles on his desk, along with an L.A. Yellow Pages. First, he looked up the address of the Bel-Air Hotel in the phone book and found its position on the map. He marked that with a highlighter, then began looking for airports. There were lots of them in the L.A. area, but the two that were nearest the hotel were Burbank and Santa Monica, with Santa Monica being closer. He started there.

He opened the yellow pages to the air charters listings and made a list of the ones that seemed to be at Santa Monica Airport, the ones with the 310 area code. There were an even dozen, and he went at them alphabetically. All of them denied sending an airplane to Napa County the night before, but with one, he had a flutter of disbelief; it was a guy called Barnum.

"Barnum Air Service, speak to me."

"Is that Mr. Barnum?" Wheeler asked.

"You got him. What can I do you for?"

"Mr. Barnum, my name is Wheeler; I'm a deputy sheriff of Napa County."

There was silence at the other end of the line.

Wheeler thought the silence was odd. "Mr. Barnum, did you do a charter to Napa County California last night?"

"No, sir," Barnum said, then was silent again.

"Have you ever had a customer named Martindale?"

"No, sir."

Wheeler was accustomed to a little more chat from possible witnesses. "Have you ever flown into Napa County Airport?"

"No, sir."

Wheeler sighed. "Thanks for your cooperation," he said, and hung up. He shook his head and finished his calls to Santa Monica Airport, then started working the Burbank list. When he was finished, only the call to Barnum struck him as not quite right. He looked up the main number for Santa Monica Airport and asked for the tower, then explained who he was.

"How can I help you, deputy?" the woman who'd answered asked.

"Do you keep any records of airplanes that take off and land at your airport?"

"We keep a log for a month, then we throw it away. Air traffic control would have a computer record, if there was a flight plan filed."

"Can you fly out of your airport without filing a flight plan?"

"Yes, you can depart VFR, that's under visual flight rules, and not file."

"Can you tell me if any airplanes departed VFR last night between, say, seven and ten?"

"Can you hang on for a minute?"

"Sure." Wheeler tapped his fingers impatiently on his desk while he waited.

Shortly, the woman came back. "Last night between eight and midnight we had only one VFR departure, and that was a twin Cessna, registration November one, two, three, tango, foxtrot."

Wheeler wrote down the number. "Can you tell me if it returned last night?"

"Just a minute." Another minute's wait. "Yes, it landed shortly after midnight."

"Is that particular airplane familiar to you and your coworkers?"

"There are an awful lot of airplanes based on this field."

"How would I find out who that airplane is registered to?"

"You'd have to call the FAA registration office in Wichita; hang on, I'll give you the number."

Wheeler wrote down the number, thanked the woman and called the FAA. He was connected to registrations, gave them the number, and asked to whom it was registered.

After a short delay, the clerk came back onto the line. "We show that aircraft as not a Cessna twin, but a Beech Bonanza, which is a single, and it's registered to a corporation with an address in Santa Fe, New Mexico." She gave him the name and address.

Sheriff Ferris walked into the station and stopped at Wheeler's desk. "What are you up to?" he asked. "Shouldn't you be patrolling the north sector?"

"Norm, I got to thinking about Martindale, and how Mrs. Kinsolving said he could easily get out of the Bel-

Air Hotel, so I called all the charter services at Santa Monica and Burbank airports to see if anybody had run a flight up here last night."

"And?"

"And everybody denied such a flight, but I got the impression that one guy wasn't being truthful with me. I figure it's possible that Martindale hired the guy, then paid him extra not to talk to anybody."

"That's hard to prove."

"Then I talked to the tower and found out that only one airplane took off from there last night without filing a flight plan, a twin-engine Cessna, and the registration number for that airplane turns out to be a Beech single, from New Mexico. The airplane took off early in the evening and returned after midnight."

"So what's your conclusion?"

"Well, my *hypothesis* is that Martindale hired this guy Barnum to fly him up here and back, and the guy gave the tower a false tail number when he took off and landed. And from the time he took off until about forty minutes after he landed, nobody saw Martindale at the Bel-Air Hotel."

"I suppose he could have landed at Napa County, but then he'd have to have a car to get to the Kinsolving property; it would be a good eight miles."

"I've got an idea about that, too," Wheeler said. "The Milburn Winery has a private strip, and that property borders the Kinsolving place. I bet the strip is less than half a mile from Kinsolving's house. I called the Milburn office, but nobody lives on the place, and the night watchman doesn't remember a plane landing. He could have been on the other side of the property."

"But Barnum denies flying up here last night?"

"That's right, but he sounded funny to me."

"Okay," the sheriff said, "let's see what you got: You got a suspect says he was in his hotel room, but he had opportunity to get out unseen and charter an airplane. You got an airplane that takes off from Santa Monica, but gives the wrong tail number to the tower; then it returns later, and the roundtrip flying time makes sense. And you got a suspected pilot who denies everything. It's all circumstantial, and you haven't got a single witness to support your theory, right?"

"Right, but I'd like an opportunity to crack the pilot."

"What do you want to do?"

"I want to fly down there in the county airplane and talk to the guy face to face."

The sheriff looked at his watch. "All right, if the county manager will approve it, and nobody else is using the airplane, and the pilot's available to go. Don't stay overnight, come right back; I'm not signing any expense reports."

"That's just what I'll do," Wheeler replied. He picked up the phone and called the county manager's office.

CHAPTER

55

S andy walked Sam Warren and his wife to their rental car. After taking the morning easy he was feeling much better.

"Sandy, you don't have to see us off," Warren protested as they walked down the front steps of the house. "You ought to be in bed."

"Really, Sam, I feel quite well now; I wish you could stay for lunch, so we could talk more."

"I really do have to get back to New York. You're not my only client, you know."

"I know, but you always make me feel that I am."

The two men shook hands, and Warren drove away. Sandy walked slowly back into the house and met Cara, who was coming down the stairs.

"I woke up, and there was nobody in bed with me," she pouted. "You shouldn't be up."

"I feel fine now," he said. "Except that I'm very angry."

"You have every right to be," she said. "He's violated our home, tried to harm us both. And I think he's too smart for the police, at least for the Napa County sheriff's department. I mean, the sheriff is a sort of bumpkin, and that deputy who's supposed to be investigating can't be more than twenty-five."

"You realize what Peter was trying to do, don't you?"

"Frighten us, I expect."

"No, he was trying to kill you, then blame it on me."

Cara paled slightly.

"That would be his idea of the perfect revenge, wouldn't it?"

"I'm afraid it would," she said.

"You know him; do you think he'd try again?"

"It wouldn't surprise me; I told you he was obsessive, and I don't think he could let this go, particularly after we humiliated him publicly. Maybe the suit was a mistake."

"Not as far as I'm concerned," Sandy said. "I hope you're wrong about the police."

"It's not the police that make me think he won't get caught. Peter is extremely clever; he wouldn't have done what he did unless he was convinced he would get away with it. It's not like Peter to put himself at risk."

"You said it was unlike him to provoke a physical confrontation, too," Sandy said, "but that's exactly what he did last night."

Cara shook her head. "He thought he had an advantage; he thought he could disable you in the dark, then have me all to himself. I told you he had no compunctions about attacking a woman. His plan went wrong, but only because he failed to hit you hard enough, and I was lucky enough to get my arm inside his noose."

"I see your point," Sandy said. "So you think he's still afraid of confrontation?"

"I know he is," she replied.

"Then," said Sandy, "I think the thing to do is to confront him."

Cara looked at him narrowly. "Sandy, what are you thinking of doing?"

"I'm thinking of confronting him."

She came to him and put her arms around his waist. "Listen to me, my darling," she said. "If you kill Peter, you'll simply put yourself in still more jeopardy. I mean, Peter is a problem, sure, but if you become a murderer you'll have to deal with the police, and that could be infinitely more difficult than dealing with Peter."

"I don't think I have to kill him," Sandy said. "I think, if he's the coward you believe him to be, it will be enough for me to make him *believe* that I'll kill him, that he's made me desperate enough to do that."

"I don't like this," Cara said.

"Neither do I," Sandy replied, "but I don't know what else to do." He went to the phone, got the number of the gallery from the operator and dialed the number.

"Hello?" Peter Martindale's voice said.

Sandy took a deep breath. "This is Bart," he said. "We have to meet."

There was a long silence, then Martindale spoke. "Where?" he asked.

"At the same place we met the first time out here. Take the four o'clock boat."

"All right," Martindale replied.

Sandy hung up and turned to Cara. "I have to go to San Francisco," he said.

"I'm coming with you."

"No, it's better if you aren't involved."

"But I *am* involved, right up to my ears."

"I'm going to take your car."

"Sandy, I'm coming with you."

Sandy shook his head and got her car keys from the hall table.

"*Sandy—*"

"No, my darling," he replied. He kissed her, then got a raincoat from the hall closet. "The forecast is for cool in the city today," he said, then left the house. He walked to the car, then stopped. He was unarmed. He walked around the house and, peeking through a window to see that Cara was not in the kitchen, he entered through the back door. Half a dozen knife handles protruded from a wooden block on a counter. He chose a slim, sharp boning knife, wrapped the blade in some paper towels, put the knife in his raincoat pocket, and returned to the car.

CHAPTER

56

T ony Wheeler sat in the copilot's seat of the old Beech Baron, relishing the flight to Santa Monica. He had eleven hours of dual instruction under his belt, and his instructor, Bert Corley, was his pilot today.

"How long do you reckon, Bert?" Tony asked as they leveled off at their cruising altitude.

"Couple hours," Bert replied. "You want to fly her for a while? It's not all that different from the trainer you've been flying, just heavier."

"Thanks, but I have to think about what I'm going to ask this guy," he said.

"What is it you want to know from him?"

"Well, I think he flew a guy up here last night and gave the Santa Monica tower a wrong tail number to keep anybody from finding out. He didn't file a flight plan, either."

Bert nodded. "That would be easy enough to do," he said. "How you going to get him to admit it?"

"I don't know," Tony admitted.

They landed at Santa Monica on schedule and pulled off the runway and into Cloverfield Aviation. Bert cut the engines. "You know where this guy's place is?"

"Nope."

They got out of the airplane, and Bert flagged down the fuel truck and had a word with him. He thanked the man and came back to where Tony waited. "Down this way a couple hundred yards," he said, pointing. "Let's just walk down the taxiway."

"Okay."

A short time later they were approaching the tin shed that housed Barnum Flying Service. An airplane's nose poked out from the hangar.

"He's got a Baron," Bert said, "like ours, only newer." He pointed at the airplane in the hangar next to the office.

Tony nodded. "I'll go on in and talk to him."

"I'll hang around out here," Bert said. "I want to have a look at his airplane."

Tony opened the door and walked in. There was a tiny reception area, with a couple of seedy armchairs and a lot of posters having to do with flying; there was a door with Shorty Barnum's name on it, and Tony opened that. Barnum, who had been dozing with his feet on the desk, started.

"Oops," he said. "Caught me catching forty winks. What can I . . . " Then he saw Tony's badge, and he didn't seem happy about it.

"My name's Tony Wheeler," the deputy said. "From the Napa sheriff's office; we spoke this morning."

"Yeah? Well, what brings you down here, deputy?"

Barnum took his feet off the desk, but he didn't offer Tony a chair.

Tony took one anyway. He wanted to begin in a way that would put Barnum at a disadvantage right away, but he was more nervous than he had planned. "You told me this morning that you didn't make a flight to Napa last night, didn't you?"

"That's what I told you," Barnum said, then he looked at the door.

Tony followed his gaze and found Bert standing there.

"Can I see you a minute?" Bert asked.

"Sure." Tony stepped into the little reception area and closed the door behind him. "What's up?"

"I had a look in the airplane," Bert said. "His logbook shows no flight last night, but his Hobbs meter—the little dial that records engine times—shows four point two hours more than his logbook total shows."

"Thank *you*, Bert," Tony said. He opened the office door and returned to his chair.

Shorty Barnum was looking at him with concern. "What's going on?" he asked.

"I thought I'd let you tell me," Tony replied. "Listen, Shorty, it makes a difference if you didn't know what the guy was going to do."

"I don't know what you're talking about," Shorty said.

"All right, I'll spell it out for you," Tony replied. "Last night, 'round eight, eight-thirty, you took off from Santa Monica VFR, after telling the tower you were a twin Cessna and giving them a wrong tail number. Then you flew up to Napa County and landed at the Wilburn Winery's private strip, and after a while, you flew back to Santa Monica and gave them the wrong tail number again."

Shorty shook his head. "You're full of shit, fella."

"Shorty, as far as I'm concerned, you haven't committed a crime, yet, unless using a wrong tail number is a crime. But if you lie to me, it's a whole new ball game. You can tell me what happened, and I won't have any reason to arrest you, unless you helped the guy do it."

"What'd he do?" Shorty asked, looking worried. "I mean, what did this alleged guy do after I allegedly flew him up there?"

"He tried to murder somebody, but it didn't work."

Shorty shook his head again. "Look, I know you got your job to do, but I can't help you, pal."

"Shorty, let's have a look at your logbook," Tony said.

"What for? It won't show any flight last night. I didn't go anywhere."

"Then why does your Hobbs meter show a flight of four-point-two hours?"

Shorty was suddenly at a loss for words.

"Come on, Shorty, was the guy a friend of yours? I mean, he couldn't have paid you enough for you to risk becoming an accessory to aggravated battery and attempted murder."

Shorty's shoulders sagged. "You're right," he said. "He didn't pay me enough for that."

"How much did he pay you?"

"Five thousand. I was in a hole, and I needed to get out."

Tony raised a placating hand. "I understand, and I'm not looking to break your back. I just want to know about the guy. Did you know him?"

Shorty shook his head. "Never saw him before; said

his name was Prendergast, but I didn't really believe him."

"Why not?"

"Well, a guy comes around with a lot of cash, says he wants to make a *very* confidential flight, and he's wearing what looks to me like a false beard and a wig."

"No kidding?" Tony was excited now.

"Looked phony to me."

"Describe the guy as best you can."

"He was a *lot* taller than me—I'm not called Shorty for nothing—six-two, six-three, on the skinny side, I think. He was wearing a black raincoat and a floppy hat. And black gloves."

Tony was writing fast in his notebook. "What kind of nose?"

"Uh, straight and kinda long."

"You notice the color of his eyebrows?"

"Dark, I think; not all that different from the color of the wig."

"Any kind of accent?"

"Funny you should mention it; he didn't sound quite American—maybe Canadian, English. His phraseology was a little on the English side, you know?"

"What did he do after you landed at the Wilburn strip?"

"He took off into the woods with a flashlight."

"In which direction?"

"Let's see, the strip ran northeast–southwest, so it would have been to the north."

"How long was he gone?"

"I'm not too sure about that; I dozed off for a while."

"How did he behave when he came back?"

"I can't help you there; he got into the backseat, sat right behind me, facing aft. He did want to get out of there in a hurry, though, and after we took off, I saw a police car or an ambulance headed in the direction he'd come from."

"That was probably me," Tony said. "I caught the call. Did he say anything after you landed?"

"He was out of the airplane before I had time to cut the engines, drove off."

"Did you see the car?"

"Yeah, but only from a distance going away. I don't know what it was, sort of mid-sized, maybe."

"You hear from him again?"

"Nope, and I don't think I will."

Tony stood up. "If you do, don't tell him we talked, okay?"

"Okay. Am I going to have to testify or anything?"

"Probably. I'm going to have to talk to the sheriff about arranging some sort of lineup, so you may have to come to Napa. We'll pay your expenses, though."

Shorty shrugged. "It's not like I'm all that busy," he said.

"You think you could recognize him if you saw him again?"

"Beats me. I mean, he was wearing the beard and all."

"You'll be hearing from me," Tony said, laying a card on the desk. "Call me if you hear from the guy again."

CHAPTER

57

T ony Wheeler and Sheriff Ferris sat in the district
attorney's office, and the D.A. listened patiently
while Tony told of his interrogation of Shorty
Barnum.

"So," Tony said, "to sum up, we've got the L.A.P.D's
report that Martindale could have left his room unseen
any time after seven-thirty and returned any time before
twelve-fifty A.M.; Barnum's description of the man he flew
up here matches Martindale, right down to the accent;
Barnum saw him go off into the woods less than half a
mile from Kinsolving's house; Mrs. Kinsolving said the
man smelled like her ex-husband but had a beard, which
tallies with Barnum's description of his passenger; and
finally, Martindale has an excellent motive—he had just
been forced by Kinsolving to admit that he'd sold a fake
painting and to pay eighty-five thousand dollars in restitution. Add to that, Mr. and Mrs. Kinsolving both threw

drinks at him at a party in San Francisco, in front of everybody that Martindale does business with." Tony sat back, looked at the sheriff for support and waited.

"What do you think, Dan?" the sheriff asked.

"I like the motive," the D.A. said. "You forgot to mention that Kinsolving had just married Martindale's ex-wife; that makes it an extra-good motive."

"Good," the sheriff said.

"We've got opportunity, too," the D.A. said, "but there we run into trouble. What we'd be telling a jury is that Martindale *could* have sneaked out of his hotel room, *could* have chartered an airplane for cash, and *could* have run through the woods, hit Kinsolving over the head and tried to strangle his wife. I mean, it's opportunity, but it wouldn't take much of a defense attorney to point out that there's *lots* of room for reasonable doubt."

"What I want to do is to bring Barnum and Martindale up here and run Martindale through a lineup," Tony said. "If Barnum picks him, we're home free, aren't we?"

"Yeah, but what if he *doesn't* pick him, deputy?" the D.A. said. "Then, no matter what other evidence we were able to develop over time, the defense would always have the fact that Barnum couldn't identify the man. And it sounds like to me that the guy was just well enough disguised that Barnum couldn't nail him in a lineup of similar-sized men."

"How about his voice?"

The D.A. shook his head. "Sounds to me like Martindale, who's English, was faking an American accent. You're not going to be able to get him to do that at a lineup, and I'm not going to be able to get him to do it on the stand, in the unlikely event that his attorney was crazy enough to let him take the stand."

Tony sat and stared at the D.A.'s desktop. "How

about if we brought him up here in handcuffs, throw what we've got at him, and see if he cracks?"

The D.A. shook his head again. "You're dealing with a pretty cool customer here, deputy, the kind who'd have the sense to clam up until his attorney arrived."

The sheriff tried to be helpful. "What if we subpoenaed his bank records. If there's a big enough withdrawal to account for the five thousand dollars he paid Barnum, that would help, wouldn't it?"

"It might help," the D.A. said, "but it would hardly be conclusive. I mean, I might be willing to go with less than an airtight case, but I want more than this in a trial that's going to attract a lot of media attention to the county. Is there any physical evidence at all?"

Tony shook his head. "I dusted the likely spots at the Kinsolving place, but there was nothing usable."

"How about Barnum's airplane? He could have touched something there, couldn't he?"

Tony shook his head. "Barnum said the man wore gloves."

The D.A. shrugged. "Well, I'm always ready to listen, if you come up with something else."

The sheriff stood up. "Thanks, Dan, we appreciate your time." He looked at Tony and made a motion with his head toward the door.

Tony got up and trudged after him.

On the front steps of the courthouse, the sheriff stopped. "You got any other leads on this one? Anything at all?"

Tony shook his head. "I've wracked my brain; I don't know where to go from here."

"I've thought about it, too," the sheriff said, "and I agree; there isn't anywhere else to go, unless somebody comes to us with something else."

Tony nodded. "There's always that hope, I guess."

"Listen, son," the sheriff said, placing a fatherly hand on the younger man's shoulder, "there a great truth about law enforcement that may not have sunk in with you yet."

"What's that?"

"We don't solve 'em all. We do pretty good, I think, but sometimes we just don't have enough to go on, and this could turn out to be one of those times. At least nobody got seriously hurt."

"I hate to let it get away," Tony said, "when we've got so much already."

"Maybe it won't get away," the sheriff said. "Maybe you'll find another way."

"How 'bout if I took Shorty Barnum to San Francisco, to where he could get a look at Martindale? A kind of preview to a lineup?" Tony asked hopefully.

The sheriff shook his head. "That wouldn't be an I.D. that would stand up in court, son, and it's not the way I do business, either. You don't want to start shaving off corners at this stage of your career; it gets to be habit forming."

"You're right, Norm, and I'm sorry I brought it up."

"That's okay; we all need somebody to steer us around the rough spots at times. I just wish I could be of more help to you on this one. I'd like to see Martindale get locked up, myself. He's a smartass who thinks he's always a step ahead of us, and I'd love to tag him."

"So would I," Tony replied.

"Well," the sheriff said, squaring his hat, "let's get back to work. I've got a lot of paperwork looking at me, and you're due back riding the north end of the county."

Driving north, Tony Wheeler struck the steering wheel of his patrol car several times, venting his very considerable frustration.

CHAPTER

58

Tony Wheeler drove north more slowly than he usually did when he patrolled. The case was eating at him, and he tried to figure out why. It was more than that he had almost nailed Martindale; he might nail Martindale yet, after all. It was more than what bothered the sheriff—that Martindale was a smartass who thought the police couldn't nail him. What bothered him, Tony decided, was that Martindale was a cold, calculating potential murderer, and that, having failed once, he would almost certainly try again. At that moment, the radio came alive.

"Napa Four, this is base." It was the sheriff's voice.

Tony picked up the microphone. "Base, Napa Four."

"Tony, it's Norm."

"Yeah, Norm?"

"What's your position?"

"Two, two-and-a-half miles north of town."

"Good. The desk had a call from Mrs. Kinsolving a
couple of minutes ago. She sounded upset, wanted to
speak to somebody. I just got in, and I called her, but
there's no answer. You wheel by there, and see if she's
all right."

"Wilco," Tony said. "I'll be there in three minutes."

"Let me know if she's all right."

"Wilco. Out."

Tony made a U-turn and stepped on it. He turned
into the driveway at what was now called the
Kinsolving Vineyards and drove quickly up to the
house. Mrs. Kinsolving, to his surprise, was on her
hands and knees in a flower bed near the driveway,
furiously pulling up weeds. He got out of the car.
"Good afternoon, Mrs. Kinsolving," he said. "I'm
Deputy Wheeler."

"Yes, I remember," she said. She was standing now,
and both hands were filled with weeds.

"The sheriff said you called; is everything all right?"

Tears began to roll down her face. "No, everything is
not all right. I'm out here pulling weeds, and I'm afraid
Sandy's in terrible trouble."

It dawned on Tony that the woman was very nearly
hysterical. "What kind of trouble, ma'am?"

"He's gone to meet Peter."

"Peter Martindale?"

She nodded. "I'm afraid of what might happen."

Tony was afraid, too. "Where is he meeting
Martindale?"

"He called him and said they should meet at the first
place they met."

"And where's that, ma'am?"

"I think at Alcatraz."

"Alcatraz?"

"Sandy told me that Peter had once insisted that they meet at Alcatraz."

"How long has your husband been gone?"

"I don't know, exactly. At least an hour, maybe two."

"Ma'am, thank you for telling me this; now you're going to have to excuse me, if I'm going to be able to do anything about it."

He ran for his patrol car, got it started, and pointed it toward town. He grabbed the microphone. "Base, Napa Four."

"Napa Four, base."

"The sheriff there?"

"No, Tony, he went off with the county manager in his car."

"Okay, listen carefully; I want you to call the airport and get hold of Bert, the pilot. Tell him I'm on my way out there right now, and I'll be there in about six or seven minutes. Tell him to have the police helicopter fueled and running when I get there, that we're going to San Francisco."

"Tony, you ought to talk to the sheriff about this."

"I don't have time to find the sheriff; you just call Bert and tell him that, and I'll take the responsibility, do you read me?"

"I read you, Tony, but remember, it's on your head."

"That's fine with me," Tony replied. He put the microphone back on its clip, flipped on the lights and siren, and stood on the accelerator.

Sandy drove across the Golden Gate Bridge feeling a mixture of emotions. He was apprehensive about this meeting, but glad that he was bringing the situation to a head. He was determined to make Martindale under-

stand that by continuing with this madness he was
putting his own life in jeopardy. He knew he could kill
Martindale now. He could squash the man like a bug
and never feel a moment's guilt about it. But he would
make one more effort to reason with him; today's effort.

He looked out toward the Pacific and his vision did
not go far; a fog bank covered everything to seaward—
one of those midsummer phenomena that were so characteristic of this stretch of water. The bridge was in
bright, cold sunshine at the moment, but soon it might
be enveloped in the dense mists.

Sandy glanced at his watch as he drove off the
bridge; he was in good time. As he parked the car he
looked around for Martindale's Lincoln, but it was
nowhere in sight. He bought a ticket and got aboard the
boat. Halfway to the island, Sandy looked toward the
Golden Gate Bridge, and it was gone. The bright, sunlit
wall of fog had crept into the harbor and was making
its way inland.

As he stepped ashore Sandy looked up and saw that,
since his last visit, a section of the stout Alcatraz wall
had collapsed. He was reminded of some ruined castle
in Ireland. An elderly tour guide was waiting to greet
the group, and Sandy pointed at the wall. "What happened up there?" he asked.

"The old girl is falling down," the guide said.
"There's no money to keep her repaired. One of these
days she'll be a complete wreck."

Sandy let himself fall to the rear of the group as it
formed.

"Now," said the guide, "my name is Wembly, and
for the last four years of this structure's life as a maxi-
mum-security prison, I was a guard here. I know every
nook and cranny of this place, and I'm going to show it

to you. Please don't hesitate to ask any questions." He led the group through the gate and toward the main body of the prison.

Sandy stayed a few steps to the rear of the group, not bothering to listen to the guide, thinking about what he was going to say to Peter Martindale.

Tony skidded to a stop on the tarmac at Napa County Airport. Bert was leaning against the helicopter, waiting for him.

Tony got out of the car and, as an afterthought, grabbed a shotgun, then ran for the passenger seat. "Bert, I told them to tell you to have this thing running."

"Well, I just got it fueled," Bert said petulantly. "Now where you want to go, and who authorized it?"

"Alcatraz," Tony said.

"Alcatraz? Are you outta your fucking mind? Who would authorize that?"

"I'm authorizing it. Bert, if you don't get this thing going right now, I'm going to shoot you," Tony said. "You can tell your boss I said that."

Bert got the thing going.

It was as before. As the crowd moved out of the cell block, Sandy hung back and looked at the cells to his right. Peter Martindale stood inside one, waiting.

"How much longer?" Tony said into the intercom.

"About ten, eleven minutes," Bert said. "Hang on, I gotta call in." He punched the push-to-talk button. "San Francisco approach, Napa One police helicopter."

"Napa One," a controller said.

"I'm five miles north of class B airspace at one thousand feet, squawking one, two, zero, zero, heading two, zero, zero."

"Napa One, what is your destination?"

"Alcatraz."

"Napa One, say again your destination."

"San Francisco approach, Napa One; my destination is Alcatraz. Request vectors."

"Napa One, do you intend landing at Alcatraz?"

"Affirmative."

"Is this an emergency?"

Bert looked at Tony; Tony nodded.

"Affirmative, San Francisco, this is a police emergency."

"Napa One, understand police emergency. Come left to one, niner, zero. Alcatraz is seventeen miles at twelve o'clock. Report Alcatraz in sight."

"Wilco," Bert said. He turned to Tony. "This better be good," he said.

"Napa One, San Francisco approach."

"This is Napa One.

"The coast guard has advised us that a fog bank has developed over San Francisco Bay and is currently estimated to be one-half mile west of Alcatraz, moving slowly east."

"Roger, San Francisco." Bert turned again to Tony. "You give me the most entertaining fucking flying, you really do."

CHAPTER

59

Sandy sat on the steel bunk and looked at Martindale, who sat opposite him. There was something in the man's face that he hadn't seen there before. Desperation, maybe; determination, probably; madness, certainly.

"Peter," he said, "I want you to listen to me very carefully. We have to end this—today, now, this minute."

"That is my intention, Sandy," Martindale replied. His voice was low, soft, steely.

"Peter, if you persist in this, you will destroy yourself."

"Yes, Sandy, I know that; but I will destroy you first, and then Helena."

"Peter, think. Why must you have this vendetta in your mind? Helena has given you everything you have—your home, your business—everything."

"And together, you and Helena have taken it away."

"What?"

"In order to raise the money I paid you, I gave the apartment and the business as collateral. But since you have now gutted my reputation, I will never, *never* be able to earn the money to repay the loan. First, the gallery will go, and since its value has been greatly depreciated by this business, it will bring very little. Then, since I won't have an income, the apartment will have to go, and the real estate market is terrible at the moment. I'll lose *everything!*" He seemed to realize that he had begun to shout, and he brought his voice down. "Everything," he repeated.

"Peter, can't you take responsibility for your own actions? Can't you see that you've painted yourself into this corner?"

"It's your doing," Martindale said.

"Peter—"

"Enough talking," Martindale said. "Stand up." He drew his hand from his coat pocket and in it was a silenced revolver.

Sandy had seen it before. He stood up and slipped his hand into his raincoat pocket.

Martindale pressed the barrel of the pistol up under Sandy's chin. "Take your hands out of your pockets," he said.

Sandy obeyed.

Martindale patted Sandy's pockets, reached in, and came out with the knife. "My, my," he said. "You came prepared, didn't you?"

"San Francisco approach, Napa One. I have Alcatraz in sight."

"Napa One, San Francisco approach. Do you see the landing pad on top of the main building?"

"Affirmative. It's faded, but I can see it."

"Napa One, cleared to land at Alcatraz."

"Roger." Bert turned to Tony. "Shouldn't you let the San Francisco police know about this?"

"Jesus, I hadn't thought of that," Tony admitted. "Yeah, ask them to call the cops. Oh, and they'd better call the FBI, too; this place is federal property."

"San Francisco approach, Napa One. Request you alert the San Francisco police and the FBI of the emergency."

"Roger, Napa One. What is the nature of your emergency?"

Bert looked at Tony. "Well?"

"Uh, hang on a second." Tony thought about it. "Tell them we're going in to prevent a possible murder."

"San Francisco approach, Napa One. We are intervening to prevent a possible homicide."

"Roger, Napa One. We'll call in the cavalry."

"Now we're really in the shit," Bert said. "There'll be no sneaking in and out of there."

"Bert," Tony said, "don't land yet. First, let's fly over the yard and see what the hell's going on."

Sandy walked across the yard ahead of Peter, wondering what to do next.

"Head for those stairs," Martindale said. "The ones to the guard tower."

Sandy looked the twenty yards ahead of him. A chain stretched across the bottom of the stairs, and a sign hung on it. "No Entry," it said.

"Unhook the chain," Martindale said as they reached it.

Sandy unhooked the chain and started up the stairs. From behind them came a shout, and Sandy looked back to see the group of tourists emerging from the cell block. The guide, Wembly, was running toward them.

"Stop!" he yelled. "It's dangerous up there!"

Martindale turned, raised his arm, and fired a shot into the dirt near the guide. Wembly stopped.

Sandy moved to reach for the gun, but Martindale swung around and pointed it at him again.

"Climb," he said.

Sandy trudged on up the stairs. At the top, the door to the guard tower was missing, and so was the door on the other side of the little room. Beyond it, a walkway stretched along the top of the wall, behind a waist-high parapet. A patch of fog blew across the top of the wall, momentarily obliterating it before blowing away. Sandy's mouth was very dry.

"Keep going along the wall," Martindale said.

Sandy looked over the edge of the parapet; it was a good seventy or eighty feet down, with pavement at the bottom. He stopped and turned around to face Martindale. He was farther behind than Sandy had thought. "Stop this, Peter. Put the gun down." A noise distracted him, and he looked up, across the yard. A helicopter was a hundred yards away, moving slowly toward them.

Suddenly, Martindale was gone. Sandy could see nothing but fog.

"There!" Tony said. "On top of the wall—two men!"

"I saw them for a second, but now they're gone," Bert replied. "It's the fog; I can't see a damned thing."

"Keep going in that direction," Tony demanded. "I think one of them had a gun."

Now the helicopter was enveloped in fog.

"Oh, shit!" Bert yelled.

Sandy suddenly realized that if he couldn't see Martindale, Martindale couldn't see him. It seemed the best idea to put as much distance as possible between himself and the gun. He turned and began to run, and as he did, he heard two quick, muffled reports, and something ricocheted off the masonry next to him. He threw himself to the opposite side of the walkway, and the action saved his life; another noise came, and a piece of masonry flew off the wall at the spot where he had been standing. Sandy stopped and tried to see ahead. The fog didn't seem any worse, but now he couldn't see the path in front of him.

"Stand still!" Martindale yelled.

A hole in the fog had come upon them, and Sandy could see Peter, no more than four feet away, pointing the pistol at him. He made to run, but as he turned, he saw that he was on the brink of an abyss. He was standing at the spot where the wall of the prison had collapsed.

"There!" Tony yelled. "I see them! Put my side of this thing as close to them as you can!" He tightened his seatbelt, opened the door on his side, lifted it off its pins, and tossed it into the backseat. "Closer!" he shouted, grabbing his shotgun and pumping a round into the chamber. It was an Ithaca riot gun with an eighteen-inch barrel, so the shot would spread quickly. "Closer, godammit!"

"Who are you planning to shoot?" Bert asked.

"The one with the gun, Bert," Tony said, exasperated. "*If* you can get me a shot at him."

Sandy stared into the uplifted gun barrel, into the silencer; he had gone as far as he could go and, to make matters worse, he felt the wall begin to sink under his feet. The helicopter was so close, now, he strained against the gale of wind from its rotors.

"Now it's over for you, Sandy," Martindale said. He pulled the trigger.

Sandy flinched and threw up a hand, but nothing happened. There was only a loud click. Misfire.

Martindale looked at the pistol, annoyed, then aimed it and pulled the trigger a second time. Nothing.

No more chances, Sandy thought. He felt the wall give way beneath him. The only thing to grab hold of was Martindale's gun. He reached for the barrel and pulled himself toward safety.

Martindale seemed surprised by this move, but he held on to the pistol.

Sandy had hold of his wrist now and, to his astonishment, Martindale moved forward, and a sort of do-si-do ensued. The two men changed places.

"Watch out!" Sandy yelled as Martindale stepped on to the sinking part of the wall.

And at that moment, a loud report came from the helicopter, and, simultaneously, Martindale's head snapped to one side as bloody flecks appeared on his face and neck. He let go of the pistol.

Sandy stood, his arm outstretched, still holding on to the gun's barrel. Then, the wall beneath Martindale gave way, and he plunged with the rubble all the way to the hard surface below.

Sandy's knees seemed no longer willing to support his weight. He backed away from the abyss, put his back to the wall and slowly slid down to a sitting position. What had happened? Why was he not dead? He pressed a button on the side of the pistol, and the cylinder fell open. Each of the six cartridges bore a mark from the firing pin. Sandy counted. Martindale had fired one shot at the guide, then, what—three at him? That was only four.

Then it came to him. This was the pistol that Martindale had given him to kill his wife. Sandy had fired two of the shots, himself, into a stack of cardboard boxes. He had saved his own life.

Now a loudspeaker barked at him. "Mr. Kinsolving!" the voice boomed.

Sandy struggled to his feet and looked over the parapet. That deputy—Wheeler—was holding a shotgun and speaking to him.

"Are you hurt?" he asked, and his voice echoed around the prison's walls.

Sandy shook his head. Wheeler was pointing back toward the tower.

"Go that way!" he said.

Sandy turned and walked back toward the tower, where Wembly was waiting for him.

"Are you all right, sir?" Wembly asked.

"I think I am," Sandy said, handing him the pistol. "In fact, I'm very sure of it."

Sandy spent the rest of the day at Alcatraz, talking to the San Francisco police and the FBI. Tony Wheeler was very helpful in filling in the background of what had occurred. It was simple, he told his law-enforcment colleagues: trouble between two men over a woman and a lawsuit; one of them took it hard and got a gun. He had been investigating.

As dark approached, Bert, the pilot, walked over to where Sandy and Tony stood. "Tony, I want to get back to Napa while I've got light to get out of here," he said. He had landed the helicopter in the prison yard.

"Mister Kinsolving," Tony said, "can you give me a lift back to Napa?"

"Of course, deputy," Sandy replied.

"You go ahead, Bert; I'll be along," Tony said.

It began to rain during the drive back to Napa.

"Deputy, I'm very grateful for what you did this afternoon," Sandy said.

"No problem," Tony replied. "Mr. Kinsolving," the deputy said, "will you tell me exactly what the hell has been going on?"

"It was just as you told the police and the FBI," Sandy said. "Jealousy over a woman, pique over a lawsuit. Martindale took it hard."

"Somehow, I think there's more to it," Tony said.

"Believe me, that's the whole story," Sandy lied.

CHAPTER

60

S andy sat at his desk above the wine shop, coun-
tersigning purchase orders for French wines. He
had been back in New York for a week now, feeling relaxed and happy, except for his conscience. The
phone buzzed.

"Yes?"

"He's here, Mr. Kinsolving."

"Please send him in." He watched as Detective Alain
Duvivier walked alone into the room. The two men
shook hands perfunctorily, and Sandy offered the man
a seat.

"Why did you want to see me, Mr. Kinsolving? And
why without my partner?"

Sandy looked at his watch. "Are you off duty now?"

"More or less. Officially, I'm never off duty."

"Then let me offer you a glass of wine."

Duvivier blinked. "All right," he said.

Sandy opened a bottle of red on his desk and poured them both a glass, then he sat down. "This is a particularly nice burgundy that I import," he said, raising his glass and taking a sip. "A Clos de Vougeot, 1978, from the shippers, Bouchard, Père et Fils."

Duvivier sipped from his glass. "It's excellent," he said. "But why did you want to see me?" He smiled a little. "Are you ready to confess?"

"As a matter of fact," Sandy said, "I am."

Duvivier's mouth fell open.

When Sandy had finished his story, and the two of them had finished the bottle, Duvivier finally spoke. "Do you feel better now?"

"I feel very much better," Sandy said. "You can arrest me, if you like."

"For what?" Duvivier asked. "About the most I could charge you with would be obstruction of justice—concealing the facts of a murder—but I doubt if it would stick. After all, you acted under duress."

Sandy shrugged.

"Anyway, I didn't read you your rights, so your confession would be inadmissible in court."

Sandy smiled. "I rather thought that might be the case. I just wanted to tell you; somehow, I felt you had a right to know the truth."

"Thank you. If you'd told me the facts at the beginning, it might have saved you a great deal of pain."

"I've thought about that, and you're right, I suppose, but there's no changing what's past. I'll just have to learn to live with the consequences of my actions."

Duvivier stood up. "Well, I'd better be getting home; my wife will have dinner ready."

Sandy stood up and took another bottle of the wine

from his desk. "Take this with my compliments—and, my apologies."

"Is this a bribe?" Duvivier asked.

"Probably."

"Don't worry, your story won't go any further. And my wife will enjoy the wine very much."

"I hope she does."

Duvivier stuck out his hand. "You know, you and your wife are very lucky. It could have ended differently."

"I know," Sandy said. "My wife and I are very, very lucky."

ACKNOWLEDGMENTS

I am grateful to my editor, HarperCollins Vice President and Associate Publisher Gladys Justin Carr, and to her staff for their hard work in the editing and preparation of this book; to all the other people at HarperCollins who have worked for the book's success; to my agent, Morton Janklow, his principal associate, Anne Sibbald, and all their colleagues at Janklow & Nesbit who have been so important to my career; and to my wife, Chris, for her help, understanding, and love.

Finally, I owe a special gratitude to Patricia Highsmith and Alfred Hitchcock, who have inspired so many, especially me.